I0708010

UNEXPECTED COWBOY DAD

HEATHERLY BELL

For my Family

Beau looked down at his baby. She smiled at him again and something in his chest shifted. Then the door closed, and his mother was gone.

Beau turned to Lucy. "Don't leave me. Don't you freaking dare leave me, Larry!"

Lucy gave him a long look, like she was bored, then took the baby from him. "Give me here."

She expertly took the baby, moved to the couch with her, and reached for the stack of diapers Rachel had left. Lucy proceeded to put a diaper on Charlotte with smooth and easy moves.

"What's this? You've been holding out on me?"

"Look, I'm a bartender, cut hair, and run a ride share service. I can do a little bit of everything. You don't think I've had my turn at babysitting? It was my first job."

"Why didn't I know that?"

"Guess you were too busy chasing girls."

Read on as two friends navigate life with a small baby and fall in love in the process…

Prologue

Well! We had recently recovered from the scandal involving Colton only to find ourselves with a brand new shiny one.

What's happened in Stone Ridge *now*, you ask? Let me tell you.

Our very own Beau Stephens has got himself in *quite* a bind. I hate to say, "I told you so" but…apparently Beau will pay dearly for his previous (ahem) "escapades." In fact, I'll bet the fun times are over for good. Children have a way of slowing, then strapping you down. Oh, he'll find out. Heh, heh, heh.

It's about time Beau settled down and gave up his "friendly" ways. We've been trying to get him married off for years! The right woman is here for him, I just know it, even if it apparently won't be the mother of his child. This is a shame, I tell you, but that's what he gets for not sticking to one of the wonderful women we have right here. The mother of his child dropped the baby off without so much as a "how dee do," I hear. Now poor Beau is trying to manage his small ranch, work his contractor business, and handle unexpected first-time fatherhood.

It's a tall order and it's going to take a special woman to put up with ~~him~~ it. I have my idea of the perfect match for him, of course, though for now I'm keeping quiet. Yes, that's right, go ahead and laugh. I can be silent when it suits me! This time I'm keeping my matchmaking ways to myself. I know the perfect woman for Beau if he'll just open his eyes. She's a special lady to all of us.

Why yes, she's been here all along, right under his nose.

Unfortunately, she's got plans to leave us for Seattle. All I know about that city is that it rains a lot. There's also coffee and computers and not a single cowboy! But folks, I don't need to tell you that we can't afford to lose one of our women and she's one of our best. It's going to take some fancy footwork on our part to keep her here, but none of us intend on letting her go quietly. We just have to make staying here in our huge man cave a whole lot more attractive to a young singleton ready to settle down. Which is all to say this has become a lot more complicated than it used to be. But we're up to the task!

You may have heard there aren't many women in our small town, and it's still true by my account, but we're keeping all the women who moved to town for the *Mr. Cowboy* reality show. Many of them are still trying to find their eligible cowboy. Don't worry, young ladies, we still have plenty of them to go around, though you might want to cross Beau off your list. Unless y'all like the idea of a ready-made family.

In that case, step right up. The water's warm and Beau is desperate.

~ BEULAH HAYES, President of SORROW (Society of Reasonable, Respectable, Orderly Women), and keeper of the *Men of Stone Ridge* bible, tenth edition. ~

Chapter 1

Once upon a time, Beau Stephens thought being in the center of a group of beautiful women would be a fantasy come true.

Their attention would be on him. Women to his right, women to his left, women everywhere he cast his gaze. Smiling and craving *him*. Like his own personal harem. Those were the foolish thoughts of a man who'd grown up in a town with few women. For decades, Stone Ridge, Texas, was a cattle town filled with a majority of men and not many eligible women.

About six months ago, however, his dream came true.

In a way.

These days, it all felt like a bit of a nightmare.

With his father in semiretirement, playing vintner on his two-acre vineyard, Beau found himself the head of Stephens Construction. He couldn't complain. It was a good income for a single man and though he wasn't one to flash his money with fancy cars or heavily tooled boots, belts, and buckles, Beau had the resources to do it now should he choose. Back when his father invested in a parcel of land along Lupine Lake and built a couple of cabins for rental income, he'd never imagined what a gold mine it would be. But with the influx of single ladies moving here after the *Mr. Cowboy* reality show broadcasted, Beau and his crew couldn't build the cabins fast enough.

At this point, he could buy himself a luxury truck with all the bells and whistles if he wanted. Instead, he still drove his old and dusty green pickup, which still ran. He'd saved and three years ago bought several acres of land where he built his home. Eventually he planned to raise thoroughbred horses, but he was still saving money for the first six-figure horse he'd purchase from Mr. Truehart.

Still, Beau couldn't do it all and dealing with these rentals was taking too much of his precious time. He was going to campaign heavily for his father to invest in a property manager. With ten new renters, and more coming every few months, it was time.

The cabins were nothing special, built to specifications, but each one was solid. Beau took pride in his workmanship. They were meant to be starter homes, one large room with a bathroom and little kitchenette. Each had an A-frame with a small wraparound porch and steps leading up to the front door. In a city, this would be the equivalent of a studio apartment.

Now, he stood in front of one of the cabins while his renter, Valerie, complained. His thoughts turned to a gorgeous one-year-old paint mare he'd wanted to purchase at the last Truehart auction, but the price had gone too high. Some of his friends called him a part-time cowboy, but they wouldn't say that once he had a prize-winning horse collection.

"Are you even listening to me?" The soft feminine voice came to him, disturbing his thoughts.

"Yep. I'm listening, darlin'. You were saying the water heater isn't working."

"I know you checked it once but this morning…" *Blah blah blah blah.*

The children of this paint would have been exceptional. Beau always fancied himself a cowboy even if he hadn't grown up like his cattle-ranching brother-in-law and best friend, Lincoln Carver. Point being, Beau was a cowboy at heart. Always had been, always would be. He had three passions in life: women, building showcase homes, and horses.

Not necessarily in that order.

"*So?* What do you say about that?" The feminine voice once more pulled him from his thoughts.

"Huh?"

Valerie went hand on hip. "Don't you 'huh' me, Beau Stephens! Just because we made out that one time and you're a good kisser doesn't mean I'm going to give you any excuses. My cabin might only be a rental but as such I am *entitled* to running water—"

"You *have* running water."

This was so annoying. City people should *not* move to the country. This was Exhibit A.

"*Hot* running water."

She crossed her arms, in that single move pushing up her bosom so it threatened to fall out of her small tee. She gave him a smirk when his eyes followed to the lush bare skin. He was only human, and as previously stated, women were in his top three.

Beau cleared his throat. "I put that water heater in myself. It's brand new. Checked it last week. But, as I've told you, we have a well. Not only that but every water heater made is going to run out of hot water if you use too much. You just need to give it at least twenty minutes to heat up again."

"Beau, I'm glad you're here," Sarah said, running out of her cabin next door wearing nothing but a loosely tied bathrobe. "I was just going to call you."

"*I'm* talkin' to him right now," Valerie said. "Get in line."

"But something is wrong with the Wi-Fi."

"I'll tell you what's wrong with it," Valerie said. "We don't *have* any out here. Didn't you read the brochure?"

Sarah smiled. "Oh yes. A cowboy paradise, with cabins situated in an idyllic lakeside community."

"I didn't *write* that," Beau protested.

Beulah Hayes had created those pamphlets, which sold the lakeside community just to get more women to move to Stone Ridge.

"I was promised my own cowboy." Sarah reached to ruffle his hair. "Are we still going out Friday night?"

"Yeah, sure, sweetheart. I'll pick you up at eight."

She'd asked him out on their first meeting, and he'd agreed, but at the moment she was showing her city ways and he had second thoughts. Granted, he'd never been around this many young women in his *life*, so he didn't know what to do half the time but smile. Still, there were plenty of cowboys around. He just happened to be front and center at the lakeside community where most of the women who'd moved here had rented his cabins.

"Oh, so you're going out with Sarah?" Valerie said. "What about us?"

"*Us?* We had one date. And last week you were hanging out with Andy. The week before that it was Jeremy. The week before that—"

"You're keeping track?" Valerie said. "The truth is, I

can't make up my mind. There are so many of you. I have *options*."

"In the meantime, I'll be keeping him warm." Sarah linked her arm through Beau's.

"Shouldn't you get *dressed*?" Valerie scowled and pointed at Sarah's bathrobe.

"I will as soon as Beau leaves."

Beau swallowed. It didn't look like she had anything on under there and his imagination went a little wild. If he had a weakness, it was women. He loved everything about them. Soft mouths headed the top of a long list, and he could see numbers two and three on his list poking through Sarah's bathrobe. Clearly, she was cold.

He shook her off and tipped his hat to both ladies. "Got to get going. Lots to do."

Hopping in his truck, he grabbed the satellite phone and dialed his father.

"Hello, son!"

"You have to hire a property manager. *Now*."

"What for? That's just a waste of money. This is a Stephens Construction project. We can handle it."

Beau sighed at his frugal father. He meant *Beau* could handle it. His mother was busy running her gourmet peach jam business and his sister, Sadie, was raising a son, with another child on the way. And of course, his dad fancied himself a *wine maker* these days.

Beau rubbed the spot between his eyebrows. "You've got me all over the place and if you and Mom are serious about me settling down and finding a wife, I need time for my personal life. *And* my ranch."

"Alrighty then, just call me next time there's a complaint of any kind and I'll go out there and see what's what."

Beau wasn't sure he meant it. Every other time he'd

made some last-minute lame excuse and sent Beau anyway.

"They're still adjusting to no Wi-Fi. You're going to hear a lot of complaints, none of which are about the cabins we built. Just people getting used to life in the country."

"Sounds about right. Your work was solid. There's no better carpenter in all of Texas."

Exactly. Beau prided himself in his work and didn't see that changing anytime soon. The cabins were built with every modern convenience available, and the rent was reasonable. Until he'd saved up enough to buy his land, he used to live in one of these cabins situated a bit closer to the lake, as did his sister, Sadie, before she got married.

He hung up with his father, satisfied for the moment he wasn't alone in this venture.

The January afternoon was crisp and clear, one of the few chilly days in Texas. He didn't mind calling it a day a little earlier than normal. Turning on the road toward downtown, he headed to the Shady Grind looking for a cold beer, and the company of good friends.

LUCY LORENZO PULLED another draft beer and set it down in front of Jeremy Pine.

She made a face. "You might want to try something *else* for a change."

"Why would I?" Jeremy took a gulp and set it down with a big "ahh." "Nothin' like a nice cold beer after a long hard day."

"Because it wouldn't kill you, that's why." She gave the bar a wipe between customers.

What was the point of learning how to make every popular cocktail known to man when all these cowboys ever wanted was a cold beer. On tap, in a bottle, domestic, or IPA. Always a beer. Boring. Any minute now a new group of them would all waltz in, en masse, done from their day of ranching. They'd be looking to unwind with a beer, the game on the flat screen, or a round of pool. There were already some women waiting in anticipation for when they strolled in with their tight jeans and tipped hats. These ladies loved a cowboy and Stone Ridge happened to be full of them.

Lucy, on the other hand, had lived here all her life and was sick of cowboys.

Just one more month before she'd be out of this small town and living in the big city of Seattle. She'd saved her money for months and would find a job and eventually get an apartment of her own. She'd have a brand-new beginning, which was exactly what she needed. At first, she'd stay with her old high school classmate, Dottie, who'd moved there a few years ago for a high-tech job.

Not a cowboy in sight, she reported. Plenty of bars, too, where someone like Lucy could drown in the tips from the techie high rollers. Lucy would go from there and choose what to do with the rest of her life. She was good at so many things it was hard to pick one. She wanted to get married eventually and have kids, too, but she wasn't going to meet anyone but a cowboy in Stone Ridge. Facts were, she'd known many of the men here her entire life. Chased by many, she'd dated quite a few. None of them were the right man.

Time to move on.

The decibel noise level shifted when a group of cowboys entered to a chorus of greetings. In the middle of that group, towering above everyone else, was the man who headlined the reason Lucy wanted to leave town.

Beau Stephens.

It was never easy to see him, but particularly tonight, his golden hair curling slightly at the ends. He needed a haircut again. The strays spilled out of his hat, which he kept readjusting. Beau never cared much what he looked like and his was an effortless kind of handsome, like it had been tied up in knots in his DNA and would never leave him. This afternoon he had beard stubble and scruff. With Beau, you knew the scruffy look wasn't intentional. Throw in the smolder, which he wielded like a lasso, and the women fell at his feet. She'd been on the other end of his smoldering once.

Only *once* and it was still a sharp memory.

She flashed back to the last time she'd given her best friend Sadie's big brother a haircut. It had been in her kitchen nearly three years ago, because the next day was Sadie's wedding to Lincoln. Beau had forgotten to get a haircut. *Again.* It was either run out an hour to Kerrville and try to get a last-minute appointment or let Lucy do it. He chose Lucy naturally, as he'd done over the years when in a pinch. Haircuts were one of her many random skills, which came in handy with her friends, besides assuming bartender duties at a party. No matter what happened among their friends, someone would almost always say: I bet Lucy knows how to do that, and if not, she'll figure it out. Ask Lucy. She was the Jane of many trades, master of none.

She'd had Beau straddling a chair, a towel draped around him to catch the errant hairs. With him, there was an intimacy surrounding cutting his hair, the air between them crackling with energy. Her, throbbing with stupid longing. She could bop him in the head to make him turn his head the way she wanted him to, like Sadie might have done. But Lucy grabbed his chin and forced him to look at her. Those deep hazel-green eyes met hers, a hint of mischief in them.

"Stop movin' or I'll get this wrong," she'd said when he'd squirmed again. "Do you want me to cut your hair crooked? It's like you're allergic to *scissors*."

"Or maybe I'm allergic to a beautiful woman holding something sharp that close to my neck."

By then she was smart enough not to let the "beautiful woman" affect her. Beau tossed the words around far too easily. He loved women, maybe a little *too* much. Words like *darlin'*, *beautiful*, and *sweetheart* were throwaway words to him.

"Paranoid? What have you done now? Have you got some jealous woman ready to key your truck again?"

Beau was notorious for disappointing women, and he didn't restrict himself to the few eligible ones in town. With construction work that occasionally took him out of Stone Ridge, word was Beau dated…a lot. More than Lucy preferred to think about.

"There goes Beau Stephens," Beulah Hayes was fond of saying. "His poor mama. That boy will *never* settle down. Uh-huh. Bless his heart."

Beulah was almost always right, and Lucy was screwed six ways to Sunday. She didn't have a thing for *cowboys*.

Just Beau.

She pulled drafts for the crop of cowboys gathered around the bar, except for some of the ranch hands who wanted to try a bottled IPA.

"If any one of you ever wants a *real* drink, you just let me know." She crossed her arms.

Beau straddled a stool and slapped the bar. "I'm going to make your day. Give me a cocktail."

"Care you to be specific? You name it, I can make it."

Lenny, their resident old-timer, joined them, squeezing

between Beau and Jeremy. "This little lady can make anything you ask. I ordered a mojito last week because I saw it on that spy show I watch. I thought, why not? YOLO. She even put a little umbrella in it. It was like having a sweet soda with a punch."

"That's a good way to describe a cocktail." Lucy gave him a smile. "Mine have a *heck* of a punch. More like a wallop."

"I've been walloped a time or two and you should know." There was Beau's easy smile. "How about Sex on the Beach?"

Lenny clapped Beau's shoulder. "Son, now that ain't no way to talk to a lady."

Lucy snorted and bent to reach the Peach Schnapps. "That's fine. It's a cocktail."

"What will you kids think of next?" Lenny strolled off, laughing hard enough to hack up a lung.

Beau leaned in closer. "Are you sure you have all the ingredients? I wouldn't want you to skimp on the sex."

"Why, I wouldn't dream of it, Beau Stephens." Lucy batted her eyelashes and put the back of her hand to her forehead like she'd swoon. "How's that for an imitation of all the women who fall for your terrible lines?"

"Not bad, Lorenzo. Not bad."

Beau often called her by her last name. Sometimes he called her by the nickname "Larry." Once she'd asked him why he did that and he'd answered, "because you're such a pal and one of the guys." Lucy never imagined being tall, athletic, and good at a little bit of everything would make her one of the guys but there it was.

"Good thing I'm making you this drink tonight. You never know, it might be your last chance at a Lucy Lorenzo cocktail."

"Why? Are you quitting this job?"

Lucy set the vodka bottle down. "Are you *kidding* me? Did you already forget? I'm moving! Remember?"

"You were serious about that?"

"Yes! I told you at your nephew's birthday party. Don't you remember? Sadie's throwing me a big going-away party next month. You already said you'd come!"

He scratched his temple. "Of course, I will. Well, where you moving to?"

"Dottie's going to let me stay with her in Seattle until I get settled."

"I don't think that's such a good idea." He wrinkled his brow. "It rains there all the time and you hate the rain."

"I'll get used to it." She added vodka, then the ice and shook all the ingredients together.

"Well, if you insist, I'll help you move."

"No need, I'm fine. I've rented a U-Haul."

"That's a waste of money when I can do it."

"In all your spare time? You're going to drive me all the way to Washington? I don't think so." She poured, then set the chilled glass in front of Beau. "Try this. You're going to love it."

"It's sex on the beach. How bad can it be?" He grinned, took a sip, and fought against a grimace.

She'd known him long enough to tell he wanted to gag. "Too sweet for you?"

"No, no." He cleared his throat. "I…kind of like it."

Lucy smirked, opened a bottle of his favorite IPA, and set it down.

"On the house. Hey, at least you tried."

"Thanks, Larry. You're a pal."

Yeah, and that was the problem.

Chapter 2

Beau's night was ruined.

It didn't matter that Sex on the Beach didn't live up to its name. Way too sweet and it could never be Lucy's fault. She knew how to make a drink. The cocktail wasn't the real problem.

Just when the day couldn't get much worse, now Lucy was leaving. It was yet another blow.

Lucy Lorenzo, the best woman he'd ever known. She could cut hair, bartend, waitress, bake pies, change the oil in a truck, go fishing with him and scale them, too. She could hunt, even if she didn't anymore on principle. Lucy, whom he'd known since he was an eight-year-old pulling on a girl's pigtails. She'd been his and Sadie's friend since elementary school when they all rode the bus together into Kerrville before they had a school in Stone Ridge.

She was leaving, and he didn't know how to keep her. What was he supposed to say: it won't be the same here without you? That wouldn't work. She wanted to live in a city for a change and if that's what she wanted, she would get it. He'd *give* her the big city and large life if he could.

Anything she wanted. He wasn't selfish, just hated the idea of not being able to see her every day.

Now he was to go to a party next month to celebrate her leaving. He liked to think he could be a good actor when he needed to be, but he didn't have the chops to act happy when Lucy was *leaving*.

For that reason alone, he made excuses and slid away from the bar. He played a round of pool with the fellas, tried to pay attention to the football game, and chatted with a new woman in town, Eloisa. Lulu for short. She was surrounded by no fewer than five cowboys vying for her attention. Beau wasn't up to the challenge tonight and a couple of hours in, he made his excuses. He'd been here long enough and had to get home to check on his animals.

As he left, Lucy was laughing at something Jeremy said. A spike of a strange emotion flared through him. Was this what some people called *jealousy*? Beau didn't have a jealous molecule in his body. And he was used to seeing men surrounding her. When she wasn't behind the bar, the cowboys were on her like flies on a horse. She was tall and beautiful with big brown-amber eyes and long dark hair she wore in a high ponytail. For a while, she and Levi Cooper had dated on and off again. They seemed well suited for each other because he was the horse whisperer around here and among all her many skills, Lucy had an exceptional seat. Beulah and her gang practically had them married off but for some reason they broke it off a few months ago. He'd always been curious what happened there, but Lucy would never tell him a thing. She'd simply said "it didn't work out" or "we're not right for each other" or "we're better off as friends" but never the actual reason why.

Before Levi, she'd dated quite a few men, but none

seemed to stick. Then sometime last year she'd announced she was sick of cowboys.

"I want a man to look at me like a cowboy looks at his horse. Or his *truck*. Is that too much to ask?" Lucy had tossed her hands in the air. "All we have around here are cowboys. I don't want one."

Not *him*, in other words. They would have been impossible anyway because Beau didn't do well with expectations. And disappointing Lucy would have killed him. Now he'd never have the chance, which was just as well.

The January night was much colder when he left, and he drove home with the heater on for the first time in months. Wonder what would happen if, before Lucy left, he hauled her to him and kissed her. Shocking, he'd bet. It would sure give her something to *think* about all the way in Seattle. But she'd either slap him silly or rest the back of her warm hand against his cheek the way she did when she gave him a haircut. But instead of "be still" she'd say: "Oh Beau, have you been pining away for me all this time?"

Not *all* of it, he'd protest. Just mostly the last few years, since the first time she'd given him a haircut, when he was one of her willing guinea pigs. All she'd done was touch him and shrill alarm bells went off in his head. A parade with symbols crashing. Firecrackers. A woman singing the "Star-Spangled Banner." He'd thought he might be either having a seizure or dying. It had scared the stink off him. He'd left the next day for a long job out of town and by the time he came back two weeks later Lucy was dating someone new.

He threw off his hat and shoved a hand through his unruly mop. He needed a haircut, but *she* hadn't noticed. Why would she care when he was just a regular old plain cowboy, not some high-tech mogul from the rainy state.

Driving up the dirt road to his property, Beau pulled

over near the barn and went straight to his evening chores. He checked on the chickens, gathered fresh eggs, then fed the goats. He'd built the barn and horse stalls but no horses yet. He wanted to be ready for them. Among so many other things, horses were expensive. Their upkeep, food, and maintenance. He'd done what he could afford. The rest would have to wait a short while. He almost had enough saved for the next big horse auction.

Beau would never live anywhere but Hill Country and didn't understand why anyone would leave. The smells of freshly cut grass, even the wind filled his lungs with the best oxygen in Texas. It was quiet out here, the only sounds being the clucks of his chickens and the occasional howl of a coyote in the distance.

Inside, he checked his messages, discovering a customer had texted him about a meeting Tuesday so they could go over a few things. Beau had a renovation going on, so he'd have to massage his schedule and make that work. He'd phone their office manager in the morning. She had a handle on all of the things, spun magic, and could nearly turn water into wine. If she couldn't figure out a way for him to be in two places at once, it couldn't be done.

The microwave dinged, announcing his dinner was ready. Frozen peas and meatloaf. What he wouldn't give for some home cooking but for that he'd have to go to his mother's or have an accident. If he got injured, the ladies from the Society of Reasonable, Respectable, Orderly Women (SORROW) would bring him casseroles for weeks. That was one of the many ways they managed this town, including coming together for wedding showers and quilt making.

He ate alone on the couch, watching the ten o'clock news. Midway through he switched to something more cheerful, a horror movie. Every once in a while, Beau pictured a totally different kind of life. A wife next to him, a couple of kids snuggled on either side of them. When they fell asleep watching TV, he'd carry each child to bed the way his father used to do with him and Sadie.

But most nights, he comforted himself with the knowledge he was a free man who could do whatever he liked without answering to anyone. His bed was his own without having to share it with a cover-hogging, feet-like-ice woman. Some nights he ate cereal for dinner followed by a bowl of ice cream, and no one questioned his dietary habits. While the dream of a family with the right woman was attractive, he hadn't met her yet. Maybe he never would.

From what he'd seen, and the way he looked at it, a family with the wrong woman was worse than no family at all.

THE POUNDING WOKE HIM.

Beau had fallen asleep and slept all night on the couch. No wonder it felt like someone had dropped a two-by-four on his neck. He sat up, rubbed, and groaned. Someone was knocking on his front door, and they didn't seem to be going away. It might be someone with news about the coyote who'd been roaming. Around here, they tended to look out for each other and warn others.

"Hang on," Beau muttered, grabbing a hat to shove it on his bed hair. "I'm coming."

A glance at the wall clock told him it was early for a visitor. There had to be something wrong. Maybe the coyote who'd killed his neighbor's chickens last week was back. The thought had him sprinting toward the front door, eyeing the rifle he kept nearby. He swung the door open to a blast from his past.

A woman with whom he'd had one crazy night in San Antonio over a year ago and never seen again.

"*Rachel?* What are *you* doing here?"

"You weren't that tough to find."

"I wasn't trying to hide." He stared from her to the infant car seat she toted in her right hand. "You had a baby?"

"*Your* baby."

"*What?*" The words made him stumble back a step.

He'd been ready to deal with news of a coyote doing his damage, yet somehow this was even worse. A jolt of awareness coursed through him like he'd slammed five cups of coffee. He was wide awake.

"Don't act so surprised."

"But we—"

She shrugged. "I guess the condom was expired."

And there it was. They'd used *her* condom. The thought had haunted him for a year.

The memory of that day, when she'd pulled him from the job and walked him to her on-site office wanting to discuss a permit issue. Rachel was the property manager at the complex where Stephens Construction bid and won. He'd worked with her for several weeks, appreciating her professionalism and attention to detail. Beau didn't think there could be a permit issue and he got ready to argue the point. He was thorough about his permits, the way his father had taught him. But she'd walked him into her office and locked the door.

Afterward Beau felt embarrassed and humiliated at his lack of self-control and alarming unprofessionalism. It didn't matter that she'd started it, he'd finished it. It was wrong even if there were two consenting adults involved. He'd walked away from the ordeal feeling the lowest he ever had. From that point forward, although he doubted anyone would believe him, he'd pretty much been a monk. A few dates, a few heavy make-out sessions but nothing more.

"Are you s-sure the baby is mine?" He stammered.

"We can have all the tests if you're going to put me through that."

Beau waved her and the baby inside. "Do you, um, want something to drink? Coffee?"

"I'm not staying long." She set the car seat and bag down.

Didn't she mean "*we* are not staying long"? "Okay. L-look, if this is my child—"

"Oh, it is." She crossed her arms. "I'm sure."

"I'll of course take care of you both."

A bead of sweat rolled down his jawline and he wiped it away. He thought of what his parents would say when they heard the news. Hell, the whole town. They would all be disappointed in him. Now he'd disappoint everyone collectively instead of just one at a time. He was getting better at it. Last night he'd been dreaming of having a family, someday, but it hadn't looked anything like *this*.

The woman he pictured certainly hadn't been Rachel. He'd worked hard to forget her and the mistake they'd made.

"Why did you take so long to contact me? How old is he?"

"*She* is six months old. Her name is Charlotte. Charlotte Rae Stephens."

She had his name. His *daughter* had his name. There was only one thing left to do to make his parents proud and possibly salvage this ugliness. It wasn't the baby's fault. Though Beau's stomach recoiled he had to do the right thing after the wrong thing.

He had to fix this. His world had just caved in on him.

"Then I guess we should get married."

Rachel laughed so hard the baby startled and so did Beau.

"You're so old-fashioned. You cowboys are all alike. But no, *thanks*. I'm not getting married to you or anyone else."

The relief that swept through shamed him. "Then I don't understand why you're here. Did you want me to meet her? We could have coordinated this better."

He nearly snorted at his use of the word "coordinated." Yes, he *should* have coordinated this better. Should have used his own condom. Should have pulled up his pants and walked out, exercising a little something called restraint.

She quirked a brow. "I'm here because now it's *your* turn."

"M-my turn?" *That* sounded ominous.

"I did the tough part. The first few weeks were a killer, let me tell you. And I'm not even talkin' about the approximately eighteen *months* I was pregnant."

"Isn't it nine—"

"It felt like eighteen, okay?"

"I'm sorry." He held up his palms.

He really was sorry, even if it had nothing to do with how long a pregnancy took. Facts were, he didn't feel comfortable talking like this in front of the baby. She'd been sitting in her car seat this entire time, kicking her little feet.

She waved a hand dismissively. "Don't worry. You can make it up to me. I'm going on vacation, and you can take care of our daughter."

All the blood rushed out of his head. *"Excuse me?"*

"I brought everything you'll need. Help me get the

portable crib out of the car." She nudged her chin toward the front door and started walking.

"You can't be serious."

Beau hadn't worked up a good mad in a while. The last time had been last year when that crazy stalker after Colton's wife, Jennifer, put a bullet hole in one of his new cabins. As a rule, and the way he'd been raised, he never raised his voice to women. Never said a curse word in their presence, but he was about to let loose with a volley of them.

"You can't *do* this. The baby doesn't even know me—"

"Her name is *Charlotte*." Rachel popped the trunk of her car and reached inside.

"Here, let me."

Never let it be said he wasn't a gentleman but after taking this contraption out, he intended to put it right back in, too. Carrying it, he rushed back inside the house, afraid of what might happen to little Charlotte, left unattended. Did she know how to crawl yet? Could she get herself out of that seat?

"You're leaving her with a stranger. *Charlotte* doesn't know me."

"What better way for you to get to know your own child? Think of it as baby boot camp. You two have already been kept apart for too long. I'm sorry I didn't tell you sooner, but I tried to work it out with my ex. When I got pregnant, well, I figured the baby might be his."

"What makes you think—"

"He took a paternity test. It was wishful thinking on my part. I made him jealous alright, but Charlotte wasn't supposed to be part of the deal. Anyway, can you honestly look at her and not *know* she's yours?" Rachel hooked her thumb toward the baby.

Beau glanced down at her, rosy alabaster skin, and

Cupid's bow mouth. So pure and innocent his chest constricted. She *did* look like him, damn it. More specifically, she looked like his sister, Sadie. Wavy blond hair and hazel-green eyes.

Then Charlotte made a squeaky sound, like she'd noticed two giants had lowered their heads to look her over and she wanted to say "hi."

"What's wrong? Why'd she make that sound?"

"Oh, that's a happy sound!" Rachel crouched near the car seat and unbuckled the baby. "You're lucky. She's a good baby, the first few months of colic are behind her. Charlotte, meet your daddy."

She stared at Beau with wide eyes, like she actually understood the words. But she couldn't. She was too small to realize her daddy didn't even know about her until ten minutes ago.

I'm sorry, little one. I wasn't there for you and I'm sorry.

"Okay, I'm off. I've left you my phone number in case of any dire emergency and I do mean *emergency*. Don't you dare call me if she cries a little. That's what babies do. I left you a list of what her days look like, what she likes and doesn't like. All her formula, diapers, and a pacifier. You really shouldn't need anything." She turned to leave.

"Wait. You can't just…you can't *leave* me here."

"I can't just leave her with her father? You'll figure this out, Beau, the same way I did. And you'll probably have more help."

"When will you be back?"

"In a week. It will go by in a flash."

When she walked out the door, Beau resisted the urge to lasso her. But he had a baby in his arms, and no rope, which severely limited him. Also, he appeared to be short on brain power. Somewhere he had an argument as to why she shouldn't do this, but nothing was coming to him.

"I don't know anything about babies...this is a mistake...let's talk about this..."

He tried to get her to see reason and followed her out. Watched her open the car door.

"You'll figure it out. I had to figure it out and you will, too. It's not just something women can do. Men are perfectly capable. Don't worry, I'll be back. I'm not abandoning her and don't you dare think I am."

He almost told her that he had to work, but a lot of women had to work and take care of their babies. Rachel probably had. Before getting in the car, she turned and took a few steps back to them. Beau tried to hand the baby back to her and for a few minutes they tussled, the baby between them, as he tried to move her into Rachel's arms, and she moved the baby back into his. Rachel then gave her a kiss, called her a sweet baby, and released her.

Beau had the choice to either drop or hold her.

He was not going to start off parenthood by dropping his baby.

"You can't do this," he kept saying, as she continued to do it. She waved one last time and drove off.

Beau cursed and kicked the ground, then realized what he'd done.

"Oh, shitfire, I mean...I'm sorry I cursed, baby girl. Jesus. What am I going to do now?"

Charlotte, none the wiser that she'd been practically abandoned, made a gurgling sound and reached for Beau's hat. Dodging her tiny fingers, he carried her into the house, picked up the landline, and dialed Sadie. His sister would know what to do. She would also help him figure out a gentle way to tell their parents.

Maybe, if he turned up the dial on his charm, Sadie would even watch Charlotte for him while Rachel was gone. She already had Sammy, what was one more kid? By now she was an expert.

Later on, he'd figure out what to do about the fact he was now apparently a father.

It was probably not too early to start a college fund. He swallowed. There went his horse. The voice mail went on, Sadie's bright voice telling him she, Linc, or Sammy couldn't get to the phone, so he left a coded message.

"Hey. Can you come over? I have a *big* little problem."

Chapter 3

Sadie Carver held the hand of her husband, Lincoln, as they stared at the monitor showing the ultrasound picture of their baby. The last few days had been terrifying ones, Sadie spotting at thirty-five weeks with way too many Braxton-Hicks contractions for comfort. This was false labor, the doctor said, but it felt a lot like the real thing, which she'd already experienced once. She hadn't had these types of contractions with Sammy, but Trixie, the midwife, and Dr. Judson Grant said every pregnancy was unique.

And, of course, this one might be a girl. She certainly hoped and prayed because she did not want to go through this a *third* time. She thought she was large with Sammy, but she was even bigger now. Embarrassingly so. She couldn't even see her feet and kept thinking Lincoln was going to look and think of her differently. But just like first time, he never did.

She'd certainly fallen for an exceptional cowboy.

Trixie, the midwife at the local Women's Center, rolled the wand over Sadie's huge belly. "The baby looks fine."

Lincoln let out a breath and lowered his head to kiss Sadie's temple. "Told ya."

"But—" Trixie said.

Sadie squeezed Linc's hand. "But? But *what*?"

"Sadie," Trixie said with the calm that made her so accomplished a medical professional. "It's *you* I'm worried about. As I said before, your blood pressure is too high. That can happen sometimes."

"It didn't happen with Sammy!"

"Every pregnancy is—"

"Different." Sadie was dangerously close to tears, and she glanced at Lincoln for strength, as she always did.

But he looked pale, his brow furrowed as whenever there was a problem on the ranch. Last week, a coyote prowling around. The week before, his horse, Lucky, had colic and nearly died. It was always something on a ranch.

"But I thought you said the Braxton-Hicks were nothing to worry about," Lincoln said.

Trixie used a warm cloth to remove the goop on Sadie's belly. "They aren't. I'm *far* more worried about Sadie's high blood pressure."

"My father has high blood pressure, and he takes pills," Lincoln said.

"This is pregnancy-induced high blood pressure and the danger would be preeclampsia which can, in addition to delivering a baby prematurely, be risky for the mother." She waved her hand dismissively. "But that won't happen. You know me, I prefer as little medical intervention as possible in the natural process of childbirth. That's not to say Dr. Grant can't prescribe medication to stop labor if it gets to that point. You're in the best place to have all your medical needs addressed right here."

"Well, what can we do to stop it before I need meds?" Sadie said.

"Bed rest is what we recommend first," Trixie said. "I know you have a toddler, which makes this challenging, but I'd like you to stay off your feet for the next week and we'll check again next week. Let's see if we can get that blood pressure under control naturally."

"Believe me, her feet won't touch the floor."

When they got home after picking Sammy up from her mother's house, Lincoln showed her he wasn't kidding. He carried her inside and *Sammy* walked.

"What wrong with Mama?" Sammy said.

"Nothing, sugar. Daddy is just reliving the 1950s," Sadie said, tipping his hat. "Or that awful movie my grandmother loved, *Love Story*. We're eternal newlyweds."

"Off your feet, you heard Trixie." Lincoln deposited her on the couch. "Don't worry, Sammy. We're going to do something fun for a while. It's our turn to take care of Mama the way she always takes care of us."

"Yay!" Sammy raised his hands above his head. "My tuwn."

"Linc, I don't think—"

Lincoln held up a finger. "We're doing this."

This wasn't going to last, but she'd let him feel like he was helping. "Supper's in the crockpot."

"Okay, Sammy!" He crouched to fist bump with their son. "Let's go get us supper."

Sadie sighed and reached for the handset to check for any messages. There was one from Eve asking about the baby shower, one from Lucy confirming plans they'd made to shop for stuff she might need in Seattle, and one from Beau. He sounded mysterious and so she called him back first.

Big little problem?

"Is this a riddle?" she asked when Beau picked up the

phone. "How can you have a big little problem? Which one is it, big or little?"

"Both."

"Alright, I give. What's wrong?"

As Sadie listened, she went from shock to outrage to joy, going back to shock, joy, and outrage and landing there.

What kind of woman left her baby? Beau sure could pick them.

"Oh, lord. Where did she *go?*"

"I don't know. In all the confusion, I forgot to ask," he said. "On vacation?"

"Vacation. Someone forgot to tell her mothers don't *get* vacation time. This is incredible."

"I know. It happened again."

"But this is different."

They were both quiet for a long moment.

Sadie's mind flashed back to another abandoned baby, left at the old Trinity church in Stone Ridge. But that was decades ago before fire stations had safe havens for babies, no questions asked. The baby could have died but survived due to the intentions of all the good folks in Stone Ridge. It was a long time ago, but every year on the Fourth of July they all celebrated the town's miracle baby on the birthday they'd chosen for her.

Sadie heard the sound of a baby fussing in the background. Beau said the mother had left everything Beau might need but *he* was technically a virtual stranger. What she'd done sounded…illegal. And even if it wasn't illegal, it was unethical and almost certainly abandonment.

"I can't believe this happened now. What timing. Just when I can't help you."

"Why can't you help me?"

"I'm supposed to stay off my feet as of today. I have

high blood pressure and Lincoln isn't going to let me get up for a while. Don't worry, he'll get over it in a few days and maybe I can help you then."

"You have to stay off your feet?"

"Safety first. Nothing's wrong with the baby, but the high blood pressure can be dangerous for both of us."

She didn't want anyone to worry about her, but she'd read a lot of baby books when she had Sammy. In the old days preeclampsia was the number one cause of maternal death. But it wouldn't happen to her. They had medical interventions now. She'd get her blood pressure under control with careful monitoring, although this situation wasn't helping.

"Damn. Can you call Mom and Dad for me and explain the situation? Use your most gentle teacher voice to talk Mom off the ledge. Then send her my way."

Sadie snorted. "I see. You want me to do the heavy lifting."

"No, the heavy work will be watching Charlotte."

"I'd rather babysit a sweet baby any day than lie here on the couch like a useless lump."

"Mom and Dad are going to freak out. I asked, well, suggested, but Rachel won't marry me."

"I guess not, since she left for vacation."

"Hey, I tried to do the right thing."

"You should have done the right *thing* over a year ago."

"Tell me about it."

Poor Beau. She'd never heard her happy-go-lucky extroverted brother sound worse. He'd never met a woman he didn't like, but this sure might cure him.

"Don't worry. We're going to help you. This is Stone Ridge, after all. We all pull together in a crisis, don't we? You've always been there to haul cattle stuck in mud, fix a fence, or lasso a runaway horse. Now it's your turn."

She hung up with Beau and dialed Beulah Hayes. Sadie had never started the phone tree because someone else always did before she could. It was almost always over the need for a few good men of which they had plenty. Now, it was an honor to do this small thing for her brother and make the type of call last made over thirty years ago.

"Hello, Beulah, my brother needs help. Alert the women."

Chapter 4

Lucy taped another box shut, used her black marker, and labeled it "summer clothes," then added it to the pile of boxes in her small living room. The boxes made this official. This was *happening*. She was leaving her hometown at last when she'd never ventured farther than San Antonio. Now she would find out who she was without the safe cushion of her family and small town. There was no doubt she'd needed this town and in a very real way the people here had saved her. But sometimes a girl had to leave the place that gave her comfort to find herself.

Lucy loved her parents, but they only saw her as an extension of themselves. They were far too protective and suffocating. She'd always been independent and fighting them since she was sixteen, explaining she had her own mind, and would make her own choices. When she'd moved out at age twenty to live with a friend, only two miles from them, they'd professed broken hearts and called her fifty times a day. It was tough being an only child and the worst part of it was that no one else understood. All of her friends were from huge families and thought Lucy was the lucky one.

It would be tough to start over, but she'd become too complacent here. Besides, maybe it was silly, but when she left, certain *people* might miss her.

She hoped.

The phone buzzed and she picked it up when she saw the caller ID for Sadie.

"Hey there, about time you called me back."

"I've been busy."

"Are we still going shopping next week? I've started to pack."

"I don't know anymore. So much happened today. I have terrible news."

"What's wrong now?"

She'd heard about the coyote last week, sniffing around the cattle to the point where one night Lincoln laid awake outside all night with a rifle.

"It's Beau. You won't believe this! Or maybe you will. He just learned today he's a *father*. The woman just showed up with the baby and dropped her off, can you believe it? Poor thing."

Lucy sat down with a thud. This was it. Any dreams she'd had of Beau in the possible future were gone.

"When are they gettin' married?"

"No, they're not getting *married*! Keep up. She just left! Left the baby with him, said it was his turn now, and too bad if he didn't like it. Poor Beau has no idea what to do with a little baby girl."

A girl. Beau had a daughter. The ladies of SORROW would probably erect a statue in his honor. The news was shocking, but at least Lucy wouldn't have to attend a shotgun wedding. At least she wouldn't have to watch Beau *marry* someone. Not that it mattered. She was leaving.

"I see. So, I guess you'll have to help him until the mother gets back," Lucy muttered.

"I can't."

Sadie explained the rest. High blood pressure, off her feet, a ridiculously attentive and overprotective husband to deal with. Lucy should have such problems.

Well, the high blood pressure she could do without.

"Alright, I'll go over and see how I can help him."

Even if the thought of tending to a baby who'd been abandoned freaked her out a little bit.

"Thank you! This is asking a lot of you, and I know that. Now I have to call my mother and explain all this to her. And my blood pressure is already high."

Mrs. Stephens would *not* be pleased. She wanted Beau to settle down and get married, *then* have children. And fair to say, nobody in Stone Ridge wanted *another* abandoned baby. One had been more than enough.

"Have you already started the phone tree?" Lucy said.

"Yes, I called Beulah. She went down memory lane with me for a few minutes."

"I'll just bet she did."

"Well, she was there when it happened."

Lucy would probably get a call anyway in a few minutes but since she was an *L* it usually took a while before they got to her. She hung up and slid the scissors at the seam of a box she'd packed yesterday with her books and important papers. She cut it back open, reached inside, and shuffled things around until she came to the old newspaper edition of the *Stone Ridge Gazette*, almost thirty-two years to the date.

Abandoned Baby found at Trinity Church
By Leonard "Lenny" Gray, roving reporter

On Wednesday at precisely seven a.m. an infant girl was found in a Moses basket. She'd been left unattended. The child is approximately two to three months old and otherwise appears to be in good health. For now, she's staying at the home of Marge and Calvin Henderson, who are foster parents registered with the county court system. We are still trying to locate the mother or gain any more information about the child.

Anyone with information should contact the local authorities. The Ladies of **SORROW** are holding a fundraiser, date TBA.

The only information known about the child thus far is that her name is Lucy.

WHEN LUCY ARRIVED at Beau's ranch only thirty minutes later, there were already three vehicles crowding the long driveway. She'd rushed over as if Beau actually needed her, but she wasn't at all surprised to find Beulah and her gang had already beat her there.

This could be awkward, the town's first and only abandoned baby meeting the latest.

Maybe the ladies wanted her here, the old giving way to the new. She had hoped this would never happen again. It wasn't the *same*, of course. Lucy's mother never came back for her, and had never been located, where presumably this mother would return. And she'd had the presence of mind to leave her with her father, and not in a basket in front of an empty church building.

Beau was a *father*.

It was going to take some time to get used to the idea.

Maybe she could be of some help here, too. She should remind some people that this baby wouldn't *owe* them anything no matter what happened. They should never make her feel obligated because they'd rescued her from a difficult situation. This was all temporary, anyway. The baby's mother would be back for her and was probably only trying to teach Beau a lesson.

Lucy cradled the plate of covered brownies she'd brought over. It was unthinkable to come to these gatherings without bringing food and the brownies were all she had left in the house. She'd baked them two nights ago when she'd needed a little cheering up after packing yet another box. Lucy didn't usually have to cook for herself since her mother, Esperanza, still brought over full dinners for her. She'd tried to get her to stop, claiming her independence, but of course she'd looked so dejected that Lucy couldn't argue.

The door was open and from inside Lucy could hear all the clucking from the women, the praises of the beautiful baby, how lucky Beau was to have a healthy baby, didn't he know it?

Lucy walked inside and the moment Beulah saw her all conversation stopped.

"Oh, there she is!" Beulah clapped. "Stone Ridge's very own baby girl. Proof that these terrible things work out sometimes. Come on in, sugar. See what we've got here."

Maybelle took the plate of brownies from her, but not before giving her a huge hug, then went to add it to the table filled with casseroles. Lucy spied covered lasagna, macaroni and cheese, broccoli and chicken bake, and Spanish rice and chicken. Fruit, crackers and cheese, pies, and now brownies. Good grief. Beau would be eating this food for weeks. This was similar to the time Wade Cruz came home after a rodeo injury and the ladies took care of him until he was fully recovered.

"Come see the baby!" Lillian Carver, Lincoln's grandmother, beckoned.

Lucy approached slowly, like she might a snake that could suddenly coil, rise up, and strike. Silly. This was just a *baby*. Helpless. She couldn't hurt Lucy. It was simply her existence that had changed everything. Beau was a father. She had the distinct impression none of their lives would ever be the same again and wondered if that's how everyone had felt when they'd found *her*.

Abandoned by a mother who hadn't wanted her.

The baby was in Delores's arms, surrounded by four women looking at her as though she was the Eighth Wonder of the World.

Oh lord she *was* cute.

"Isn't she precious?" Beulah remarked. "Little Charlotte. She's our own little princess."

She looked like Sadie. Or Beau. Some version of Beau. Maybe Beau if he'd been a girl. Lucy swallowed against the pebble lodged in her throat. She couldn't understand why it was so upsetting that Beau had a baby. Everything would change but this wasn't her problem. She was leaving. Now they might have a new baby to dote on for a while, or maybe longer. She could stop feeling so…obligated to everyone for having saved her years ago. When she left Stone Ridge behind, it could be with zero guilt now.

"She's…so little," Lucy said.

"You were smaller," Lucy's mother said. "A precious baby who needed a home and parents."

Lucy hadn't noticed her truck, so she must have hitched a ride with one of the ladies.

As usual, her mother commanded the room with her presence. Esperanza was petite but that didn't matter. Even her voice demanded attention. High and pitchy. She usually walked into a room and immediately took charge. Wherever she went, things were always better when she left. She'd fluff pillows, straighten blankets, clean dishes, put them away. A born caretaker. Her mother hadn't been built to sit still. Even now, she hovered over the baby, as if *she* was the one in charge.

"She'll know who her birth parents are," Lucy said. "It's not the same."

"No, it's not," Beulah said. "But she still needs our help, poor lamb."

"More like Beau needs your help. This is actually his responsibility."

Maybelle snorted. "Good lord, sugar. You don't think he can handle this baby *on his own*?"

"Why not?" Lucy crossed her arms, directing this to all of them. "It's time y'all understand that Beau is perfectly capable of doing a lot more than you give him credit for."

Esperanza quirked a brow. "I think it's safe to say we're now well aware of what he's capable."

The ladies giggled at the comment and added "you got that right," and "uh-huh."

But Lucy pressed her point. "If we all jump in and rescue him, what's he going to learn?"

"He'll learn, but at whose expense?" her mother said. "Thank God Marge and Cal knew exactly what they were doing when they took you in, and of course I'd been ready for a baby for years."

Yes, and she'd *chosen* Lucy. She'd heard it all over the years. Not discarded or thrown away. Chosen.

"Oh, Lucy came around at just the right time, didn't she?" Maybelle cooed.

Everyone was ignoring the fact that someone had given Lucy up. It wasn't so glorious, from her perspective. Yes, she'd wound up in a better situation, probably, but she'd never actually know.

Somedays, that knowledge was a dark hole that couldn't be filled.

"Sooner or later, he'll have to learn." Lucy glanced around the room. "Where is he? Y'all didn't chase him out? Or did he already run?"

"Sugar, now, we wouldn't let him *run*," Beulah said, shaking her head.

"He went out to feed the goats," Delores said, then held the baby out, presumably so someone else could have a turn.

Maybelle took her up on it. Sooner or later, however, everyone would have to leave, and playtime would be over. Lucy walked back to the kitchen, unwrapped her brownie plate and had one. Chewed and thought about getting herself a glass of milk.

This whole kerfuffle was making her stress eat.

"Lucy. Thank God."

She jumped when Beau pulled her by the elbow and led her away from the kitchen toward the adjacent sliding doors leading to his patio. Funny, he looked no different though everything had changed. But his golden-boy looks, strong forearms, and square jaw still made him almost movie-star handsome.

"Sadie called me," she said.

"I almost did. But the ladies showed up shortly after, and I haven't been able to get a word in since then." He sighed and leaned against the outdoor grill. "Colic, teething, vaccinations. It sounds like a heifer but scarier. A *baby*. She's so little. Helpless. What if I drop her?"

"You won't."

"How do you know that?" He held out his hands. "I'm used to holding much bigger things. My nephew was *never* this small. She must weigh two pounds. Is that normal?"

Lucy almost laughed and bit her lower lip to keep from

smiling. "I'm sure that's not true, Beau, or she'd be very sick."

"She weighs nothing."

"She looks perfectly healthy."

Beau dragged a hand through his overgrown hair. Without his ever-present straw hat, he looked far more… vulnerable, somehow.

She gave herself permission to touch him again, like she did with purpose whenever she gave him a haircut. It was the only reason she'd ever had to touch him. Her excuse now was that she would offer him comfort. The back of her palm slid over his jaw, and she took his chin in her hands like she did when she stilled him.

Beau was a force in perpetual motion. He'd been that way since she'd known him.

"It's going to be okay."

"No, it isn't. I'm…sorry this happened."

"You're not the first man to wind up in this situation. Remember Riggs and Winona?"

"But I don't want this…I'm not ready."

He shook his head and for a moment she saw the face of the little boy he'd been. The boy who'd pushed her on the swing before she could figure out how to do it herself. He'd always been there, and the thought of how this would change them all had her throat narrowing and constricting.

"I don't want to marry her, but I know I should."

Everything in Lucy stilled. "You're *getting married?* I thought—?"

"Beulah thinks I should try asking her again when she comes back. And if I've done a good job with Charlotte, she'll be forced to reconsider." He shook his head and scowled. "I know it's the right thing to do."

"Is that actually the right thing to do? Get married when you don't love each other just because you have a baby together? You can also be partners and co-parent the way the rest of the country does it."

"Hell, Lucy, that sounds like some Hollywood mumbo jumbo. I kind of like it." Beau grinned and winked. "Don't let the ladies catch you saying it."

"They're hopelessly old-fashioned! You know me. I'm a free thinker. Maybe it's because I'm not originally from Stone Ridge even if I have no idea where I'm from." She tugged on a lock of his hair and wrapped it around her finger, surprising herself. "And you need a haircut."

A moment passed between them, a little snippet of memory filled with friendship and tenderness, and a little bit of…something else entirely. Something wild. Forbidden. Unexpected.

She might stay if he'd ask her to, but he never would. Beau didn't make huge proclamations. He usually asked very little of people, an easygoing, carefree kind of cowboy who took care of himself. He'd never asked her for help.

And it was worthy to realize that he still hadn't.

Outside a door slammed, breaking the spell. Beau walked to see the car that had just pulled up behind all the others. And there was his mother, nearly falling out of the driver's side of her truck.

"I'm here! I'm here, baby girl. Grandma is here!" She ran toward the house, losing her footing only once.

"That's good." From behind Beau, she lightly put a hand on his shoulder and squeezed. "She looks happy."

"Yeah." Beau dragged a hand over his face. "Here we go."

Chapter 5

"She looks just like you, Wanda!"

"Look at that pretty blond hair and those hazel-green eyes."

"Oh, isn't she a beauty!"

Beau met his mother at the door, but she'd bypassed him like he was made out of paper, shoved him aside, and rushed like a defensive player on the twenty-yard line. Now, she sat in the place of honor on the couch holding Charlotte, counting fingers and toes as if no one else had thought to do that.

Actually, he hadn't, and it wasn't until Lillian Carver started counting that Beau even realized this was a thing.

"I have a granddaughter, and Stone Ridge has another girl. Leave it to Beau. Thank you, darling boy."

Thank you? Thank you for knocking up a virtual stranger and not even realizing it until his child showed up on his doorstep? Lucy gave him a smirk like she was thinking the same thing. The so-called gentleman rules appeared to have been relaxed when it came to a baby. Any baby, but particularly a girl.

"You're welcome," he said, and Lucy pinched his elbow. "Ow."

"You're going to learn so much." His mother continued to gaze at the baby, holding and kissing her little hand.

"I am?" He cleared his throat. "Well, I only have a few days with her."

"After which you will have a lifetime," his mother said dreamily.

"That's right," said Esperanza. "A lifetime of love."

"Uh, didn't they tell you?" Beau said. "I tried. Rachel won't marry me."

At this, his mother raised her head to meet his gaze. "She won't *marry you*? What's *wrong* with this woman?"

"We don't know," Esperanza said. "I was thinking the same thing. Who would turn *Beau Stephens* down?"

He exchanged a quick look with Lucy. She knew better than most that he'd never been serious enough about a woman to want to get married. He had no idea who might turn him down since he'd never asked. But, he'd guessed, *plenty* would. Women in Stone Ridge had their choice of men, and they married the ones least likely to disappoint them. Starting with Lucy, who had her choice of men, and who'd been eyeing him with a mixture of surprise and disappointment since she'd arrived.

Familiar territory.

"Oh it's just nerves," Maybelle said, waving her hands dismissively. "That's the only reason she said no."

"Exactly," said Delores. "And the poor thing needed a break, don't you know. When she comes back well rested and rejuvenated, she will see our handsome Beau in a brand-new light and be unable to resist his charms."

All the ladies joined his mother and proclaimed his virtues (some of which were outright lies) and all of them demonstrated enthusiasm for this prospective marriage of convenience. After all, it had worked once before when Riggs Henderson married Nashville superstar Winona James. But that was different.

"I don't think Beau should marry her!" Lucy suddenly blurted out.

Dead silence ensued as the ladies shifted their attentions from Charlotte to Lucy. Their lips were pursed, their brows quirked.

She had the floor.

He also wanted to hear what Lucy had to say. Why did it matter to her, anyway? She was leaving him.

Esperanza quirked a brow and crossed her arms. "And why not?"

They continued to stare at Lucy, and, for several empty seconds she didn't say a word. Then the words spilled out from her like from a broken hose.

"There's not just *one* reason! To start with, oh, let me see: she doesn't love him. He doesn't love her. All they have in common is a baby and that's *not enough*. Next, have y'all considered the woman who would keep her baby a secret for over six months, then just drop her off when she needed a break? I don't think she'll make a good wife to Beau." Lucy let out an exasperated breath. "And that's just for starters."

"Well, now." Beulah said, a smile tugging at her lips. "Those are all valid points."

"Thank you," said Lucy. "I think so."

"How do you *know* she doesn't love him?" Esperanza said, hands on hips.

"I don't...I...I..." Lucy stammered.

"She's right," Beau interrupted. "Rachel doesn't love me, and I don't love her."

"That's a shame," Esperanza said. "Then I agree with

Lucy. It's always best if a couple has a solid relationship first before they become parents. It's a good foundation for a family."

"I don't disagree with that," Lillian said. "Why, look at my Lincoln, my Jackson, and my Daisy."

"Yes, well, I have a different spin," Delores said. "Just look at my Riggs and Winona. They didn't love each other in the beginning, but Riggs did the right thing. Now, they love each other so much it's embarrassing."

Everyone then called up examples of couples they'd known over the years who tried, and in some cases succeeded, with a marriage for the sake of a child.

"Great!" Beau announced, sick of hearing about this. "I think we've established sometimes this kind of thing can work."

"And sometimes it just doesn't," Lucy added, arms crossed. "Something to think about."

If Beau didn't know any better, he'd think Lucy had a personal interest in the outcome of this situation. But that wasn't because Lucy had any interest in *him*. They'd been friends for so many years, even as children, that the whole thing was almost unthinkable. Still, they'd had the one small moment just now in the patio. The one that reminded him of the first time she'd cut his hair and touched him, really *touched* him for the first time. He'd wanted to leap out of his chair and kiss her. But he hadn't, and now he'd missed his chance. There was another woman he should put first. The mother of his child.

And the truth was he and Lucy had plenty of small moments over the years but none of them added up to anything big enough to change the trajectory of a friendship that had lasted over two decades.

It made sense that she wouldn't want him now because he had an obligation to someone else.

For the rest of the afternoon, Beau was instructed on how to change a diaper, and how to mix, then properly warm up a bottle of formula for Charlotte. Delores, who'd had the most recent experience with Riggs's little girl, Mary, showed him how to work all those snaps on the sleepers she wore. He began to get worried, however, because though naturally it was a good idea for him to know all this, it seemed they believed he could manage this on his own.

They were wrong.

Slowly, one by one, all the ladies left, wishing him well. Thank God he still had his mother.

That lasted about ten more minutes.

"Before I leave, I should show you how to give her a bath."

"Leave? You're *leaving*?"

"I have to get home and start dinner." His mother handed him the baby and rolled up her sleeves.

"Let Dad learn how to cook. He should have done that years ago."

"That's hilarious." She moved toward the kitchen sink.

Lucy, who'd been hovering over the plate of brownies, moved aside.

"You can't be serious. Bathe her in the *sink*?"

He'd had dirty dishes in there not long ago. This couldn't be sanitary. For his dishes, or the baby.

She rinsed the sink down. "It's not perfect but it will do temporarily. I see the mother didn't leave a little tub for her."

"Well, she'll be back soon. Maybe she thought I wouldn't need it?"

"But what if she has a bad accident and you need to clean her up?"

The idea of an accident horrified him. Yeah, he

couldn't do this. She was too small. One false move and she'd break. Why were people trusting him like this? They should all know better. Once, when he was twelve, he'd forgotten to feed his dog for a week.

"If she has an accident, shouldn't I take her to the clinic or the hospital?"

Suddenly his mother burst into laughter as if the idea of an accident was funny! Beau exchanged a look with Lucy, who shrugged as if she didn't understand, either.

"What's so *funny*?"

"Not that kind of an accident!" While he held the baby, she started unsnapping the outfit he'd just finished snapping closed a few minutes ago. "Sometimes the diapers can't hold in a particularly *large* bowel movement. It doesn't happen often, but it can go out the sides, down her legs and up her little back. The best way to clean that up quickly is a little bath and the sink will do just fine for that."

He glanced at Lucy, who, she couldn't kid him, was holding back a laugh behind her hand.

"*What* did you just say? Why won't the diaper work? What good are they if they can't hold it in?"

"Don't worry, it's unusual. It probably won't happen, but just in case." She slipped the sleeper off one of Charlotte's arms and then the next while Beau balanced his daughter as if she was made of crystal. "You *should* know how to do this."

"Yeah, Beau," Lucy said. "You should know how. Anyway, you're a cowboy and you've been through far worse than baby poop."

"Good point, Lucy." His mother removed the diaper and sat Charlotte down in the water.

She widened her eyes in surprise but then her hands started splashing in the water. Damn, she already knew how to do that. She was a cute little thing. But he didn't know how to keep her alive, for the love of God. Why couldn't anyone see that?

He had goats and chickens. *That* he could handle.

"Mom, can't you stay here with me for a few days at least?"

"Oh, honey. I'll help you out here and there, of course I will, but you need to do this on your own. It will be good for you. You're a father now."

"Trial by fire," Lucy said, chewing on another brownie.

Beau wished she'd either help him or shut up. He glared at her.

"See? Just a little dip is all she needs, and she's all fresh and clean." His mother turned to him as if he'd forgotten something vital. "Towel?"

Beau rushed to his bathroom and grabbed one of his clean bath towels. When he brought it back his mother took Charlotte out of the sink and wrapped her in it. It was big enough to go around her three times.

She handed the bundled baby to him and frowned. "I don't suppose she thought to leave towels for her, either."

"Mrs. Stephens." Lucy shuffled from one foot to another. "I didn't want to say anything while my mother and the ladies were all here, but shouldn't we...I don't know, shouldn't Beau *call* someone?"

"Like whom?" she said.

"Um." Lucy chewed on her lower lip. "The police?"

The idea surprised Beau. Even he hadn't thought to call the police. This was his responsibility, so he knew how that conversation might go.

Officer, this is my child, apparently, and the mother left her with me! Shouldn't that be against the law?

He could already see the smirk on Taylor, the town's only deputy. He drove all over the county. If he had to come here for such a nothing burger, he'd probably want to give Beau a ticket for disturbing *his* peace.

But Lucy was especially sensitive to the situation. He wasn't sure how this whole thing would affect her, though it wasn't at all the same. He'd been a toddler when Lucy's ordeal happened but over the years, they'd all heard the story plenty of times.

In Lucy's case, the police *had* been called. They'd investigated but never located the mother.

"Oh no, honey. Listen, I know what you must be feeling. Your mind can't help but go back to what happened to you," his mother said. "Leaving a baby like this does seem a little…impulsive."

"A *little*? It's just wrong."

Now she was speaking Beau's language and he had to pipe in with his support. "I agree."

"You both forget that she didn't just deposit her outside in a basket, but instead knocked on the door of her *father's* house"—at this she turned to Beau—"who really should take his turn."

"I would have taken my turn," Beau protested, "had I even known she existed!"

In his arms, Charlotte made a little sound like that of a bird and gave him a drooly smile.

"Oh, look how happy she is in her daddy's arms." His mother clapped her hands. "And on that happy note, I'm going home."

"Seriously?" He followed her as she gathered her purse. "C'mon!"

"Go put a diaper on her right now." She pointed to the baby in his arms. "She's probably already peed twice while we've been talking."

Beau looked down at his baby. She smiled at him again

and something in his chest shifted. Then the door closed, and his mother was gone.

Beau turned to Lucy. "Don't leave me. Don't you freaking dare leave me, Larry!"

Lucy gave him a long look, like she was bored, then took the baby from him. "Give me here."

She expertly took the baby, moved to the couch with her, and reached for the stack of diapers Rachel had left. Lucy proceeded to put a diaper on Charlotte with smooth and easy moves.

"What's this? You've been holding out on me?"

"Look, I'm a bartender, cut hair, and run a rideshare service. I can do a little bit of everything. You don't think I've had my turn at babysitting? It was my first job."

"Why didn't I know that?"

"Guess you were too busy chasing girls." Lucy made a face. "There. All done."

"You're a genius."

"Jane of all trades, master of none." She lifted Charlotte as if to hand her back.

Beau put up his palms. "You're better at this than I am."

"That's not a compliment. It doesn't take much to be better than you." She stuck out her tongue but stood to sway Charlotte in her arms.

He watched as she rocked and swayed, lulling the baby until her eyes closed. "Hey, that's pretty good. Teach me how to do that."

"You need hips." She eyed him. "And a sense of rhythm."

Beau covered his eyes. "This is hopeless. I have a business to run so I can't call in sick or schedule a vacation unless I pay someone to do my job. No parental leave for me. How am I supposed to hire a babysitter with such short notice?"

"These are the kinds of problems that single mothers all over the country are dealing with."

"And they have at least nine months to line up help. I have, what, nine hours?"

"Cry me a river." Lucy cradled the baby to her shoulder, rubbing her back. "Welcome to parenthood."

"You sound like you're on Rachel's side!"

No matter what conflict they'd been through, he and Lucy always took each other's side. The thought she'd go against him now was a betrayal of the highest order.

"No." Lucy shook her head. "I'm *always* on your side."

"It doesn't sound like it."

He plopped down on the couch beside all the diapers and detritus of a baby. "Lucy, I have a meeting tomorrow morning I can't miss. It's a final walk-through for the house I personally designed, and my crew and I built for Mr. Truehart. His dream house. I need you to be on my side."

"I am on your side." She was quiet for several seconds, then sat down beside him, holding a now sleeping Charlotte. "How long have you known her?"

She meant Rachel, of course. It was uncomfortable discussing this with Lucy. Much worse than with Sadie. For some reason, Beau had always wanted to impress Lucy. And this wasn't the way to do it.

The humiliation spiked through him all over again. "I…hardly know her."

"So…just the one time?"

"Yeah."

"Thought it might be something like that." She whistled. "Hoo boy. Some powerful sperm you're packin'. If only breeders bought male sperm like they do bull, you could be rich overnight."

"That's not funny."

"Was I right? You don't love her? Because if there's even some small whisper of a possibility, you should—"

"I don't think I even like her very much." Beau shook his head slowly. "And yes, I know how terrible that sounds."

Silence stayed between them for several long seconds.

"I'll help you. You know I will."

Relief spread through him like butter over a warm flapjack. "It will take time away from your jobs and packing for Seattle."

"Don't worry about all that."

Beau didn't know what it would take to convince Lucy, but he was ready to go down on bended knee for something he truly wanted.

"I'll pay you well. Whatever it takes. Would you do it?"

"Do *what*?" She met his eyes, her own shimmering.

The sight of her sitting and holding his baby threw him, the view from here doing all manner of wicked things to his heart. He could almost feel it pulsing, growing, beating loudly in his ears. She didn't know how many times she'd saved him in the past, when she'd shown him a tenderness he didn't deserve.

When it often felt she was the one person in his life he had never disappointed.

A record he'd never wanted to ruin.

"Save my life and be my nanny."

Chapter 6

"You're an idiot," Lucy muttered as she drove to pick up a passenger.

Before she left, she'd agreed to be back at Beau's in the morning.

He'd given her those puppy-dog eyes, then clinched the deal when he promised her more money than she could make with her rideshare business and bartending combined. Beau knew she'd been saving money for months for her big move. She needed everything she could earn in these last few weeks before leaving for Seattle. And the way she looked at it, she could take the occasional fare *and* watch Charlotte. The problem would be her bartending shifts, but Beau would be home in the evenings anyway.

She really should have said no. *Hell, no.* No to watching Beau's "love" child with another woman. *Are you crazy, Lucy Lorenzo? Why would you do this to yourself?* Sadie would say those very words to her, if she had any indication that Lucy still had feelings for Beau. She thought those feelings were long buried, Beau's many casual affairs having beaten them out of her. The truth, however, was far more complicated.

Beau had never disappointed *her*, or lied to *her*, or promised *her* anything he didn't deliver. The very opposite was true. He'd always been her friend. Always her champion and defender against the men that toyed with her affections. A bright light, an unexpected gift, an undeserved joy.

By the time she arrived at the Shady Grind, her passengers had been waiting for half an hour. First, there was the whole issue with cell service. Fortunately, around here, people were grateful enough to have an option other than Lenny, who only drove a golf cart around town. The app might not work well around here, but landlines did, and Lucy checked her answering machine messages often. The Shady Grind location was where she picked up most of her regulars.

The couple was huddled outside together against the January chill.

"I hope you haven't been waiting long." Lucy pulled over and unclicked the door locks in her old sedan.

However long it had been, it probably wouldn't have seemed so to Colton Henderson and Jennifer, his new bride. Lucy had a special place in her heart for Colton, the youngest Henderson brother. She and all the Henderson brothers had the same wonderful foster parents, but not at the same time. They'd come a bit later, after Lucy had already been adopted by Esperanza and Arturo Lorenzo. The Henderson brothers, Riggs, Sean, and Colton were older when they'd come to Marge and Calvin, and later all three were adopted. Had things gone another way, they'd have been her brothers growing up. Lucy might not remember her time on the Henderson Grange, but she did remember Marge and Cal in the years that followed. They'd always called her "their special girl."

A rumor in town had circulated for a while that Marge and Cal had wanted to adopt Lucy, too, but in the end, Esperanza was much younger and deemed a better fit. It was true, because Cal and Marge were long gone now, though Lucy still wondered what life would have been like growing up with three older brothers. For one thing, she wouldn't have been an only child. But thinking of what might have been served no purpose. She'd bet that right now Beau had thoughts along those same lines. Too late now. He faced the next eighteen years co-parenting with a woman he didn't love.

Colton opened the door and waited for Jennifer to get inside. "Sean and Bonnie Lee wanted to go home early, and we rode here with them."

"That's what I'm here for. I'm just sorry if I'm a bit late. We need a better system."

"Where's the fun in that?" Colton joked.

"There's something special about a town that feels like a blast from the past." Jennifer said, and curled into Colton's arms, reminding Lucy to turn up the dial on the heater.

"I'm kind of looking forward to Seattle and finally using all those apps."

"You're seriously moving?" Colton said, catching her eyes in the mirror.

"Absolutely."

Why didn't anyone believe her? Alright, so it was possible that she'd cried "wolf" one too many times. Sure, Lucy had *tried* to move in the past, but the timing hadn't ever been perfect. Whether her father had knee surgery and her mother needed her help, Sadie was getting married and wanted her to be in the wedding, or Beau asked her if she'd help him do one thing or another, there was always a reason to stay. But she wasn't going to let this latest debacle intervene with her plans. Not this time.

Not everyone left Stone Ridge, of course, but no one had started their life somewhere else. She'd started her life in a place she knew nothing about and had no hope of ever discovering. Every connection to that past was gone.

"We're going to miss you around here," Colton said, cuddling Jennifer close. "Feels like I just got back, and now you're leaving."

"It's not my fault you've been all over the world with the Army while I've been stuck here for years."

"Well, you're too special to let go," Colton said. "Jen, did you know Lucy was a miracle baby?"

Jennifer sat up straighter. "Why didn't anyone tell me?"

Lucy adored Colton, but, in the moment, she resented him bringing up the "miracle" story. Still, she didn't interrupt, as in the quiet of the car, Colton explained how Lucy had been found in a Moses basket outside Trinity Church over thirty years ago. She was considered a miracle, because while no one could be 100 percent certain, it appeared Lucy may have spent the night outside. Alone.

"Lenny found her." Colton finished the story. "He also reported the story in the paper."

"Yep. Good ol' Lenny," Lucy said. "Man of many jobs. He still considers himself my spiritual father."

"That's a great story," Jennifer said. "It's no wonder no one wants you to leave."

"Right. I'm like the town's mascot." Lucy snort laughed. "But that might change soon. I don't suppose y'all have heard yet, but you will by tomorrow morning."

She told them all about Beau's baby, how she'd been summarily dropped off without any warning.

Colton let out a low whistle. "Poor dude."

Lucy pulled over in front of their house on the hill of the Henderson Grange. "Don't feel too bad for him. He's already got me to agree to be the baby's nanny."

"You're such a pal."

No need to tell her. She was always the pal. The buddy. In the past, she'd been hunting and fishing with the Henderson brothers.

"Believe me, he's paying me well."

"Good." Before getting out, Colton reached forward to squeeze her shoulder, and handed her a generous tip, too.

"Lucy, I want to tell your story." Jennifer leaned into the driver's side window. "It would make such an interesting slice of Americana. People need to hear more from small towns like Stone Ridge and how we take care of our own. They've already heard my story. This place saved me, too."

"Oh, I don't know. Really, I'm leaving soon, and I have so much to do…"

"Well, think about it, please. I'm running out of material out here." She glanced over at the handsome Colton, who stood waiting for her, hands stuck in his jacket. "There's only so much I can do with a cowboy who loves to *cook*."

"I wouldn't complain." Colton grabbed her by the waist and got a little handsy. "Unless you want me to declare a strike. *You'll* have to learn how to cook."

Jennifer laughed. "It would be cruel to subject myself to my own cooking."

"Okay, you newlyweds." Lucy glanced in her rearview, ready to back up. "I'll see you next time. Thank you for using my service, and feel free to leave a review but it's not like I have any competition."

"Five stars!" Jennifer held up her splayed hand. "And

please think about it. I love podcasts about ordinary people who survive despite great odds."

"That's me." Lucy saluted, then waved. "I promise I'll think about it."

But she drove away, knowing she wouldn't. Lord knew she'd done enough time shedding the "miracle baby all grown up" label. No need to further reinforce it with a podcast with thousands of listeners all over the country.

Before coming to Stone Ridge, Jennifer had a popular, well-known podcast called "Truth Salad," which she broadcast from where she'd lived in Los Angeles. After she'd acquired an unhinged fan who became her stalker, she had to end it. Now, listeners were told she was coming to them from an "undisclosed location" in Hill Country.

Either way, her new podcast was heard all the way in Seattle, and the last thing Lucy wanted was to start her new life bringing with her a sordid past.

SUN RAYS STREAMED through Beau's curtains, but it was too quiet. *Scary* quiet, like the silence after a hurricane's devastation. Or after a bomb. He peeked into the crib and Charlotte was sound asleep.

Last night before she'd left him, he and Lucy had set up the fold-up crib beside his bed. Then she left, promising upon pain of death to be back in the morning. Around eight o'clock that evening, after he and Charlotte stared at each other for what seemed like hours, he'd changed her diaper like he'd been taught. It didn't go badly but he was used to working with his hands. This was just working with soft material and little tabs. For two seconds, he thought he might be able to do this. *Only one week. Only one week*, his mind replayed like a mantra.

And then *the rest of your life*, the left side of his brain shouted!

He'd laid Charlotte down in her crib and told her it was time to go to sleep. When he shut off the light, she let out such a piercing wail that he, *Beau Stephens*, called his mother.

"I think I hurt her," Beau explained. "You better come over and check."

"What happened?" his mother asked.

Once he explained, she had another laugh at his expense. "She's fine. You might have to rock her to sleep. Just pick her up and sway her back and forth like we were all doing this afternoon."

Beau didn't like that answer. He called Lucy a bit later when Charlotte still wouldn't stop crying.

"I don't know," he explained. "I might have hurt her when I laid her down in the crib."

The truth was he'd laid her down so carefully he almost fell in himself.

"I'm sure you didn't," Lucy said, a thickness in her voice that made it sound like she'd been sleeping.

"How do you know for sure? That's when she started crying. When I put her down."

"Haven't you heard? Babies *cry*. Especially when you stop holding them. That's what they do." With that, she hung up.

He didn't like that answer, either. All night long, Charlotte laid awake, crying. And it was like she could sense the fear in him, the same way animals did. She didn't realize they were biologically related, like a creature would in the wild. They'd smell each other and know they were related. From the same tribe. They'd find comfort in biology. No such luck here.

Beau didn't doubt the poor baby missed her mother.

Her *irresponsible* mother, who'd left her baby with a stranger. After two hours of the weeping, he fished out Rachel's phone number from where she'd left it. She said *emergency*, well, this qualified. He'd call, let her listen to a wailing Charlotte. Maybe she'd be back by tomorrow morning with any luck. He'd done his best. No harm, no foul. The baby just didn't like him and hey guess what, she didn't know him. He wasn't going to take this personally. The child clearly wanted her mother. He was on the verge of wanting *his* mother and he was thirty-four.

But instead of Rachel's voice, he got voice mail.

Hey, I'm busy right now, but leave a message and I'll call you back!

Ding.

"Hey, sorry you're *busy* but Charlotte is crying. Hear her? I'm not sure how you could hear anything else!" He shouted. "I think she misses you. Call me back when you get this message."

But now that *eternity* had passed, the sun was up, and Charlotte was asleep.

Beau leaned over to check that she was still breathing. Then, satisfied, he hopped in the shower and set the coffee to brewing. Lucy would be here soon, and he'd be able to make the appointment he had with John Truehart, the richest man in their county. The home he'd commissioned was Beau's crowning achievement. He'd labored over the design and blueprints, then headed the crew that built it from the ground up. The whole project was some of the best work Stephens Construction had ever done.

Beau's father had built his contracting business from the ground up, with his first jobs in Stone Ridge and a very few in the closest neighboring town of Nothing. The town was named well for a reason, but Stephens Construction had designed and constructed the only building: the church. In Stone Ridge, they'd also built the new Trinity Church, the new school, and dozens of homes in addition to the lakeside cabins. The firm grew quickly, and once Beau joined his father with his architectural degree, they took on more work with a larger crew. Now, Beau was the head contractor and President of Stephens Construction, and he took great pride in their work. By now he'd done a bit of everything in design and construction, but Beau's passion remained the single-family home and building the place where a couple would cook, talk, play, make love, and live their lives. It did something for his soul that almost nothing else did.

He and his father and their crew had also built the Henderson brothers' homes, with Colton's starting construction later this month. Beau had built a spacious home on the Carver ranch for Nashville celebrity Jackson and his wife, Eve. And when the wealthiest man in town, John Truehart, owner of the largest horse ranch in the state, wanted a second home, Beau was more than happy to bid. He won, too, and had spent much of the year on the custom-made home.

All to say, he would not be late for this walk-through and exchange of keys.

He was on his third cup of coffee and buzzing around his house, gathering papers and blueprints, when the doorbell rang.

He threw open the door to find Lucy. She stood, arms crossed, sunglasses covering her eyes. She wore an Astros cap over her long dark hair.

"I see you *survived*." Her voice dripped with sarcasm he did not appreciate.

"Barely. She didn't sleep last night, so neither did I. Not until around three in the morning. She's still sleeping."

Lucy waltzed in past him and went straight to the

kitchen where she grabbed a mug and poured some coffee. "You can take off. Just keep your pager on in case of an emergency and—"

"What *kind* of an emergency?"

Lucy lowered her glasses and peered over the rims. "Any kind. But don't worry, I've got this."

"Yeah. You've got this."

She gave him a double thumbs-up.

His stride suddenly a lot peppier, he did his best to walk, not run, out the door.

Chapter 7

Beau pulled over at the end of the street so he could get the best view. From here, anyone would know this home belonged to a family who had money. With the kind of budget he'd had to play with Beau created the shining diamond Mr. Truehart had ordered. The walkway to the home was paved with beautiful flagstone imported from Italy. The same stone accented the outer walls and the log cabin architecture. The roof was A-framed, the back of the home a wall of windows reaching to the top of the pitched roof. Beau had built around the crops of trees, giving it a woodsy appeal, and the views were incredible. This was his opus. His masterpiece.

He let himself inside with the key, always the first to arrive to these final walk-throughs. Inside he once again admired the open beams, and cathedral ceilings with more floor-to-ceiling windows allowing beams of sunlight to shower through. No need to be concerned with privacy on Mr. Truehart's land where he owned everything for miles. Beau wouldn't have ever designed all those windows for his personal home, but more due to practical purposes. The maintenance had to be a nightmare, but Trueharts didn't have to worry about that sort of thing.

The painters were last, scheduled two days ago, and Beau found a stray plastic piece of wrap they'd missed. On the granite kitchen countertop, he found a lone screwdriver and picked it up, shoving it in his back pocket. There was always something to put away, and he strived for perfection when the owner first feasted his eyes on the finished product. He was no different than an artist, unveiling his painting.

Thirty minutes later, Beau heard the car door slam outside and walked to the window. He wanted to enjoy the moment when the owner feasted his eyes on the home. In many cases, such as the house he'd soon be building for Colton, the owners not only checked in daily but often assisted. But Truehart had been gone for a while, on one of his frequent business trips, and hadn't met with Beau since the time he presented him with the design and blueprints for final approval.

Now, the elderly man slowly walked up the flagstone pathway next to his far younger wife. Beau lost count which wife the man was on now. Fourth? Fifth? Beau didn't judge. All he cared about was the wide smiles he observed on both their faces as they pointed to all the special touches outside, like the outdoor grill built into a wall of stone. Beau didn't discriminate when it came to who would live in the homes he built. When a client had a huge budget to work with, they got the best he had to offer in materials. But no matter who he built a home for, Beau threw in his expertise and all his heart and creativity.

He greeted them both at their door and handed Mr. Truehart the keys.

"Welcome to your new home."

Damn, he loved saying those words.

Truehart shook his hand with surprising strength for an octogenarian. "Thank you, son! Thank you."

"We're so excited to begin our new lives here." Darcy, who had been Miss Texas ten years ago, clung to Truehart. "I want to start having babies right away."

Mr. Truehart turned in a circle in the marbled entryway, the light spilling in through the windows from all angles. "Damn, I don't mind telling you: this was worth every penny."

"Thank you, sir."

"Sweetheart, Beau Stephens is the best architect in the entire state. And he built our dream home. How do you like that?" He threw off his hat, and it sailed until it landed on the gleaming wood floors leading to the living room.

"I'm sure going to have fun decorating." She waltzed into the kitchen, and Truehart followed, Beau staying behind to give the couple their privacy.

He'd learned from his real estate agent friend that couples liked to have their alone time as they pictured living the rest of their lives in their dream house.

"I'll be over here if there are any questions, but everything is just as we talked about last week."

Glancing at the phone he'd set to vibrate he saw a missed call. *Rachel.* At last, she was calling him back, but he never had decent reception out here. He'd have to grab his satellite phone from his truck or drive further into town to talk on his cell. Anxious to talk to her anyway, he walked outside and found an open area away from the crop of trees. He searched for a bar of service.

He had two and that was worth a shot.

Rachel picked up after the first ring. "You called me? Is Charlotte okay?"

"Yeah. Listen, she misses you. It only makes sense she would. You're probably all she knows. I was thinking we need to talk anyway. There are things we need to discuss. Child support." Beau winced. "Visitation. We're wasting valuable time here."

"You.. know…its…wait…and now you…"

"What? You're breaking up. Hang on."

Beau walked further outside, holding his phone up, looking for bars. He was down to one now. One lousy bar. And if he'd heard one-word answers from Rachel, what were the odds she heard anything he said? He hung up, deciding he'd call her later from his satellite phone or downtown at the Shady Grind where he could always depend on regular service.

Mr. Truehart beckoned him from the front door and Beau rushed over, expecting a question or problem.

"How are we doing?" Beau said. "Everything good?"

"Fantastic." Mr. Truehart patted the pocket of his jacket. "Love your work, always have. And expect a little something extra from me this time."

"You didn't have to do that."

"Consider it my gift to you, a bonus. If you'll excuse me, my wife is excited and we're going to bless the rooms if you know what I mean." He cleared his throat and winked. "Got to get started on those babies."

"Yes, sir. Y'all have a good time, or a blessed…um, well…good luck."

"Won't need luck, I took the little blue pill earlier." He shut the door.

Beau drove away from the healthiest and happiest elderly man he'd ever met. Already the father of four sons and one daughter, he apparently wanted more.

The first meeting of the day accomplished, he checked his schedule. To make a few calls from his truck, he pulled over once he reached downtown reception and checked in with his office manager.

His father answered the phone.

"*Dad?* What are you doing in the office?"

"Working, of course. Don't worry about a thing. I'm taking over for a while."

"What? You are?" He'd simply wanted help managing the cabins, but everything else he had fully under control. "But I—"

"Don't worry, your mother explained everything. Congratulations. I'm not thrilled with the way it happened but you're a father now. Your life is forever changed. Welcome to parenthood."

He made it sound so *depressing.*

*Not thrilled…your life…forever changed…*Beau liked his life just fine and hated change.

"Well, as it turns out Lucy agreed to be my nanny. I hired her. So, all's well in that department."

"No, no, no. You need to take this time off and adjust to being a father."

"No, I do not."

"Well, that's what your mother says. Many hands make light work. We're all pitching in here."

"You'll take care of the cabins?"

Beau considered how this would be good for him if his father took the calls from all the women who were unhappy with the mosquitoes and lack of Wi-Fi by the lake. People said his father resembled Sam Elliot, and maybe if they saw him ambling toward them like an old-time gunslinger, they'd think twice about complaining.

"Don't worry about a thing."

"I appreciate it. I haven't had a week off since Sadie's wedding."

"You're overdue."

That didn't mean Beau had to stay home and be a baby daddy. He had Lucy to help, and this meant more time for his personal projects. He might actually finish working on his outdoor deck. Contractors were notoriously bad about working on their own homes. Beau had no wife to nag him, which if you went by all his married contractor friends, was the only way to get it done. Yeah, this would be good. Lucy would take care of Charlotte during the day, and he'd get plenty of his own work done.

The perfect solution.

"EVERYTHING OKAY BACK THERE?" Lucy glanced through the rearview mirror.

She'd just picked up Pamela Ann, who needed a ride to the Vet clinic. Lucy's one request was that she ride in the back with Charlotte. Once upon a time, Lucy and Pamela Ann had been good friends. Then along came her husband, Derek, in high school and she and Lucy parted ways. They weren't enemies. Stone Ridge was far too small a town for two of the few women to be enemies. They just weren't particularly friendly with each other anymore. Pamela Ann tended to speak her mind and that mind was often far too much in other people's business.

"She's fine," said Pamela Ann. "Very interested in the puppy, that's for sure."

Charlotte's little legs were kicking, and that's all Lucy could see. Charlotte was strapped in the rear-facing infant car seat so Lucy couldn't get a good look at her, but she'd been quiet since they started the drive. She liked the car. The baby had mostly been quiet all morning, actually, only fussing once or twice when she was hungry.

"So, the rumors are true," Pamela Ann said. "Beau has a daughter."

It never took news long to get around their town and this was particularly juicy gossip. Juicy enough that Pamela

Ann might have scheduled the ride just to get the latest, but there was no way she could have known Lucy was babysitting her.

Now, of course, *everyone* would.

Lucy shifted in her seat. "It's all true. This is Charlotte."

"And what are *you* doing with her?"

"Beau hired me to be her nanny."

"He…*hired* you?"

"Why? Is that so odd? You know me, I do a little bit of everything to make a living. I get antsy just doing one thing."

"I thought you might have helped out…for free. I mean, you and Beau…you're tight."

Lucy bristled. "Yeah, well, I'm moving to Seattle, remember? I'm saving every penny. Believe me, Beau understands."

Pamela Ann sighed. "Oh, Lucy."

"What?" Lucy sat up straighter and met Pamela Ann's eyes in the rearview mirror.

She was petting the puppy's head, who sat in her lap, panting, looking out the half-rolled-down window. "You're not really leaving, and we both know it. Just…stop."

"Okay, wow. Just because I've said it before and it didn't happen doesn't mean it's not going to this time."

"All I'm saying is it would be a lot cheaper and less trouble to tell him how you feel."

The car didn't screech to a halt, but Lucy's thoughts did. Her hands gripped the steering wheel so tight her knuckles were white.

"How I feel?" She hated where this conversation was headed. "About *what?*"

"My lord, Lucy, you've been in love with Beau Stephens since we were in fifth grade. Give me a break.

The whole town knows it! He's the only one who probably doesn't because he's a typical clueless male."

"Pamela Ann!"

"*What?*"

"Just…just mind your own beeswax!"

"I have for years, but I'm getting tired of this soap opera. Either you have to tell him, or I will!"

"Don't you *dare*!"

Pamela Ann pouted. "You should be begging me to do it."

"What are we, still in fifth grade? Think I need you to pass him a note in class? You let me deal with my own love life or lack of!"

"That's just the point. You have men here that would die to be with you and you're moving to Seattle? What's up with that?"

"There are men there, too, you know, and none of them are cowboys."

"So what? I guarantee you none of them will be Beau. He's right here, and you don't need to move."

"It's too late now even if I wanted to. He's got a baby and will probably marry the mother."

"See what happened? You waited so long it's too late."

"I didn't wait. There was nothing to wait for. Beau and I are just good friends."

"Because you never told him you wanted anything more, did you?" The question was posed as a challenge.

It reminded Lucy of schoolyard taunting. *Did you? Did you? Did you?*

Did not!

"There's nothing to *tell* him."

Crossing the line from friends to lovers with Beau would be like crossing yellow police tape, a clear barricade serving as a warning to reasonable people. You might be curious, you might be dying to cross and see what was behind that barrier, but whatever you found would change you. Whatever you saw couldn't be "unseen." Proceed with *caution.* Better yet, keep out.

"I have a suggestion," Pamela Ann said when Lucy pulled into a space near the Vet clinic.

"And I didn't ask you for one."

"You're getting it anyway, because even though we're not friends anymore I still remember that time we went on a field trip, and you lent me the dollar I needed so I could get a gift in the shop. Tell Beau how you feel before you leave, and if he doesn't respond the way you'd like, *then* go to Seattle. You can start your new life without any regrets." She unbuckled her seat belt. "But just going so that he'll miss you isn't going to work. He won't know that's why you left, and he'll assume you're over there having a good old time meeting new people."

"I didn't…that's not why…" Lucy was speechless because she didn't know Pamela Ann was a mind-reader. She nudged her chin toward the clinic. "You better go. Don't want to make Eve wait."

Pamela Ann opened the car door. "Fine, I've said my piece. Do what you want, you always do."

"What's that supposed to—" Lucy whipped her head around.

But Pamela Ann had already shut the door.

"I don't always do what I want," Lucy muttered, with no one but the baby listening to her now. "I haven't done what *I* want for most of my life."

She'd *wanted* to go East for college, but her parents couldn't afford it, and she couldn't get a scholarship or enough financial aid to make it happen. Besides, being an only child meant her mother was paranoid, worried that Lucy would get abducted from her college campus like the girls she'd heard about on the national news. Instead, she'd wound up going to the community college and living at home. A safer bet.

She'd *wanted* to find out who her biological parents might have been but that was a dead end and Lucy gave up when Lenny discouraged her.

She'd *wanted* to tell Beau that the women he'd dated were all wrong for him, but she'd never said a word.

Lastly, she'd *never* asked to be the town's "miracle baby," but no one cared what she thought.

Chapter 8

Sadie stretched out on the living room couch. She couldn't see her feet, even when she turned to her side. Only sticking her leg out reminded her she still *had* feet. It wasn't like she was using them much. She was about to go out of her mind. Linc fussed over her, carrying her to bed, and back to the couch. The only thing he *didn't* do was carry her to the bathroom and that was because she'd glared at him and threatened they'd never have sex again.

Her heart hurt for Sammy, who probably thought his mother must be really sick to be lying down all the time. He brought her his favorite toy to cuddle, the soft plushy version of Buzz Lightyear, which made Sadie's eyes wet with tears. Yesterday, he'd taken his favorite blanket and tucked it around her. That time, Sadie *had* burst into tears and lied to Sammy, telling him she'd bitten her tongue and it hurt. This routine was not at all what he'd experienced in the first years of his life. Sadie was always a whirlwind of activity, balancing her job as a grade-school teacher with being Sammy's mother. Not only a mother and teacher, but she was also a *ranch wife* and that came with certain responsibilities, too.

She kept some of her routines with her son normalized, like reading to him every night before bed. Only she could do the character's voices to his satisfaction. But Linc was now in charge of the bath-time routine. Sadie lay on her perch and listened to it all happen. All she wanted to do was get up and walk over a few feet to watch him, her little man splashing in the water and making himself a beard with bubble soap. She was missing all of it.

Sadie's mother was over every day to take over while Lincoln was out in the field. She fussed, too, taking Sadie's blood pressure constantly.

"You need to *relax*, Sadie," she said now. "Stop worrying about Sammy, he'll be just fine and won't even remember this time."

"Does anyone ever relax when constantly reminded to *relax*?"

"You're right. Maybe we should play soothing music," her mother said. "Ocean sounds, perhaps?"

"Stop talking about ocean sounds and tell me about the baby!"

"Well, honey, as I said she definitely looks like a Stephens. Beau couldn't deny her if he tried." Mom chuckled. "She's adorable, with soft blond curls and pretty hazel-green eyes. Everyone says she looks just like me."

"I wonder who's watching her."

"Beau. But you know him, he'll probably ask for Lucy's help. Or whatever girl he's currently dating. He better not. I told him I had to help you and Sammy, and he may as well get used to being a father. I'll go over to check in on them, of course. Don't worry. I've set everything else aside to take care of my daughter and grandson."

She picked up and folded one of Sammy's shirts from the basket of laundry.

That was something Sadie didn't mind so much someone else doing for her. But the cooking and the cleaning? Only she knew how to run her household the way she wanted.

"This morning Linc fed Sammy *cereal* for breakfast," Sadie complained. "Fruity O's."

"Why do you buy them if you don't want Sammy to eat it?"

"It's a treat!"

Mom quirked a brow. "Well, does Lincoln know that?"

"No," Sadie muttered.

"It sounds like someone else is getting a crash course in raising a child," Mom chuckled. "It will be good for both of them. You'll see."

"I'm surprised y'all trust Beau to take care of a baby. He has no experience." She still remembered how nervous Linc had been to hold Sammy when he was an infant.

It wasn't until Sammy started crawling that the two really bonded.

"I taught him a lot yesterday. Some of it is instinct, and Beau has good instincts." Mom patted Sadie's leg and rose, taking the laundry basket with her.

"If you say so."

The phone rang, and Sadie picked up the handset she'd kept near her. The caller ID said Beau Stephens, but it was Lucy, whom she hadn't talked to this much in a couple of weeks. She was leaving for Seattle, and like a good friend, Sadie had tried to accept this. But it still hurt to think she'd lose a friend. Every once in a while, she pictured her and Beau getting together but that was a pipe dream. Even less likely to happen now.

"Hey, do I strike you as a person who does what she wants no matter what anyone tells her?" Lucy said.

"Well, hello, you." Sadie chuckled. "And no, you do not strike me as that person. Not even close."

"Thank you, that's what I thought. You know me best."

"Hey, why are you calling me from Beau's place?"

"This is Exhibit A, should I need one. I'm watching Charlotte today."

"Beau isn't?" Sadie sat up straighter and glanced at her mother, who was now over in the kitchen working on supper.

"He had a meeting."

"Of course. He has to work, after all."

"He offered to pay me, and you know how I've been saving every penny for Seattle."

Sadie considered how she could make this situation work for her. "Don't remind me. I'm going to miss you."

"That's the first time you've said that."

"I shouldn't have to say it. You don't think I'd miss a friend I've had since the fifth grade? C'mon! I got my period in the sixth grade and every time I miss it my *life* changes. What do you think?"

"You'll be fine. And I'll be back to visit once you have our latest little one. But…I need to get started on my life." Her voice was soft and gentle.

For such a long time, Lucy had believed her life might be better somewhere else. As a best friend, Sadie tried to understand. So had Eve, who had formed their little girl trio early on. Lucy belonged here with all of them, but her beginnings seemed to matter to her more than they did anyone else. Sadie believed only someone who'd experienced that type of abandonment could relate. Privately, she considered that might be the only reason Lucy and

Beau never got together even if they were perfect for each other in every other way.

Lucy had been abandoned, and Beau was a classic abandoner when it came to women.

Sadie kept waiting for him to change, to slow down, and notice who had been there right in front of him all along. But she certainly wasn't going to offer up her best friend's heart when Beau wasn't ready for it. So, she'd done everything in her power to discourage the two of them getting together.

But on the other hand, she and Lincoln had once been in a similar situation. Lincoln had dated a lot, too, just like Beau, including the town's runaway bride and daughter of the richest man in town, Jolette Marie. What it took for Linc to notice her was being thrown together when outside circumstances intervened. And maybe, just maybe, that's what it would take here. Sadie couldn't support Beau winding up with a woman who'd drop off her child the way Charlotte's mother had done. No preamble, no easing him into the situation.

What Sadie could do now was make sure Lucy and Beau spent this entire week together watching the baby. Throw in a romantic surprise or two (which she could easily engineer with a phone call from her couch), and this might work. She'd start with flowers, delivered by the new place in town that needed the business.

After hanging up with Lucy, Sadie went to work.

"Hi, there," Sadie said when the owner picked up the phone. "I'd like to order one dozen red roses to be delivered this afternoon. To the attention of Lucy Lorenzo."

She gave out the address of Beau's home since she expected Lucy to be there watching the baby.

"What should the card say?"

Sadie thought carefully of the language that would say

just *enough* but not too much. What was said was just as important as what was *not* said.

Then, she came up with the perfect words.

"It should be signed 'With love, Beau.'"

Next, she phoned Lenny, who loved Lucy like she was his own daughter. The second part of her plan would begin sometime tomorrow. Lenny would make sure of it.

"Heh, heh. Great idea, Sadie!" He chuckled.

How about that. It seemed Sadie could scheme best while off her feet.

BY LATE AFTERNOON, Beau still hadn't arrived home and Lucy had plenty to do at her own house. It was rude of him to take advantage of her like this when she had boxes to pack. She phoned his cell hoping he was near reception, and he picked up.

"Hey, Larry. How's it going?"

"Where *are* you?" She waited for him to lie, when she knew very well where he was, given by the noise in the background.

"Stopped by the Shady Grind for a cold beer."

"Rude! You've got to be kidding me."

"No. Why? Want me to bring you a Shady Burger and some fries?"

"I *want* you to come home and relieve me. I need a shower and I've got boxes to pack. This isn't fair, Beau!"

"Why not? I'm paying you well for this nanny gig, over-time included. Is she being a problem?"

"You're the problem, sir! You need to get over here and be her father."

"Aw hell. She doesn't like me very much."

"That's no excuse. She doesn't know you yet."

"But she likes you fine!"

"I don't know about that. She spit up all over me earlier. I had to change."

"Borrow one of my shirts," Beau said.

As if this was the answer to all her troubles!

"I already did. Get over here, or I'll drive her to you, and *you'll* have to explain why you have a baby in a bar."

"*Sweet Home Alabama*! Got it on the first try."

"We're not playing 'guess the movie.' You have ten minutes to get here, or I bring Charlotte to you." With that, she hung up on him.

Charlotte blew a raspberry from the playpen the ladies had brought over earlier today. They'd included a high chair donated by Pamela Ann and a wind-up indoor baby swing. Beau's entire house had begun to resemble a very large nursery. Lucy almost felt sorry for him. What must it feel like to have a baby dropped into your bachelor lifestyle? A child you hadn't known existed. But her sympathy was on fumes to discover he'd been hiding out at the Shady Grind like he had any business resuming his normal lifestyle. She wondered how many women had flirted with him and how they'd react to be faced with a baby and… this mess.

The doorbell rang and Lucy went to the door to find Shula standing on the other side of it holding out a bouquet of red roses. Recently, she'd decided to become a florist and given there were so many men, the business had started to take off. Some, like Levi, had standing orders. Kind of amazing no one ever tried it before.

"Hey there, Lucy! These are for you."

"For me?"

She almost never got flowers. Of course, the florist shop was new, but the General Store had always sold flowers. She occasionally received a bouquet of wildflowers or yellow mums from her dates. A few of the men who'd chased her had brought her roses. Levi used to bring her flowers every time he took her on a date. For a horse trainer, he was a romantic. Too bad he had a thing for Jolette Marie, and Lucy had a thing for Beau. Otherwise, they were a match made in heaven.

"Oh, hang on." Lucy ran to her purse and brought a tip back for Shula.

The flowers were truly lovely, the red buds perfectly formed. She found the card and read it:

You're always there for me. Thank you for everything.

With love, Beau

"Hmm, that was fast."

These couldn't have been because of their conversation two minutes ago. He must have ordered them for her earlier, knowing she'd have spent the day babysitting *his* child. At least he'd given her this small consideration.

You're always there for me. With *love*.

Well, he didn't mean it, did he? He'd just called her "Larry" a few minutes ago. Would it be nice if he'd finally notice her as a *woman*? It was too late now anyway. He was a father, and she was leaving for Seattle. That was final. The roses were nice, however. He'd at the least made up for being caught at the bar and being derelict in his duties. So, she'd forgive him. Apparently. Again, and again and again.

Because he was *Beau*. Beauregard Stephens, who'd once rescued her from a handsy ex-boyfriend, pulling him out of the car by the scruff of his neck. Beau, who whisked her away whenever her birthday came around (of which no one could be 100 percent certain, so they'd arbitrarily chosen the Fourth of July, judging by her approximate age when she'd been found). On that auspicious day, everyone wanted to talk about the morning she'd been found at the church. Of course, Lenny had most of the information.

Such a sweet baby.

She wasn't even crying.

She just looked up at me with those dark eyes and I swear to y'all, she smiled at me!

"Sorry," Beau would interrupt. "I made plans with her. Say goodbye, Larry."

And he'd pull her away from whichever old-timer wanted to talk about how they'd found her, who'd found her, who they'd called, how they wondered who could leave such a beautiful baby. How *lucky* she was to be found in Stone Ridge.

He'd take her for ice cream in Kerrville where he'd tease her for always choosing vanilla.

"Did you know vanilla is the number one choice flavor for most people? You're just like everyone else. Try something new for a change, why don't you."

It was almost as if he knew those words were the only gift she wanted on her birthday.

You're just like everyone else. Not "we have no idea *when* you were born so we'll choose a special day for you. You don't mind sharing it with the birth of our nation, do you?"

How many people had no idea when they were actually born? Her guess was not many.

Lucy used to imagine that her biological mother had been a desperate woman who'd fallen in love with a famous movie star and not known what to do when he didn't want either one of them. How her birth mother wound up so far from Hollywood was not something Lucy could explain at the age of ten. Now, with the benefits of maturity, she realized her mother was more than likely a homeless woman with few resources.

She couldn't have been from Stone Ridge or nearby. Kerrville was still a mystery because as a much larger city it had been almost impossible to locate any information on an abandoned baby. The police had checked nearby hospitals and labor and delivery for approximately three months prior (the doctor's best estimate as to Lucy's age) with no results. But this didn't discount someone who'd had a home birth or given birth out of state.

She was, simply, the girl with no birthday until one was given to her. At least she had a name, one that thankfully her parents kept as the only connection she might have to her first family. Because she'd never left the town where she was abandoned, the name would conceivably make it easier to find Lucy.

As long as someone wanted to look for her, and clearly no one did.

"You don't need anyone else," Sadie had once told Lucy when they were both about twelve. "Because you have *us*."

Then Sadie and Beau surrounded her from both sides.

"I always wanted a sister," Sadie sniffed. "Now I have one."

"I already have a sister," Beau said and when they'd both looked at him, he'd burst out laughing, his devilish grin lighting up his eyes. "But I guess you can never have too many."

Even now, the memory had her wiping away an errant tear. Leaving her friends and found family would be difficult, but if she didn't leave the safety of Stone Ridge, she'd never grow.

She'd never stretch.

She'd never find out who she was in a different setting where she could reinvent herself.

Chapter 9

Caught in the act.

Beau had been trying to run away from home and, even as a grown man, it was no less humiliating. The first time he'd run away he'd been twelve and camped out behind the Lorenzos' house for two nights, where Lucy snuck him food and drinks. They'd both been in a heap of trouble over that one. All because his father wouldn't buy him the latest PlayStation. Too bad life couldn't stay as simple as it had in childhood.

He grabbed the vanilla milkshake and Shady Burger with seasoned curly fries he'd ordered for Lucy.

Lucy greeted him at the door, holding Charlotte. "Dinner, too?"

"You deserve it." He walked inside and for a moment didn't recognize his surroundings.

His house. It looked like a…like a baby store.

"What's all…*this?*"

It seemed that the few items Rachel brought over had somehow multiplied in his absence. He set the food down on the end table and tripped over some kind of contraption.

"What the—" He rolled on to the couch, saving the milkshake by holding it up.

"That's a baby swing someone donated. The ladies took up a collection and brought things over earlier. Anyone who had baby gear they didn't need anymore gave you their old stuff."

"It makes my place look like a…like a…"

"Family home. Definitely not your bachelor pad anymore, but what did you expect?" She set Charlotte in the little bucket seat, fastened the seat belt, and cranked the swing with a lever on the side.

It played a horrible song, something that sounded like a children's nursery rhyme.

Beau covered his ears. "What is that *song*?"

"Why that, Daddy-o, is 'Three Blind Mice.' Don't you recognize it?"

"I must because I just want it to stop. I'm not a fan." He followed Lucy into the kitchen.

"Babies love those repetitive songs. Over and over and over again. The routine is comforting. Familiar."

He noticed a bouquet of red roses on the counter. That must mean Levi, flower lover, wanted another chance with Lucy. Beau was keenly aware of how much time the two had spent together. Everyone was sure Levi would pop the question and many jokes were made about the LLs getting together. He still didn't know what had happened but had a feeling Jolette Marie had something to do with it. She and Levi spent a lot of time together on her father's massive horse ranch where Levi trained their thoroughbreds. Levi training, Jolette Marie riding. But though Jo was beautiful and even Beau had dated her once (who hadn't?), she couldn't compare to Lucy. No wonder Levi wanted her back. If he managed to talk Lucy into staying here and forgetting all about Seattle, Beau would swallow his pride and shut his trap.

Beau traced the outline of a soft petal. "Red roses."

He knew exactly what *red* meant, too, having familiarized himself with the meaning of flower colors early on. Yellow for friendship, pink when you liked someone, red when you loved them. He'd never sent red roses to anyone but his mother and even that was pushing it. Yellow was his vibe, with the occasional pink thrown in.

"Yes," she said and wouldn't look at him, turning her back to him at the sink. "And they're very nice."

He swallowed thickly. Red roses. Levi had just sent Lucy red roses. Did she know what they meant? Was there any girl alive who *didn't*?

"They are. Hey, I'm sorry I was…I don't know… running away from home. It isn't fair to leave you with my mess." He waved an arm around the kitchen, doing a double take when he saw a high chair in one corner. "What the…"

"It's a high chair." Lucy crossed her arms and gazed at him from under her lashes.

"I've *seen* a high chair before, but what's it doing here in my kitchen?"

"I think the ladies figured you might need one eventually."

"She's going to be here a week. One *week*."

When Rachel came back she'd take their daughter with her. Beau never allowed himself to even contemplate the word "if" she came back. She had to, or he would definitely call the police.

"She's coming back. No one takes this good care of a baby for all these months and then just dumps her off never to return." The moment he said the words, he wanted to cut off his tongue.

Of course, that could happen.

It had happened to Lucy.

"Damn it. Lucy, I didn't mean to…"

"That's okay." Her head was now lowered over the sink where she was filling a bottle. "Except of course you *know* that's wrong. There are some parents who never come back."

Just the thought he'd have to care for Charlotte because her own mother wouldn't do it made Beau's stomach pitch. How could he possibly be everything she would need in a parent? He couldn't do this. He didn't have it in him. Even with all the help he would get, he would still have to be… her *father*.

"I guess I'm in denial."

"That's no surprise. This all happened so fast. And for all you know, she isn't actually yours. You should get a DNA test just to be sure."

"She looks like a Stephens."

"Blond? Hazel eyes? I don't think that's as rare as you might think." Lucy, facing him now, gave him a smirk.

Beau was ashamed of how much the possibility filled him with hope. Yes, he needed a DNA test. That's right. Just because Rachel claimed to have had one didn't mean anything. She might have lied about it. He tended to believe the best about people, but that hadn't always worked out so well for him, had it?

Lucy took the bottle and went back into the great room, heading back toward the baby, who hadn't made a peep in that swing. Thank God someone thought to drop it off. Wonder if she'd sleep in it. He'd put it near his bed instead of the crib, find some good ear plugs, and let it play a nursery rhyme all night. Even those songs were preferrable to her crying all night and that was saying something.

Lucy bent over the swing and unbuckled Charlotte, taking her out. She wasn't asleep.

Lucy pointed to the couch. "Sit."

He did, at which point she handed him the baby and the bottle.

"Feed her."

He fumbled, trying to settle a wriggling Charlotte in his arms, pushing the bottle's nipple closer to her mouth, angling it. At least he'd done this before even if not on a human baby. Charlotte opened her mouth and accepted the bottle, sucking on it with enthusiasm.

"See how simple this is?"

"In theory," he said, staring down at Charlotte as she guzzled. "It's like that time when we found those stray kittens in a box. Remember?"

"I believe Sadie and I didn't really let you near them to feed. We wanted to do it all. That was our first mistake."

"I've fed a couple of baby calves a time or two at Linc's ranch but well. This is different. To say the least."

"Yes, it is. She's very cute, for one thing."

Lucy sat beside him, and relief spread through that she wasn't leaving him yet. For the next few moments, they sat in the silence of Charlotte's sucking sounds and his own pounding heart.

"You don't want her, do you?" Lucy said quietly and Beau thought his heart might have stopped. "I sometimes wonder if that's what happened with me."

"Lucy," he said. "No."

"Yes, that's exactly what happened. My mother, or father for that matter, because really who knows, didn't want me."

"Or maybe they didn't feel capable of taking care of

you. That's how I feel. It isn't that I don't want her, but I wasn't expecting her."

"In my case, someone had expected me for at least nine months."

"Yeah, and they took good care of you for a few months. It could have been someone very young who didn't have resources. We know it wasn't someone from our town. Maybe she was on vacation or passing through."

"We'll never know. Hopefully Charlotte will never have to hear about this little blip in her life. Her mother will take her back, and they'll never talk about it again. But on the other hand, I sometimes wonder if there's a part of her that will always remember being left behind. They say babies don't really have memories but how do we really know that?"

"Do you remember? I didn't think you did."

"I don't remember." She touched her chest. "But sometimes, I think something in here does. Psychologically, I think I remember being abandoned. Do you think that's possible?"

"I hope not." He looked down at the baby who might well be his daughter.

Just the thought something in her might already be broken…

"The new research says that babies who are adopted as infants psychically feel that separation from their birth mothers. They cry more, they have a difficult time sleeping and eating." Lucy took a deep breath. "Imagine being ripped away from the person who carried you for nine months. From the voice you heard every day. At least I wasn't a newborn when I came here. But Marge told me when I came to them I cried a lot. Then, finally one day, I stopped, and I smiled at her for the first time. I'd adjusted and on some level I must have accepted that no one was ever coming back for me. This was my new home. Babies are resilient, at least."

"You've had a good life here."

"I know. Don't get me wrong, I'm grateful for my parents. And for Marge and Cal. For the ladies of SORROW. But…well, I've always felt indebted. Like I owe them."

"Not me. You don't feel that way about me." It wasn't phrased as a question because he wanted it to be true. *It was true, damn it.*

She rested her hand on his arm, and he felt it like a firebrand. "No, not you. Or Sadie. I guess maybe I want to find out who I am to the rest of the world."

"Lucy, if your birth parents ever come looking for you, they're going to look *here* first."

She met his eyes, hers shimmering suspiciously. "I think we both know by now that no one is ever coming for me."

Beau's heart felt hammered, like a fist had just punched it once and flattened it. He'd had no idea Lucy ever felt this way. She'd never said anything to him. This was why she wanted to leave here for Seattle. Now it was obvious to him and also clear how he'd failed her.

"That's a good thing in my mind," he answered in the only way he knew how. "Because they can't have you back. You belong to us now."

She stood and bent slightly to fondle a curl on Charlotte's head.

"The truth is I don't know where I belong."

Chapter 10

The next morning, as she showered and dressed, Lucy thought she might have been a bit dramatic last night. Call it the flowers, or the way Beau had appeared so rumpled and simply...*vulnerable* when she'd forced him to sit down and feed Charlotte. This big man holding a tiny baby. It made an interesting picture.

But she didn't appreciate the look in Beau's eyes. He couldn't fool her. That look was pity, pure and simple. Now he felt *sorry* for her, which was the last thing she'd wanted. See, there was a reason she didn't unburden herself to people the way she had last night. Everyone assumed she'd always been nothing but grateful to be found, and she was of course, but it was far more complicated. Too difficult to explain to people who had never been through the same experience. And it was likely a small club, as it should be.

All that to say it was far better to remain strong and show that she'd grown up fine despite her circumstances.

Because she had. Despite biological parents who hadn't wanted her, who had gone so far as to dump her somewhere like a stray dog, she'd had a good life. Family, both real and found, good friends, even if there had never been anyone special yet. She was thirty-two and it was time to find a special someone because she wasn't too jaded to want that. She wouldn't make the same mistakes her first parents had, or her second ones. Because holding on too tightly to a child wasn't a whole lot better than letting them go. It was all a matter of timing, and she wasn't sure her parents were ever going to accept she was a grown woman capable of making her own adult decisions.

Ironic. On one side, she had parents who'd too easily given her up, because no one could convince her otherwise. There had to have been some other options even more than three decades ago. But on the other hand, she had adoptive parents who didn't think she should wander too far away from the homestead. Either they were afraid of losing her, or maybe they were afraid she'd somehow lose herself. Neither was going to happen.

Her phone was ringing when she hopped out of the shower. Her mother.

"Can you come over for dinner Friday night? I'm making your favorite: chicken enchiladas with corn tortillas."

Interesting how her mother never assumed Lucy might have a date on Friday night. The entire time she'd dated Levi, Esperanza pretended he didn't exist. Lucy never could figure out if her mother had someone specific in mind for her, or if no one would ever be good enough. She suspected the latter.

"Oh, and bring the baby."

What the… "Mom, it's not my baby. It's Beau's."

"But you're watching her. Don't think I didn't hear *that* news."

"I was going to tell you but there hasn't been any time. It all happened so fast."

"I'm sure it did. Beau is ever so resourceful." The snark in her mother's tone was thick enough to cut.

"He's *paying* me and as you know—"

"I know. You're saving every dollar for Seattle." She sighed loudly.

"It's an expensive city."

"Which is why you shouldn't move there. You're not *rich*."

They weren't getting anywhere. "I have to go now but sure, I think I can make dinner on Friday. The green enchilada sauce?"

"Of course. See you then."

Lucy raced around the room, packing her bag, rushing to get to Beau's on time. Last night, he hadn't mentioned any appointments he had, but he usually had to be on the job fairly early. It wasn't until she stepped outside and locked the front door that she found Lenny standing nearby wearing his gray "exterminator" coveralls.

"Bug Killers, Licensed to Kill—Literally" the tag read. Among his many jobs since retiring from the post office, he worked in pest control. He'd sprayed her rental house a time or two for ants and spiders, but she'd had no issues for a while.

He was staring up at the eaves, rubbing his chin, muttering to himself. "Not good. No. Not good at all."

"Lenny? What's up?"

"Oh hey there. Good mornin'." He wandered over, shaking his head, arms crossed. "Bad news. Terrible."

"What's wrong?" She followed his eyes as he gazed at a shingle.

His finger swiped at the side paneling with his glove. "See that?"

She saw absolutely nothing but old dried dirt on his glove. "No. What is it?"

"That right there is a *termite.*"

"Where? I don't see anything."

"They're tiny. Invisible to the naked eye."

"Then how can *you* see them?"

"Experience." He nodded sagely.

Lucy cringed at the thought of tiny invisible bugs crawling all over the house where she lived and slept. And *ate*. "So…you're going to spray?"

"Yup. We're going to have to tent this puppy."

"Tent? You mean like when they put a hideous cover over your entire house?"

"Exacta-mundo." Lenny nodded, shoving his hands in his pockets, and tipping back on his heels. "This is going to have to be done immediately."

"Of course. Do you think I want to be living in a house infested with termites? Get them out, Lenny! They must be all over everything."

She tried not to scream, picturing invisible bugs latching on to her suitcase and hitching a ride with her to Seattle.

"Will do, will do." He waved his hand over the house. "You'll need to move out for a few days, that's all."

She pictured spending the night in her old bedroom, which her mother hadn't done anything to change in years. Lucy told her to turn it into a workout or sewing room, but her mother said it would always be Lucy's room in case she ever changed her mind and wanted to move back home. As if. She did not want to go back home even now. Freedom was sweet.

"I was already moving, so I have a lot of boxes packed but where am I supposed to go now?"

"I'd offer my house but as you know I have very little room since Polly moved back in with her children."

"No, I couldn't bother you. That's fine. Maybe I'll stay

with my parents. My mother is always begging me to come home."

Lenny held up three fingers. "Just give me three days and I'll have every termite killed. Exterminated. Oh it won't be pretty, but it has to be done."

"Thank you."

Lucy hurried back inside and packed an overnight bag and a few necessities. She arrived at Beau's a few minutes later and knocked on the door ready to apologize for being late. But he opened the door clearly not ready to *go* anywhere. For one thing, he wasn't wearing a shirt.

"Hey." He left the door open and walked back into the kitchen with Charlotte. "I was just getting her a bottle."

"I'm sorry I'm late." Lucy followed him. "But my mother phoned and then I wound up chatting with Lenny for several minutes. He says my place has termites. Can you believe it?"

Beau squinted. *"Termites?"*

"Here, let me take her. You look like you're running late, too."

He hadn't even shaved, stubble covering his jawline. He wore jeans and without the ever-present hat, she could see how badly he needed that haircut. If he didn't do something soon he'd be able to put it in a ponytail. She should mention something.

"It's fine. No appointments today." He filled a pan with water and stuck it in on the stove as he'd seen her do. "Believe it or not, my Dad said he'd take over this week. It's his part in helping out with this…um, situation."

"So, you don't need me?"

"I still need you."

"But…for what?" She turned in a circle. "I could clean up a little bit around here but if you're good maybe I should go get settled at my mother's house."

"Why?"

"Didn't you hear me? I have termites and they're putting on the horrible tent. I can't be inside. It's just a few days."

"Strange that house has termites. It's not an older place."

He went about his business, taking a premade bottle out of the fridge and placing it in the pan. Beau seemed strangely subdued. He always had so much energy it was usually like watching a top spin. Now he seemed to be moving as though through silly putty. He must have had another rough night with Charlotte.

She was quiet in his arms, against his bare chest. The skin on skin must be calming.

"Do you mind holding her for a minute?"

Mind? This was an odd request. She was here, after all, for the baby. "Of course not."

As soon as the handoff happened, she regretted it. Without the coverage of a baby, Beau's chest screamed like a neon sign: *Man chest! Man chest! Read all about it.* It had been a while since she'd seen Beau without a shirt on, as contrary to the romance novels she sometimes read, cowboys did not walk around shirtless.

Among other things, it was supremely impractical. Now, Lucy could see he'd added *another* tattoo on his left arm. He now had a half sleeve. Nothing else had changed, however. He still had those glistening six-pack abs and the light smattering of chest hair leading in an enticing line to his navel. Lucy wished she didn't notice such things.

"Just going to take a quick shower. Then, if that's okay with you, I want to work on the deck. I never have time for my own projects."

"Oh, sure. Um, yeah. That's…that's fine."

"But I don't want you to think I'm dodging Charlotte.

I'll give you a break during the day and we'll do this together. Alright?"

"Sure."

She might be staring and stammering a little bit just trying to get her bearings and read the latest tattoo. Part of the lettering wrapped around his bicep and into his shoulder.

He tossed up his hands. "I heard what you said last night and I'm not shirking from my responsibilities. I don't want…well, I don't want Charlotte growing up feeling on some…what did you call it?"

"Psychic?"

"Yeah, psychic level that her father didn't want her."

Oh. That was nice, to think her own history had helped someone else. Especially a sweet little baby who happened to look a lot like her two best friends. She didn't know if it would make a difference because the real issue was her *mother* abandoning her. But it was nice that Beau wanted to try.

"Anyway, I fully intend to help you out with her today. I just want a little help, here and there so I might get something done. I rarely have time off for my own projects."

He probably also realized she'd started to count on the extra money for Seattle. She appreciated that, too. She cocked her head, still trying to read his new tattoo.

"Did you...um, already feed the animals?"

"Yeah." He stopped walking and a slow smile spread across his lips. "Are you okay?"

"Yes, it's just the…terminate situation. Very unsettling."

"Gotcha." Then he disappeared down the hallway into his bedroom.

Lucy buckled Charlotte into the swing and phoned her mother. "Apparently, I have termites."

"Oh dear. Lenny is *never* wrong."

"I'll need to stay over with you for a few nights while they tent. Hope that's okay."

"Oh, sugar, no. I'm so sorry. But you can't."

"*Excuse* me?"

Stop the presses. Her mother didn't want her home. She'd just invited her over for dinner and yet she didn't want her staying over a few nights. It was as if something had changed between their earlier phone call and this one. Wonder what was wrong in the cosmos. Mercury might be in retrograde.

Mom laughed. "I know it sounds silly, but um, I'm painting. And we just started today. It's going to be a few days, that's all. Everything is moved around, and the room is in a state. The entire house is all cattywampus. We should be fine by Friday."

"I'll just call Sadie. She will appreciate the extra help, I'm sure."

"Why don't you just stay over at Beau's? I'm sure he has the room. And you'll be such a help to him, maybe grab some nanny overtime."

This was yet another odd thing, her mother encouraging her to spend the night in a man's house. Even if it was just Beau, it was still highly unusual.

"Bye, Mom," Lucy said and hung up, a bit irritated, then phoned Sadie.

Mrs. Stephens answered the phone. "Sadie's taking a nap. Can I help you?"

"Um, well, how's she doing?"

Lucy felt a big selfish asking her friend for a favor now of all times. Sadie had Lincoln to take care of her most nights and that's when Lucy would be there anyway. She could help Lincoln with Sammy, she guessed, not that he needed it.

"Much better. She hopes the doctor will take her off bed rest next visit! By the way, thank you for helping Beau. I know he appreciates it."

"Believe it or not, I think he's figuring this father thing out for himself."

It always semi-irritated Lucy that Beau and Sadie's mother didn't expect much from her son. She gave him a pass when it came to many household chores but that was the way of so many older ladies in Stone Ridge. The younger ones, like Sadie and Eve, had changed all that. She knew for a fact that both Lincoln and Jackson helped out more with the household than their father ever had. The same could be said for Wade, Daisy's husband.

"Um…would you give Sadie a message? I have termites and I need to stay somewhere for a couple of nights while Lenny tents the house."

"Why not stay with Beau? He has that guest room and you're already there most of the day. It's perfect."

Okay, what was the deal with *two* mothers wanting Lucy to stay with Beau? If she didn't know any better Lucy would think they were matchmaking but that couldn't be the case. Neither one of them had ever been even slightly encouraging and now that she was leaving they couldn't wait to get her and Beau together. Well, she wasn't falling for that. She was leaving for Seattle and that was final. Her own mother was probably behind this, and she'd bet that she wasn't even painting her old room!

She hung up with Mrs. Stephens and picked up a fussy Charlotte, patting her back. "There, there."

It didn't matter what they tried to do, Beau wasn't interested in Lucy, and she'd known that for many years. Living right under his nose and behaving all maternal with his baby like she was auditioning for the part of fairy step-mother wasn't going to change a thing.

. . .

THE UNMISTAKABLE SOUND of a horse trailer pulling up outside put a giddyup in Beau's step. But he wasn't expecting anyone other than Lucy and had been so happy to see her he could have kissed her. After last night and Lucy's talk about her origins, he'd done a lot of thinking. Lucy had a point. Charlotte would be going back with her mother and might never remember this strange period of time. But she *would* remember having a father who'd lost touch, or who didn't care to know her. He may have said the right words to everyone, and he would do what was expected of him. But up until last night he'd been prepared to do it without any heart in the equation. With little emotion. That clearly wasn't going to be enough.

Beau pulled on a shirt and jeans and quickly toed on his boots.

Lucy was already staring out the wide-paned window facing the driveway, holding Charlotte.

"Who's here?" Beau rushed to the front door and swung it open. "What the…"

The trailer was clearly marked. *Truehart Horse Ranch* the rig read in the large letters and logo brand seen everywhere horse breeding mattered. They pulled up near the barn and the driver got out.

Beau ran out to meet him. "Did you lose your way, partner?"

"Nope. You're Beau Stephens, I take it?" He held some paperwork in his hands.

"That's me, but—"

He hooked his finger to the trailer. "This is your horse. Mr. Truehart said she was to be delivered straight to your ranch."

"You're kidding." Beau took the papers when they were

handed to him and looked them over. It didn't appear to be a mistake.

"Hang on." Beau stuck his palm out to stop this. He's just semi-inherited a baby, and a horse at this time was not going to work. "I can't afford this."

"Well, she's yours. I don't know what to tell ya."

The driver, whose shirt name tag said "Ike" went about his business as if Beau hadn't just tried to stop him. He walked around to the back of his truck and Beau rushed inside.

"Did you buy a *horse*?" Lucy said with wide eyes. "This hardly seems like the time."

She was judging him for lousy timing and poor decision making. He couldn't say that he blamed her. Everyone in Stone Ridge knew the significance of a Truehart horse. They were always thoroughbreds for racing and other lofty pursuits.

He grabbed the handset phone and dialed the Truehart Ranch operations. "Are you kidding? As if I could afford a Truehart horse. I've been saving up but nowhere near and now with Charlotte…"

It took a few transfers as Beau explained the situation to a receptionist, a staff member at the ranch, and finally Mr. Truehart himself.

"How do you like her?" Truehart's booming voice came through the other end of the line like he was in the next room of Beau's home.

"There must be some mistake. I know we talked about possibly buying a horse from you someday, at some point, but right now I'm not in the position—"

"It's a gift."

Beau exhaled as the knowledge hit him. "*That's* the bonus you were talking about?"

"You built the home of my wife's dreams, and she's

happy, which makes me extremely happy. Happy wife, happy life. It's the least I can do."

But you paid me well to build that house, Beau wanted to say. John Truehart had a reputation for both being a tyrant and also generous with those he liked, but this seemed over the top. He was known for his thoroughbred horses from good stock, which were often worth hundreds of thousands of dollars on the open market. This was far more of a bonus than Beau deserved.

Beau looked out the window, watching the magnificent horse led down the plank.

"But…I mean, this horse has to be…"

"Worth a hundred grand? You're right about that. But it isn't just for the house you built and how much pride shows in your work. You've been a good friend to my daughter, and I appreciate that. You never took advantage of her, ahem, outgoing nature."

"Well, thanks, I—" Beau could say he wasn't exactly a saint and didn't deserve the praise, but Truehart was on a roll and who was Beau to interrupt him.

"And I heard what ya just got saddled with, too."

Beau winced. He didn't like using the word "saddled" with the baby who could very well be, and likely was, his daughter.

No doubt word was all over town. "Yes, sir. I'm going to do my duty there, don't worry."

Beau shouldn't have been surprised to hear Truehart snort. "Son, your duty is to that child but not necessarily the mother. Let me haul you into the new millennium. We're a bit old-fashioned here in Stone Ridge, and while I appreciate that, take it from me: it's not a good idea to start a marriage without love. Love doesn't always grow because you want it to. Know what I mean?"

"Yes, sir. So I've heard."

Moving between joy and unbelief, Beau hung up with Truehart. He caught himself standing in a sort of daze, rubbing at the stubble on his chin, remembering how long he'd had this dream. It was one thing to own a horse of his own, quite another to have a Truehart.

"Beau?" Lucy snapped him out of his haze. She stared at him, then set Charlotte down on the bouncy thingamajig. "What's wrong?"

"Um, apparently I've just been gifted with a Truehart horse. Out of the kindness of his heart for a job well done."

For a moment, Lucy gaped. She, of all people, would know what this meant to him.

She broke into a smile and flew into his arms before he realized it was happening.

"I'm so happy for you!"

It should have been a sisterly hug, but it wasn't. Again, that jolt of awareness coursed through him, and it felt like a live wire flowed through the veins in his arms.

The arms that were hugging her back. Tightly.

Chapter 11

Beau pulled back without letting Lucy go. He wanted to get a good look in her eyes because he knew her well enough to see the truth in them. Had she felt that sudden jolt of electricity, too, or was it just him? Because if she had, it might be a little too much happiness in one day for him.

Her eyes were beautiful, a deep and golden brown just a shade darker than amber. He'd noticed those eyes many times before, of course, but with a kind of distance that felt safe. Now it felt like there was nothing between them but oxygen and a warm rush of adrenaline, clear and bold. She felt it, too, obvious by the softness in her gaze. This moment between them was different.

It wasn't a birthday hug, a congratulations hug for clearing that rock when he jumped in the lake that one time, or for graduating from college with honors. He'd had those innocent hugs from Lucy many times over the years. This was Beau and Lucy, the adult-version hug. The one he'd waited for and fantasized about for years.

He wanted to kiss her. Would it be crazy to kiss her now? He wanted her and didn't care what other obligations were before him. Maybe he was getting greedy, but it wasn't too much to ask that he might also have…this. The only thing he'd ever really wanted but been afraid to have. His hand lowered to just below her hip and like she sensed what he was about to do, she stepped back.

She lowered her head to study her fingernails. "Um, so I take it you accepted the gift?"

He cleared his throat. Yeah, that was a *no, please* don't *kiss me*. Got it.

"I think I'd be a fool not to."

"You're right. We all know that Mr. Truehart can occasionally be the generous sort so I don't think you should feel obligated to him in any way. Like he said, it's a gift."

Beau ran a hand through his hair, grinning a bit. "He also said he was grateful I'd been a good friend to Jolette Marie. Emphasis on *friend*."

Lucy smirked. "True, you may have been the *only* guy she didn't date even once. Well, except for the Henderson brothers whom she didn't date, either."

"She dated Linc on and off before Sadie, and I always thought it would have been…weird."

Now, he stared at *his* hands, turning them over as if inspecting for cuts. It wasn't as if he'd never seen his hands before, but it was something to do to ease the tension pulsing between them.

He'd almost kissed her, and where would they be right now if he had?

Again, he was leaping without thinking when it came to women. Rushing forward. Among so many other things, he had to change that about himself in order to be a better father to Charlotte. Gone were the days of casual hookups and random dating with women he barely knew or liked. He would not be dating anyone for the foreseeable future. He'd been cured.

"I'm going to go outside and help…" He made a move to step around Lucy.

This was tricky because despite her step back she still stood rather close to him, and when she tried to move he moved the same way. Like they were in a choreographed dance, she moved in the other direction just as he did. Their timing was perfect.

Perfectly off. How telling and fiercely ironic.

The misstep happened once more before he settled his hand on her waist. "Don't move."

She held up her palms and studied the floor. "I'm not moving."

He was halfway out the door when she called out to him, "By the way, you need a haircut."

How about that. She'd finally noticed. She wasn't too busy thinking about Seattle men and good Wi-Fi to care what happened to his hair. The length of his hair always seemed so important to both Lucy and Sadie. As for him, he'd been ignoring it for weeks.

"That's what God made hats for." He grabbed one on his way out the door. "Think I can get one more Lucy Lorenzo haircut out of you before you leave the great state of Texas?"

"Lucky for you, I have my scissors in the car."

"For now, I have to go see a man about a horse." He shut the door behind him.

LUCY DIDN'T MOVE from her spot by the door for several seconds. Then Charlotte cooed from the bouncy seat where she was swatting at a rubber star in the ring of toys swinging and suspended above her. The pinging sound made Lucy startle.

For a moment, she'd almost forgotten there was a baby here. Beau's baby. Yes, let's not forget *that*. But…he'd almost kissed her. She was sure of it. There had been that soft glint in his hazel-green eyes, the "lean in," the arm around her low back. Her brain said, *he's going to kiss me*, and *yes, please God, let him do it*. She'd felt a piercing and hot sensation, not at all unpleasant, but still unlike anything she'd ever experienced before. For a moment, it was as if they were fused together. But something fragile, she'd call it doubt for now, made her take a step back.

Then the little sidestep dance where she honestly couldn't figure out which way to go. Left? Right? Center? It was as if their thoughts were perfectly aligned for once. She didn't *want* to get away from him, and maybe her body sensed that, ignoring the brain's signals telling it to move. So *why* had she stopped him from kissing her? Why had she stepped back? Did her body know something she didn't? Had it reacted of its own accord?

No, not at all. Unfortunately, her body realized what she did. She had to be honest. For once in her life, she would follow through with her plans. She was leaving Stone Ridge for Seattle, and everything had already been set in motion. She had to go. Nothing would derail her this time. Nothing.

Not even Beau.

Besides, it was too late for them, and he had obligations now. To Charlotte. To Charlotte's mother. Even if he didn't marry her they'd now forever and always be in each other's life. Co-parenting, coexisting. Sharing a precious child. She'd have no place in that situation. So, yes, a kiss would have ruined everything. She would then have had to question whether she could stay and babysit Charlotte under the new circumstances.

No, better to let this situation play itself out and go from there. Lucy was nothing if not logical. Practical to a fault. Kept emotions out of her decisions. She was, her mother used to tell her, like a boy in some ways, which Lucy didn't take as an insult. To be fair, her mother hadn't meant it as one.

Lucy picked Charlotte up when she began to fuss again and walked her to the window facing the driveway.

"See that? That's a horse. Your daddy has a new horse."

"Bababa." Charlotte kicked her legs happily.

"Yeah. More like yum," Lucy said as she watched Beau, wearing that tight-fitting shirt, walking his new horse to the barn.

She loved seeing him this happy. Beau always dreamed of owning a stable of horses from the time he'd been a boy. He'd spend weekends at the Carvers' house where he was practically an honorary brother. There he'd learned how to saddle and ride a horse and from Lincoln how to lasso like a champ. Like Lucy, Beau's family didn't have a working cattle ranch. They were just hardworking people that had lived in Stone Ridge for decades. They had land, but they used it mostly for farming small crops like peach and apricot trees until Mr. Stephens decided to try his hand at grapes.

But far from a cattle rancher, Beau's father had a construction business that kept him busy. Despite that, even she could see that Beau was a cowboy at heart. He'd been working on his dream since she could remember. Now he'd have it, along with a few other things he probably hadn't counted on.

It was several hours before Beau returned and in the

interim Lucy changed Charlotte four times, put her down for two naps, and washed and prepped more bottles of formula. She tried to straighten the room, but Beau didn't have the space for all this baby paraphernalia.

It wasn't that his house wasn't large enough, but the fact that it was decorated in the décor of American Millennial Cowboy. He told Lucy he'd built the home keeping in mind his carbon footprint. For Beau, his home was all about the land he had around him. He'd developed that land, building a barn and stables. He had a chicken coop and grew fruits and vegetables in a fenced-off area. His was a ranch-style home with one bedroom and an office on one side and two other bedrooms, functioning as guest rooms, on the other side for privacy. The two sides of the house were joined together by one common and large living area, the kitchen with an island in the center and a modest table and chairs nearby.

Beau didn't actually need half of the stuff the ladies had brought over, or at least not all at once. Lucy carried some items to the room next to his bedroom, which Beau used as an office. He'd left his bedroom door ajar, so she peeked inside. He'd made the bed, so she didn't get to see the color and guess at the thread count of his sheets. Funny, she knew so much about one of her oldest friends, but the intimate stuff had always been off-limits.

Lucy's father had never even allowed Beau inside her bedroom, even when she'd protested, "Why not? It's only *Beau!*"

"Yeah, well," her father had chortled. "Heh, heh, heh. Trust me on this one."

Honestly, she'd never fully even admitted to herself that she'd crushed on Beau when they were teenagers. She'd tried not to notice how hot he was, even when all the girls her age reminded her. Frequently. But as her own father realized early on, Beau wasn't "only Beau" and maybe he never had been.

"Hey, Lucy!" Beau said with a loud booming sound from the other room. "What should we have for dinner? You're staying, right?"

She rushed out of his bedroom only to nearly run into him. "I was just putting some stuff in your room. You really don't need to have *everything* out."

"Yeah, I noticed it looks a lot better in there. Thanks." He hooked a thumb toward the kitchen. "You want one of those casseroles? It's way too much food for just me."

"Um, sure." The truth was, she couldn't go home anyway though she'd failed to mention she still didn't have a place to stay tonight.

"Unless you have plans."

"No plans." If not for being here, she'd go home and pack another box. "I have a shift at the bar tomorrow night."

"What about the termites? Where are you staying?"

"I can't stay with my parents. My mother said something about painting my room. I don't believe her."

"What?" Beau blinked. "Why would she lie about that?"

Lucy shrugged. "No idea what she's up to."

"I think she's still trying to fix you up with someone, so you'll stay. Is it *Levi?*"

"You know what? I hope not but maybe that's also going to happen." Lucy grabbed Charlotte from the bouncy seat to put her in the high chair.

"Let me do that," Beau said, taking her. "You're off the clock."

She watched as he tucked Charlotte behind the tray

with ease, then fastened the belt. He was really getting the hang of this and, what's more, he didn't behave like he feared he might break her anymore.

"I've been practicing," Beau said, as if he heard her thoughts. "You should have seen me last night, all by myself, sliding this tray on and off like a fool. I'm pretty sure Charlotte was staring at me like I'd lost my mind."

"Practice makes perfect. I'm sure your daughter appreciates it."

Beau made a sound somewhere between a grumble and an acknowledgement. He set the table while Lucy dug two trays out of the fridge.

She presented them. "Lasagna or tuna casserole?"

"Lasagna," they both said at once.

"No brainer," Lucy said, pulling off the cellophane and sticking it in the oven to reheat.

While they waited for the food to be ready, they talked about the horse, whom Beau was considering naming Thor.

Lucy poised a fork in the air like a dagger. "If you do, I'm never speaking to you again."

"That's all it takes? Hell, you could have told me that years ago. My life would have been so much simpler."

She elbowed him in the ribs. "Your life would have been miserable without me, and you know it."

"That's true. I was just kidding. I'll think of another name."

"No, *I* was kidding. Of course you should name him Thor if that's what you want. I mean, if you want to name your horse after a Marvel character."

He grinned. "He's a *she*. Still don't like Thor?"

"Now it has possibility."

"Right. Why can't a pretty girl be named Thor?" He leaned back against the counter. "Or *Larry*."

She smiled at him because maybe this was Beau's subtle way of telling her he still thought of her as a woman, no matter *what* he occasionally called her.

The roses, and now this.

When Beau spoke again his voice was unnaturally soft. "I've been thinking about something. What if she's not?"

Lucy knew exactly what he meant. They both turned their gazes on Charlotte, who was sitting in her high chair intent on gumming a Cheerio. She was the innocent in all this, someone who'd never asked to be born. Who'd never asked to have parents who barely knew each other, or a mother who would drop her off with a stranger.

"What if she's not your daughter?"

"Yeah. I won't lie. When you first suggested that, the idea had appeal. Now? She's a cute little bug. It wouldn't be the worst thing to ever happen to me if I'm her father."

"No, definitely not. But it will change your life."

He met her gaze. "Maybe my life needed changing. Maybe I'm ready for a change."

"Yeah. So am I. That's why I'm moving."

He opened his mouth as if to say something, then shut it. The timer dinged for the lasagna and Beau grabbed a potholder, setting the Pyrex on the counter. They ate in companionable silence the way only two people who have known each other for years can do, until the phone rang.

Beau handed her the receiver. "It's for you. Sounds like Wade needs a ride."

"Oh yeah, I had my calls forwarded here."

Apparently, Wade Cruz and his wife, Daisy, needed a ride from San Antonio where they'd attended a rodeo.

"Can't they get an Uber? They've got those in San Antonio, you can't fool me," Beau said.

"Sometimes they don't want to ride all the way out

here, but I suspect Wade and Daisy want to give me the business. It's nice of them."

"You have to ride all the way there and back. I thought the point of a rideshare was picking someone up closer."

"It is normally." Lucy put her plate in the sink and grabbed her bag. "I'll see you in the morning. Thanks for dinner."

"Wait." Beau stood, hands shoved in his pants pockets. "Why don't you spend the night here?"

"Here?"

"Where else? You can't stay at the tented house, can you?"

"I'll figure something out."

"Or you can stay here, at least tonight. You're already coming back here in the morning. And now you'll be out late. It just makes sense." He shrugged.

"Okay, fine. I'll think about it."

She was out the door before he could argue with her anymore.

He was right and it made sense, but the way she'd been feeling about him reminded her of the times her father wouldn't let Beau in her bedroom. There was a reason for that, a reason that still applied to grown-up Lucy. He wasn't "just Beau." He would tempt her, and she did not want to be tempted. She did not need to make a mistake at this point in her life. She was headed to Seattle and that was final.

Anyway, this was a good fare, quite a distance, much longer than her usual and Lucy was already thinking about the money. Knowing Wade's generosity over the years, he'd hand over a sizeable tip, too. He and Daisy had a nice operation going on his land since shortly after he retired from the rodeo. Together, they ran rodeo classes and exhibitions that took them all over Texas. Apparently, one of their rigs broke down. They waited for it to be towed, then simply needed a ride home.

They were outside the event center when she got there almost an hour later. Wade opened the door for his wife to hop inside first.

"Thank you for coming out!" Daisy said, always so peppy and cheerful.

"I hope you weren't waiting too long."

"No problem, we wanted you," Wade said, cozying up to Daisy in the back.

"And we don't mind waiting," Daisy said. "Pretty soon, we won't have this option when you leave for Seattle."

"Someone else will take over, or you'll get Lenny again. He's been letting me take all the calls since I'm saving up, but you know him. He loves to keep busy."

"I have missed his tall tales," Daisy said. "Have you ever noticed how Lenny tends to exaggerate everything? And to think he was once a reporter!"

"For a small-town paper," Wade added.

It was true that Lenny did tend to hyperbole more often than not. Quite possibly he'd had a good editor at the paper who cut out all his exaggerations before they went to print.

"I heard about the baby," Daisy said. "How's poor Beau handling all this?"

"Believe it or not, he's adjusting. Though I still can't believe the mother would just drop her baby off with someone she doesn't even know."

Even as the words came out, she winced and nearly bit her tongue in half. It was late, or she might have been more aware of how this would affect Daisy. Not long ago, Daisy herself had discovered she wasn't Hank Carver's biological daughter. She, Lincoln, and Jackson had the same mother but different fathers. For years, her mother had passed Daisy off as Hank's, later abandoning her family. Daisy, who looked just like her mother, might have never known but her real father came looking for her when he was dying. The entire ordeal had been devastating for Daisy, but they had all readjusted and Daisy would never accept any other man but Hank as her father, biology be damned.

When all that happened, Lucy had been forced to admit to herself that the mother and father who raised her were the only two she'd ever consider her parents. It didn't stop the curiosity about her biological parents, but her feelings about family were clear. She'd been lucky to have two of the best parents a girl could have.

"I know all about the kind of mistakes mothers make," Daisy said, without a hint of anger or pain.

She'd already worked through all that pain with Wade's amazing support.

Lucy pretended she'd just remembered. "Oh, right, I almost forgot."

"I'll bet she regrets it someday. I only hope she comes back," Daisy said.

Lucy's stomach lurched. "You really don't think she will?"

She'd never allowed herself to believe Charlotte's mother wouldn't return, which in hindsight was stupid. No, it wasn't the same, but *her* mother hadn't returned. Neither had Daisy's.

"No, she probably will. I mean, I'm sure Beau can *find* her, anyway."

"Right, of course he can."

Lucy relaxed because in all honesty, she would not be

able to leave for Seattle if Charlotte's mother never returned.

How was she supposed to leave Beau to be a single father? He'd need her then, and all the help he could get.

If she didn't stay, would he ever forgive her for abandoning *him*?

Chapter 12

The company made the ride back to Stone Ridge go much faster and before she knew it, Lucy was pulling past the gates of the Cruz Ranch. The property was adjacent to the Henderson ranch, a place Lucy knew quite well.

For a second, she admired Wade's remodeled ranch-style home. Beau had built the house when Wade decided to raze the one he'd inherited from his mother and start from the ground up. It was a beautiful example of Beau's craftsmanship and attention to detail. He'd once told Lucy that nothing was more satisfying than building a family's home. Truthfully, she'd been jealous that he had work that he was passionate about while she enjoyed a lot of different things but wasn't truly an expert at any of them.

By the time she got back to Beau's ranch, it was nearly midnight. The lights were off, with only the soft glow of the porch light by the patio. He'd be asleep by now, and even if he'd probably left the door unlocked, she hesitated to go inside and disturb him and Charlotte. For several minutes, she just sat in her car, the cold of the night seeping through the tiny cracks in her rolled-up windows. The forecast said this January would bring a cold snap into the forties, pretty icy for Texas Hill Country.

What must it have been like to be left alone all night? To cry when no one was there to answer her needs. Thankfully, she didn't remember.

If she slept here all night, she'd know for the first time what it might be like to sleep outside when you had nowhere else to go.

No, that wasn't fair. She had plenty of places to go. Beau had offered and the warmth of his cozy home was a few feet in front of her. If she showed up at her parents, they'd let her sleep on the couch. They'd never turn her away. Why did she have this unnatural belief, this *false* belief that somehow she was unwanted? She hugged the steering wheel and leaned her head against it, sniffing back tears.

These feelings had resurfaced when Charlotte showed up. Before that, she only had to deal with her so-called "miracle baby" status once a year around her pretend birthday. At the same time plenty of summer celebrations were going on all around her. Her parents were the only ones who didn't make a big deal out of her miracle status, having long before claimed her as their own no matter her beginnings. But Lenny, Beulah, and the ladies of SORROW seemed to take joy in reminding her. In truth, they were emphasizing the positive and taking the focus off the negative fact: abandonment.

Lucy had always been curious about her biological parents, and why they would have been so desperate. But it was normal to wonder, her mother assured her. It would be strange *not* to have questions.

A rap on the window startled her and Lucy lifted her head from the steering wheel, wiping away a random tear.

Beau, a scowl on his face, rolled his index finger to indicate she should bring her window down.

She did, feeling silly. "Hi."

"What's happening here?"

He sounded irritated, his voice edgy and tight, and for a moment she tried to picture him as the father of a teenage daughter, and it took biting her lip to keep from laughing. Beau would get a helluva payback by having a daughter. One advantage was that at least he'd always be one step ahead of his daughter's admirers.

"I just got back."

"And decided to take a nap? In your *car*?"

"No, I was just sitting here thinking."

"Well, think inside. I've got the guest bed made up for you. Fresh sheets." He hooked a thumb to the house.

"I don't want to bother you."

He opened the driver's side door and unceremoniously pulled her out by her elbow. "C'mon, Larry. You're on my last nerve."

"Hey!"

But despite protesting, she went along because it was cold outside, and she'd never had any intention of spending the night in her car. Humble beginnings aside, Lucy was pretty spoiled when it came to a warm bed at night and other creature comforts.

He opened the passenger door and hauled out the overnight bag she'd packed. "This is it?"

"It's only a couple of nights."

She followed him into the house and toward the guest bedroom, where he flung open the door and set her bag down.

"Make yourself at home." He held his arm out toward the bed with a flourish.

"Sorry. I don't sleep anywhere that doesn't have 1,000-thread-count sheets."

He quirked a brow. "And yet you were about to sleep in your car."

"No, I *wasn't*. I just wanted to see what it might be like. To sleep outside because I had nowhere else to go."

His gaze and voice softened. "But you did have somewhere."

"I know. It was stupid."

He pulled back the covers to reveal sky blue sheets. "1,000 thread count. You have no excuses. Go to sleep now."

Lucy lifted a shoulder. "I was just kidding about thread count."

"I figured." Beau walked to the door. "Good night."

Before he left, she had one more thing to say. "Beau, would you please stop calling me Larry? It's not cute anymore."

"Seriously? But that's our thing." He cocked his head.

"No, it's not our thing. Not anymore. I'm a girl. A woman. A woman you almost *kissed*."

Oh damn. She hadn't meant to say that. Now it was out there, right between them, and though they'd certainly teased each other before, kissing had never been something they joked about.

Beau closed his eyes, seemingly almost instinctively, like someone had thrown an object at him.

When he opened them, he squinted. "If that made you uncomfortable, I'm sorry."

With one hand on the bed to help, Lucy found her bearings. "So…y-you admit it?"

"That I wanted to kiss you? Of course, I admit it. No use denying it. I was caught red-handed."

"Oh." Well, what was there to say now when he'd just thrown a bucket of honesty in her direction?

Beau winked at her. "Now it's up to you to decide if that was okay, because I could definitely kiss a girl named Larry."

What? What. What!

Her breath caught in her throat, and she simply stared at him without words.

"As long as she looks like you."

Then he shut the door behind him.

HOW EXACTLY WERE things supposed to stay the same, again?

Answer: they weren't. And Beau had done it again, he'd leapt, but this time some thought preceded it. Progress. Because in the end he couldn't let Lucy leave without letting her know, at least a little bit, about his feelings. And it was easier than he'd thought since his body spoke for him. These thoughts weren't going away, after all, the way they usually did whenever he crushed on a woman. He had found connections in the past with a handful of women, but nothing like *this*. No one else ever made his chest both tight and also expansive like the universe.

Last summer, Meg, a girlfriend from Kerrville, had come out to meet his friends when he had a cookout on his new patio. It took only one outdoor grill party for her to break up with Beau, because he was so clearly in love with Lucy.

"That's not true," he'd said. "I thought you weren't the jealous type."

"I'm not unless I need to be. Thank you for being

obvious before I got in too deep with you. Trust me. If you don't tell her how you feel you'll always regret it."

Beau chalked it up to yet another woman he'd disappointed, probably because he'd been a bit too friendly with Lucy. He'd been called a flirt more than once. In the end Meg had been right. And if he didn't *do* something, and soon, he'd regret it. It would either be the second coming of Levi, or she'd be gone to Seattle. Beau wasn't conceited enough to think he was going to be able to keep her here, but he'd give her something to think about if it was the last thing he did. Whether or not Charlotte was his baby, he and Lucy owed each other a chance to explore…whatever *this* was. Yes, it would be complicated. But stranger things had happened.

It turned out his daughter had a lot more in common with him than her coloring. She was also an early riser. Four a.m. was not an issue for her, and she was wide awake before the sunrise. At least she'd slept better during the night, waking him only once and going back to sleep when he stroked her back.

"You not only look, but act like a Stephens." He changed her diaper, having become adequate at the task, and changed her into a different outfit Rachel had left for her.

This one had pink hearts stamped all over it and Beau frowned. Whoever said girls always had to wear pink? His daughter would not wear only pink. How about purple and powerful? Blue was a fine color, too, and let's not forget green. Amber was a personal favorite of his, like Lucy's eyes, though he guessed no baby clothes came in amber.

"Your mom should be back in a few more days."

This was day four, and by his calculations, she should be back by Monday or Tuesday if she was serious about exactly a week. But maybe with any luck she'd be back sooner.

"Mmmmma, ma, ma," Charlotte said, batting her fists in the air.

He noticed she had a way of alternatively going between *b*'s, *m*'s, and *t*'s. He recalled Sammy had done the same about this age and Lincoln had been pretty frustrated at the lack of recognition. Suddenly, Beau could relate even if he'd called Linc a fool at the time.

"How about dada?" Beau said as he snapped the last snap.

She gave him a toothless smile and kicked her legs. Lord, she was adorable. Every day he found himself wishing and hoping she was really his. Surely Rachel wouldn't have lied. But even if the baby didn't belong to her ex-boyfriend, it still didn't mean Charlotte was *his*. He'd have to get that test done just to confirm what he already suspected.

With so much on the line right now, he had to be sure. Then, he'd make his plans accordingly.

An hour later, Beau had given Charlotte a bottle and had his coffee when he heard a truck pull up just as the sun was rising. Lincoln. About time his best friend showed up. He realized he had his own family, but Beau had been drowning here, and without Lucy stepping in and showing up for him he'd now be dead. He was fine, however, and making his way, no thanks to Lincoln.

He wrapped Charlotte in a blanket against the cool morning air and stepped outside the side door closest to the kitchen, so they wouldn't disturb Lucy. There was a small patio just outside the kitchen, and in a rare streak of homemaking, he'd bought patio furniture he rarely used. So far, he'd had only one grilling party here since building the house, but he had a meat smoker and a state-of-the-art grill outdoors. He sat on the swinging patio bench with Charlotte on his lap and waited for his best friend to stride toward them.

"Hey," Linc said, tipping his hat by way of greeting.

"Hey yourself. Finally decided to stop by, huh? Could have used your help."

He understood Sadie was on bedrest, but he'd already lost his mother's help to her. The least Linc could do was drop by and give Beau some advice.

Linc chuckled. "Oh boy, you have got yourself in a pickle this time."

"Yeah, thanks. How's Sadie?" Beau did the obligatory asking but he knew she had to be fine or Linc wouldn't be here.

"She's alright. It's driving her crazy but between me and your mom, we're forcing her to relax."

"Forcing and relax are two words that don't seem to fit together well."

"Funny, that's pretty much what she said." Linc shrugged. "I'll do whatever it takes to keep her healthy."

"I know you will." Beau would have expected no less.

Linc took a seat beside them and grabbed a hold of Charlotte's little foot. "She's a cutie."

"Yeah, well, you would say that. She looks like Sadie, doesn't she?"

"A little." Linc fished out his phone and took a picture. "Hold still. She'll want me to show her what the baby looks like. Your mom didn't get any good pictures."

Lincoln stood and snapped several photos, close-ups of Charlotte, then zooming out to get him in, too. Charlotte seemed fascinated by the big new guy in her surroundings and smiled and cooed at him as if she, too, was saying hello.

Beau grew irritated. "Never mind the damn pictures.

What am I going to *do*? Got any advice for me?"

"Well, my advice is retroactive." Ping, ping, ping went his phone.

"Not helping," Beau muttered.

Lincoln glanced at his phone. "You're not smiling in that one."

"I'm not smiling in any of them." He settled Charlotte against his shoulder. "I don't think this is fair. It would have been nice to know I had a daughter, like six months ago."

"Agreed. It isn't fair to spring her on you like this."

"Without Lucy, I wouldn't be a functioning adult right now."

"Were you ever?" Linc smirked and put away his phone.

"Listen, funny guy, I'm doing the best I can over here."

"I get it. All I can say, Beau, is you gotta make the best out of this situation. You remember Sadie and I didn't exactly plan Sammy. He was sort of a surprise."

"Not the same at all. You found out on your wedding day. Point is you were in love and *already* getting married."

"Right, and we made the best of him coming a little earlier than we wanted."

"I don't see how this is the same thing."

"Didn't say it was. But you're going to have to find a way to make the best of it. Like you've done all your life. You know how to build. I've seen you take a pile of scrap wood and turn it into a home. Just turn that ability around and build a family. It might not look like anything you ever expected but it could be good." Lincoln studied Beau. "Is there any way you can make it work with the mother? Any way at all? Can you rebuild whatever you had once before?"

He thought of Lucy, and the fact she knew he'd offered to marry Rachel. But it had been done in the moment, trying to do the right thing. Thank God she'd turned him down. If not, he might be getting ready for a wedding at Trinity Church, still pining away for Lucy. That was no way to begin a marriage.

"I might have thought so at one time, but not anymore. It's impossible. I don't want to be unfair to her and my heart isn't in it. I'll be a father to my daughter, and I guess we'll be our own little family."

"Well, that works sometimes, too."

Beau heard movement from inside. Lucy was in the kitchen, probably making her way to the coffee maker. It seemed she hadn't noticed them out here yet.

Lincoln, however, noticed her and squinted through the sliding glass doors. "Isn't that Lucy?"

"Yeah."

Lincoln whistled and quirked a brow. "She spent the night?"

"It's not like that. She stayed over because they're tenting her house. She's been helping me out with Charlotte."

"Ah yes, Lucy *can* do anything." And then, as if a lightbulb had suddenly gone on in his head, Lincoln blinked, then smiled. "Oh wait. You're kidding me. *Still?*"

"I don't want to talk about it," Beau muttered.

Once, when drunk, Beau had made the mistake of confiding in Lincoln that he thought Lucy was hotter than a jalapeno pepper if you lit it on fire.

Lincoln held up his palms. "Fine. I won't say anything. But if you're thinking it's too late for you two, it's just not. It's only too late when one of you is walking down the aisle at Trinity. Even then, hell, don't forget we are known for being the town with the greatest number of runaway brides. *Anything* is possible. Now, let me go take a look at that horse."

Chapter 13

The moment Lucy heard the muffled voices outside, she decided not to disturb Beau and Lincoln. For one thing, her bed hair was particularly alarming this morning. She first discovered this fact when she went in the guest bathroom after grabbing her coffee. Brown waves and curls were sticking out in every direction. Frizz city.

"Don't you look lovely, *Larry*." She stuck her tongue out at her reflection.

I could kiss a girl named Larry.

As long as she looks like you.

The words poured over her like sweet sticky syrup on a flapjack. She could almost feel those words, slicing and worming their way inside, through tiny air bubbles and cracks in her heart. The same need to run was now tempered by a desire to know more. Information was power. Good decisions could not be made in vacuums, and she was afraid that's how she'd made the choice to leave for Seattle. She'd consulted her own opinions and those of a homesick friend who'd talked her into exploring what the great city had to offer. Besides, when Beau discouraged her from going, all he talked about was the rain.

He'd never said: I want to kiss you.

Because that would have changed everything. Maybe.

She really wanted to eavesdrop on the men's conversation but once she heard the name Rachel the urgency with which she wanted to listen in had her backing off. Whatever she heard couldn't be *unheard*. She'd have to live with that knowledge. But first, she wanted to explore this thing with Beau and see where it led, if anywhere at all. Beau was known far and wide for his short attention span when it came to women. Lucy did not want to be in that far-from-exclusive league.

She quickly took a shower, dressed, and tried to arrange her hair in some semblance of order. Which meant a ponytail. Her usual attitude was "take me as I am, buddy." Even if some small part of her wanted to become a hoochie mama and vamp overnight to show Beau how fun she'd be to kiss, this also wouldn't be a good idea. For one thing, she didn't have the wardrobe.

Oh, she'd seen the women Beau dated. They were so *obvious*. Years ago, rumor was Beau had dated a stripper from San Antonio for a short while. He did not discriminate with women. This Rachel woman was probably the same, with her tight skinny jeans and crop tops showing off a pierced navel. With parents like Lucy's, she couldn't get a piercing until she was eighteen and by then she'd changed her mind since it had lost all its allure and she wasn't a big fan of pain. Even tattoos had been difficult, honestly, but one girl's night out she, Sadie, and Eve wound up at a parlor in the city.

At the last minute Sadie and Eve both chickened out of the matching tattoos they'd all wanted to cement their forever friendships. Lucy was just drunk enough to follow through and she had three pink and red hearts tattooed right above her hip bone. Not too many people knew about this tattoo, but it was just this side of wild, and every single time Lucy looked at it something inside her unfurled and ripped open.

So, it was a good thing she couldn't see it all the time. And, by the time she'd removed her clothes so that a man could see her hip tattoo…that was a good time to unfurl anyway.

When Lucy came out of her room dressed, Beau was sitting at the table eating cereal from a bowl while Charlotte was in the high chair gumming it.

"Hey," he said, lowering his coffee mug. "Good morning."

"I was up earlier but wanted to give you and Lincoln privacy. Charlotte seemed to be doing fine with you."

Beau nodded. "Linc wanted to see the horse."

"Word travels fast. What does he think of it?"

"He also doesn't think I should name her Thor." He shrugged.

"Well, he's a smart man." She poured herself another cup of coffee for fuel.

"Otherwise, he agrees she's a fine specimen. I'm going to saddle her up and take her for a ride in a while. If that's okay with you."

"Sure, I'll watch Charlotte. Just remember I have a shift tonight at the bar. I'll be quite late."

"That's fine. Don't you even think about sleeping in your car again, La—"

Lucy almost laughed at the way he stopped himself in time, but bit on her lower lip instead. "I won't sleep in my car. You have silky soft sheets. Your bed has won me over."

He met her eyes, his darkening. "That's not my bed. That's the guest bed."

"Well, you know what I mean."

"Let's just say if thread count is what wins you over to *my* bed, I know I did something wrong."

Lucy nearly spit her coffee out and had to swallow fast, cough, and hit her chest.

"You okay there?" Beau sent her a grin that showed his understanding of how he'd unnerved her. "I don't think I've ever seen you blush."

"I'm not blushing!" She was totally blushing. "And before I…um, were to ever test your bed out, there would first have to be at least a kiss."

"Plenty of kissing." He stood and plopped his hat on. "You're right about that."

"Exactly. It's called foreplay."

Now she'd surprised Beau.

He blinked. "Which is what you and I have been doing in some form or another for about five years."

He walked toward his bedroom, letting her sit with that.

SADIE STILL COULDN'T SEE her feet but now she was used to it.

Just a few more days. She could do this. At her next appointment, maybe Trixie would take her off bed rest. Her blood pressure was down and cooperating and the baby was happy, going by all the kicks he or she gave on a regular basis. No more pain or spotting. She was fine and wished someone would listen to her when she said she could get up. All she wanted to do was straighten up a little. But between Lincoln and her mother, she felt like a prisoner in her own home. And she had not one but *two* wardens.

Her mother had taken Sammy to the park earlier and

they would probably be gone for at least a couple of hours. Her boy loved the park. He loved climbing *everything*, even things that were not meant to be climbed. Like the slide. He went up instead of down. Once he'd tried to climb the *under* side of the slide and bumped his head before Sadie could stop him. She picked up her phone now, wondering if she should call her mom to warn her again. But her mother had raised Beau, so she knew a little something about rambunctious boys.

"Is that you, Linc?" she called out when the front door shut.

"Yep, it's me."

She could hear him bounding up the steps to their bedroom and then he bent to kiss her temple. "Hey, sweetheart."

She sat up straighter. "Did you see the baby?"

The thought cheered her. *Her baby niece.* She'd been lying around for days thinking about Charlotte and just couldn't wait to meet her. Hopefully she'd also be lucky enough to have a girl, too, and the girls could grow up together. Her daughter, and Beau's. Sadie just couldn't bring herself to regret Beau having a baby, even if it was with the wrong woman.

Lincoln propped up the pillows behind her. "Saw the baby and the horse. Both are cute. Only one of them looks like you."

"She looks like me? It's true?"

"She's one lucky little baby." Linc plopped down beside her on the bed, on top of the covers since he still had his boots on.

"Let me see."

He pulled out his phone and handed it to her. "Took plenty of photos for you."

Sadie swiped through each one, admiring the sweet

little girl, smiling so hard her face hurt. "Oh my goodness, look at Beau. Poor thing. He's not smiling in any of them."

Linc snorted. "Cut him a break. He's been out of sorts. I know he wishes we were over there helping out."

"It's only a few more days till the mother comes back. Right?"

"If she comes back."

"Oh don't say that. She'll come back for this precious baby."

But on the other hand, no one had come back for Lucy. It was probably the first thought on everyone's minds.

Sadie had never understood it. With a fervent imagination like hers, she often entertained the thought that Lucy's mother was a woman in trouble and on the run. She'd gotten mixed up with the wrong people and made a tough choice. The adventurous life she led wasn't for a baby, so she'd dropped Lucy off in a small town known to revere and protect its women. A sacrificial kind of love. A mother's love.

"Beau is going to have to ease into this fatherhood thing." Lincoln splayed his hands behind his neck and tipped his hat. "Most of us have at least nine months to get used to and ready for the situation. Beau had a few minutes. It isn't fair."

"I know. What kind of a mother would do this?" She stopped Lincoln before he could answer. "Never mind, don't answer that."

In the past Beau had dated strippers to nurses to teachers and everything in between. And he still hadn't found the right woman because she'd been here all along. Maybe it was Sadie's fault that she hadn't thrown them together before. But she was doing whatever she could now to right that wrong.

"Did you know Lucy is staying with him? She was

waking up earlier this morning while I was still talking to Beau on the patio."

"She has to stay with him because of the terminate infestation at her place."

Lincoln tipped his hat to peek at her from under it. "That's what Beau told me, but how do you know about that?"

"Um, Lenny told me?"

"When have you seen Lenny?" Lincoln propped up on his elbow. "Did he stop by? Call?"

"No, I...I..." Sadie didn't want to lie to her husband when he asked outright.

"Sadie?" Lincoln had that "what are you up to" tone in his voice. "What's going on?"

"Alright! There are no termites in her house!" She tossed up her hands, giving up.

"I thought that sounded suspicious." Lincoln grinned. "What are you saying?"

"I'm telling you I conspired with Beulah. She got Lenny to pretend he saw termites and tent the house so Lucy would have to spend the night somewhere else. Then, we got her mother to say she couldn't stay over because her room is being painted. And we got my mother to imply that we didn't have the room for her."

"We actually don't. Your mother is staying in the only spare room we have." Lincoln paused. "Oh wait. Is that why you asked your mom to stay over?"

"Maybe." Sadie felt her cheeks heat. "But I can always find room for one my dearest friends."

"But not this time."

"It just made sense she would stay with Beau since she's already helping him out."

"Of course. Makes all the sense in the world. And you think that's going to be enough? Just put her in his line of vision? She's been in his sight for years and nothing happened."

"Well, I may have helped a little more, too."

"Uh-oh." Lincoln chuckled.

"It's nothing terrible. They both just need a hard shove." She pushed her hands out to demonstrate.

"Too bad you didn't shove sooner. Like six months and nine months ago sooner."

"Lucy was dating Levi. And I've been a little busy here?" She made a gesture over her enormous girth. "You keep knocking me up."

He grinned. "What else did you do?"

"I sent red roses on his behalf with a sweet little note."

"That won't work. Beau will admit he didn't send them."

"Or *will* he?" She touched her temple.

"Hmm." Lincoln got closer and threw an arm around the section Sadie formerly referred to as her waist. "What else has my little evil wife done?"

"Nothing yet. But I have plans. Those two are not leaving that house until they both realize they're absolutely perfect for each other."

Chapter 14

Beau had put in a full day of ranching by the time he waltzed back inside to relieve Lucy. He'd fed the horses, mucked the stalls, fed the chickens, collected eggs, and finally had time for a leisurely ride. He still hadn't named the horse, calling her "sweetie" for now. Since he hadn't a chance for any input on naming his daughter, he figured he'd take his time to come up with the perfect name. Maybe he needed another Larry in his life now that Lucy had asked him never to call her that again. What was wrong with "Larry" Lorenzo? It was cute and perfect, like her. If he'd known it bothered her *that* much he would have stopped years ago.

He had silly nicknames for all his good friends. Lincoln was both Linc, LincTown, and Lucky-meister, based on the name from his rodeo days, or L-dog for short. Jackson was Jacka-roo, or J-train. Eve was Evie-Bee-V and Sadie was Sashimi. He used to call Lucy Lulu and LooLa but somehow he'd wound up calling her Larry one day for fun. And face it, he called her Larry whenever he wanted to put distance between them and the deeper attraction he had for her. Hadn't worked long term.

Today he'd made it abundantly clear that his nickname for her did not reflect on his ability to see her as a woman. His feelings for her were burning hotter every day and he congratulated himself on not acting on them. He'd let her come to him and try that for a change. Lucy probably didn't care for all the women he'd dated in the past. She'd want to know he would be different with her. He would be, but words weren't going to be enough to show her. Levi was already trying to get back into her good graces with those roses and Beau had noticed. Levi might have something else up his sleeve and Beau had to act fast. Patience in this area was not exactly his forte.

Exhibit A was currently swinging in the little infant seat playing a song that bordered on human torture for him. But one of them, him, or Levi, could talk Lucy into staying. Beau voted for himself.

A few minutes after disappearing into the guest room to change, Lucy came out in the clothes she always wore when bartending. Which is to say, she looked hot. This was the only time Lucy went out of her way to do those little things women did to attract a man's attention. She wore dark eye makeup, red-hot lipstick, and had teased her long dark hair from its usual unruly state into waves that cascaded all over her shoulders in perfect curls. Even though she wore jeans and her usual black fashion boots, her black top was tight, giving her plenty of what she called "oomph" otherwise known as "good tips." Beau called it T&A but that was beside the point.

Beau swallowed. "You look nice."

He'd said that before, he was certain, but now the words carried with them a resonance that rang between them like a clanging bell.

"Thanks." She didn't look at him, combing through her bag for something or the other. "You know how it is. It's a big night for tips."

"All *you* have to do is smile."

"I'll tell Levi you said that. We're in a contest to see who makes the most tips on any night."

That got his attention. "Levi's working tonight?"

"Yeah, he asked if I could come in a little early because he needs to talk to me."

Damn it. The red roses, and now he needed to "talk" to Lucy. It had begun to be too obvious to Beau that Levi wanted Lucy back.

"Talk to you, huh?" Beau gave the swing a little push and Charlotte squealed. "You mean he wants you back."

"What?" Lucy's head whipped up and she met Beau's eyes. "Why would you say that?"

Beau pointedly glanced at the roses then back to Lucy. "It's kind of obvious, isn't it?"

She gave him another you're-a-dumb-guy look. "No. We broke up over six months ago. That's not what he wants. He needs my help with something."

Yeah, Beau would just bet he needed her "help." The emotion coursing through him wasn't at all familiar. It took him a minute to recognize this anger mixed with confusion and desire was what some people called *jealousy*. *What the ever-lovin' hell was happening here?* He wasn't a jealous man. Never had been, swore he never would be. Jealousy was unproductive. Useless. He'd seen it in too many of his friends. Jealousy could eat a man alive with its power.

If a woman wasn't interested in him, he moved on. No harm, no foul.

No use getting all stupidly *emotional* about it.

Lucy held up her circle ring of keys. "Took me long

enough to find these. Well, I'm off. Wish me lots of tips for help with Seattle!"

"Yeah," Beau muttered. "Bye. Tell Levi I wish him luck and I hope you'll…he'll be very happy."

She gave him a quizzical look that said *okay, you dingbat.* "Sure."

With that, she was out the door, her curvy rear end swinging behind her. Beau watched her walk away from him, and then sat back down for a quiet evening with his daughter.

TONIGHT WAS ALWAYS a busy time at the Shady Grind since it had somehow unofficially been dubbed "couples' night."

This happened to be Lucy's favorite night to work because the tips were plentiful. Levi was waiting for her when she showed up, early, too, for once. He looked nervous, going shifty eyed about ten minutes after the door opened and couples started to file in.

"Something wrong?" she asked.

"No, no." He wiped his brow. "It's just…well, this is a big deal."

The way Levi looked at her, so intently, she wondered if Beau had been right. For a slice of a moment, she'd thought Beau might have been jealous earlier. After all, jealousy caused men to make unreasonable blanket statements. Because it was *unreasonable* to believe Levi suddenly wanted her back. But Beau wasn't the jealous type so there was something else going on here. Something she didn't know.

"Wh-what's happening?"

He smiled. "I have a surprise and I need you to relieve

me for a few minutes because I need to get out from behind the bar to do this. I want to do it right."

"Do…do what?"

"I can't tell you. You'll find out soon enough and it's going to shock you, but I know you're going to be happy about this. It's everything we talked about. Just wait and see."

"Um…Levi…I…"

But Levi was busy with a customer and a moment later, so was she.

While she worked, she racked her mind for their last talk. What had they talked about, exactly? They'd had a big "come to Jesus moment" months ago and resolved everything when they broke up for the last time. It was never going to work. He knew it and so did she. They'd had to admit to each other that they were simply spending time together because neither one of them liked being alone. As for him, it wasn't like he had a lot of women to choose from. She had a different situation, but Levi was someone she felt comfortable with and so for a while, she gravitated toward him.

What had she done to mislead him? Did he think her move to Seattle was to get him to step up? Because it wasn't! She'd distinctly told him last time that "Sometimes you have to take a risk to be happy" and she'd announced her move to Seattle shortly after.

For the next hour or so, Levi kept throwing her little smiles of encouragement, a little anticipatory wink here and there. And then, just as she was pouring another draft beer, she *saw* it. Everything froze and the room seemed to spin. No. This couldn't be happening. Oh. No.

In the pocket of Levi's pants, she noticed a bulge exactly the size and shape of a ring box.

"I'm taking my break," Lucy shouted to Levi, who nodded.

She threw off her apron and ran for her purse and cell. At least they had service in town, and she dialed Beau's landline.

"Beau, have you and Levi been talking recently?"

"No, I called him about my horse, which by the way still needs a name. What do you think about—"

"Stop talking about your horse," she hissed, then tucked her phone close to avoid any eavesdroppers. "Did he mention to you that…that he's going to ask me to marry him?"

Utter silence was Beau's reply.

"Hello? Hello? Are you there?" Good service was never a guarantee, and she glanced down to make certain she hadn't been disconnected.

"I'm here," Beau said after a moment. "You said he's going to ask you to marry him."

"I mean, I think so, because he has an obvious ring box in his pocket. And he wants to surprise me with a special announcement."

"You really shouldn't be surprised by this."

"Are you *kidding* me? Of course I'm surprised!"

"I don't see why."

Beau went on to say something about the roses that *he'd* sent her, and she had no idea what *that* had to do with this.

"I knew he wanted you back. The signs are all there."

"I don't know what to *do*," Lucy said. "I hate to embarrass him in front of all these people."

"What does that mean? You're going to say no to him?"

Then Levi was beckoning to her from behind the bar to hurry back. Oh my lord. He was doing this.

"I...I have to go now." She hung up with Beau, her mouth dry and her palms sweaty.

The only thing to do was act happy, say yes, then later remind him how they'd agreed they would never work. Remind him of the conversation they'd had. She hadn't meant taking a risk *with her.*

As soon as she got back behind the bar, Levi went on the other side. She caught him tapping the ring box in his pocket self-consciously like he wanted to confirm it was still there, and she had a little heart attack. This was not the way she'd wanted to change her life. Sure, she'd wanted something new and explosive. Something not so certain, but this was not it at all. *Not even close.*

And then a strange thing happened. Levi walked away from Lucy and the bar, toward the section containing the booths where people sat to eat. And for the first time, Lucy noticed that at some point Jolette Marie Truehart must have come inside with a couple friends.

Then, as if in slow motion, Levi dropped to one knee beside Jolette Marie and pulled out the box. It was a ring.

Everything stopped.

All chatter, all eating, all drinking. It seemed every couple in the bar turned their attention to the floor show. Lucy felt her heart swell with relief followed quickly by worry and fear for Levi. Jolette Marie would not be kind. If her answer was "no" it would be more like, "oh hell no," and she wouldn't care *who* she embarrassed. Levi was still Lucy's good friend even if he was no longer anything else, and she couldn't stand by and watch a friend go down in flames. Evidenced by her taking care of Charlotte, and a million other things she could name.

But Levi...he was doing this.

Lucy's hands gripped the bar, and her expression was clear enough to read.

Someone said, "Oh, damn. Lucy, I'm so sorry. Are you okay with this?"

"Shh," Lucy said, waving her hand for silence.

"Jo, you know I've loved you for years. I never thought I was good enough for you—"

"Yes you are, Levi!" This was from Jackson, seated at a nearby table with Eve and their daughter, Lily.

"Thanks, buddy." Levi waved. "Anyway, I still love you. A good friend of mine told me you have to take a risk for the things you truly want. And I don't want anything more than I want a life with you by my side as my wife, my partner."

There was a collective swoon from Jolette Marie's table. But the key was what *she* would say in response. Jo was the town's spoiled rich girl even if the Henderson brothers, and Bonnie Lee, tried to tell Lucy otherwise. She was highly misunderstood, apparently. Well, this was the time to prove Jo had a big heart in addition to a big inheritance. If she said no to Levi, or embarrassed him, Lucy would have no recourse but to take her outside and punch her lights out.

"Will you marry me?"

Lucy held her breath. After all, she'd, through no fault of her own, told him to do this and now here he was, the fool, doing it. *Listening* to her. Who did that?

She grabbed the hand of her closest patron, who happened to be Jeremy, and squeezed hard.

"Ouch," he said. "Lord, you have a grip."

"Shut up," Lucy hissed. "I need to *hear* this."

"Oh Levi," Jolette Marie said and stood from the booth. "Yes! Yes, yes!"

The entire room erupted with cheers.

Lucy practically crumbled with relief. She'd mistaken all Levi's signals. He'd been trying to tell her he was going through with *his* biggest risk, which wasn't her. They'd talked about this carefully without hurting each other's feelings. He confessed that he loved Jolette Marie and had for years, but her father was a man who did not approve of poor horse trainers like Levi. Even if he was the best in their town and possibly the entire state. Even if three previous marriages Mr. Truehart had tried to arrange with men he approved of had resulted in Jo becoming a runaway bride three times.

"Are you going to be okay?" Jeremy said, clearly mistaking her hand wrenching for despair.

He, like everyone else, knew that she and Levi had dated exclusively for a time.

"Oh yeah. I saw this coming." She could say that's why she'd broken up with him but that wasn't entirely true. "I encouraged him."

"Seriously?" Jeremy looked like he didn't believe her.

She was supposed to be jealous, she imagined, and want to claw Jolette Marie's eyes out. But this love-story happy ending was in part thanks to her convincing Levi that no woman was too good for him, not even a Truehart.

"I'm always happy for my friends. And Levi is a good friend." Lucy grabbed a glass and rubbed it clean with her towel.

The rest of the night was spent celebrating. Drinks were passed around, toasts made to Levi, Stone Ridge's very own "horse whisperer" according to Eve, a veterinarian who knew what she was talking about. As it turned out, for the past several months, Levi and Jolette Marie had once again reignited their affair. He'd kept the new flower shop in business, sending an arrangement every day for a week. They'd somehow managed to keep their relationship a secret, and after finally confessing they still loved each other, Levi knew it was time to take that last leap of faith.

"It was thanks to you and what we talked about," Levi told Lucy later that evening. "You decided to make a move to Seattle and change your life. Take a risk. That gave me courage enough to do this. I'm sorry I didn't tell you sooner, but I didn't want anyone to talk me out of it."

And Lucy would have, at least the public part of the proposal, given her reaction and fear as she'd watched. She didn't know why she'd ever thought Jolette Marie would say no, however, given by the clear adoration in her eyes.

"I was nervous on your behalf, that's for sure." She touched Levi's shoulder. "I'm happy for you."

"Thanks, pal."

"But what are you going to do about her daddy?"

"Jo says she doesn't care if she gets disinherited, she loves me enough to run away with me and live in a shack by the river."

"Oh lord, I hope you realize she doesn't mean it. She loves you, yes, but forget about the shack."

Levi rolled his eyes. "No shack. Don't worry about us. Got it covered."

For the rest of her shift, Lucy watched the happy couple accept drinks and congratulations. There was practically a glow emanating from both of them, real and palpable. To think for one second she'd imagined…she'd known better, deep down. It would have been utterly crazy for Levi to ask her to marry him. But this joy, this happiness that shimmered from both of them like rays. She *wanted* that. She'd told Levi to take a risk like she had with her plans to relocate.

Funny how she'd never for a second pictured telling Beau how she felt. She'd loved him at least as long as Levi had loved Jolette Marie. Longer.

Yet here she was, alone on couples' night. Planning on moving to Seattle to meet new people.

Because she was too terrified to act on her own feelings. Coward.

That was going to change.

Lucy drove home at the end of the night, ready and willing to blow up her life.

Chapter 15

Beau finally got Charlotte to sleep around ten o'clock for the first time. The second time, he got her to sleep around midnight.

But it made no difference because he couldn't sleep after that phone call.

Lucy was getting married.

To *Levi.*

And Beau would have to live with that. If she walked back through his front door, he was going to smile if it killed him. He would offer a hug, congratulations, ask to see the ring. All those things a good friend would do. Then, when Rachel came back, he'd show her how well he'd done with Charlotte and ask her to marry him. Because if he couldn't be with Lucy, it didn't matter who he wound up with. He wouldn't be happy either way. Better to be unhappy with the mother of his child.

He was still up at two a.m. when he heard Lucy's car roll up the driveway. It would have made more sense for her to go home with Levi, but he wasn't entirely surprised.

Lucy's sense of obligation ran deep. Marriage proposal or not, she would have finished her shift, collected her tips, then back to Beau's so she could be here early in the morning. As promised. It occurred to him, for one minute, that she might have said no to Levi. If so, poor sap. Beau almost felt sorry for him. Almost.

He stood from the kitchen table when Lucy opened the side door connecting to the patio. For once, he couldn't read her expression. She was walking fast, stopping only to set her bag down by the couch, still not looking at him.

"Did you say yes?" It was the only question he wanted answered and he wanted an answer now.

It felt like the rest of his life hinged on that information. Like the road before him had a curve and a huge dip ahead and he had to know which way to turn.

It happened so fast Beau didn't even see it coming, but Lucy continued her fast walking toward him. She didn't stop until she was in front of him, where she grabbed him by the collar, pulled him to her, and gave him a fierce kiss right on the lips.

He did not see that turn coming, but he let go, enjoying every bump and bounce on the road. Lowering his hand to her hip and kissing her back because there was no way he wasn't going to participate. Threading his fingers through silky hair, he pulled her closer, angling her face.

When she pulled back they were both breathless.

"Does that answer your question?" Shimmering amber eyes gazed at him from under lowered lashes. A hint of a smile curled her upper lip.

"Not really." He needed a real answer.

"Levi didn't *ask* me to marry him. You were way off. We both were and thank God for that."

"*What?* I don't get it. Then who…"

Beau's voice trailed off as a crazy and random thought came to him. No…

"Yes, he asked *Jolette Marie* to marry him in front of the entire bar filled with customers. That's why he wanted me there, so he could leave the back of the bar and go to her table. And maybe for moral support, who knows. He dropped to one knee and everything. The craziest thing is she said yes!"

"Wow."

"Exactly."

Beau palmed a hand down his face. This was nuts. No one in town thought that relationship was ever going to happen, but rather that Jo was simply toying with the poor horse wrangler. Now Beau could forget about Levi. He wasn't a barrier or obstacle for him anymore. And for the first time in years, he was going to step in before somebody else did. Clearly, he had a chance if this kiss was any indication.

He tugged on a lock of her hair. "What was that kiss all about?"

She was still so close, her hands wrapped around his neck, and this moment was better than any in his fantasies.

"That was me following my own advice."

"Yeah?"

"I was the one who encouraged Levi to go after Jolette Marie if that's who he wanted. The last time we broke up? In case you were still curious, that was the reason."

"Because you figured out he was in love with Jo?"

"Because we both were brutally honest with each other." She closed her eyes. "This next part is embarrassing."

"We need to have this conversation. I'm not interested in being your rebound guy. If seeing Levi ask Jo to marry him made you—"

Her eyes flew open. "No. Well, at least not in the way you think."

"Tell me." He tugged on a strand of her hair. "And be brutally honest with me, too. I can take it."

He braced himself to hear that she was still moving to Seattle after years of hanging on to someone who wasn't all that into her. He'd seen it himself, the way Levi wanted to play both sides at times. Sending flowers to keep Lucy because she was a sure thing (in his mind) but lusting after and loving Jo from a safe distance. He'd tried to figure out a way to tell Lucy that Levi was all wrong for her without sounding like a jealous guy. When they'd broken up, Beau expected to see Levi change his mind and try to win Lucy back. The roses were confusing, a mixed message, and they must have misled Lucy, too.

Lucy closed her eyes again and when she opened them, her lashes were slightly damp.

"Listen. The truth is, I've had a thing for you. I tried to get over it, I tried to move on, so I dated other guys. Levi and I clicked but it would never work. We couldn't figure out why until…I told him to go after what he wanted because…it wasn't me. I tried to follow my own advice, and for me that was moving to Seattle. Starting over."

"But—"

She put a finger to his lips. "After tonight, I couldn't outrun my feelings anymore. The minute I saw Levi go after and get who he wanted, I thought maybe…"

"Maybe?" Beau cocked his head.

"I could also go for it. See, I'm a coward when it comes to big emotions like these. I should have said something a long time ago. I could have. But you…"

"I know."

He'd been running around, chasing his own tail,

thinking he had a thousand years to settle down. And then a little bundle had caused him to reevaluate his life. Charlotte made him realize life would pass him by if he didn't slow down. She'd taught him that if you didn't choose who you wanted to spend the rest of your life with, the decision might be made for you. He could have wound up spending his life with someone he didn't love out of obligation and duty. That would have never been enough for either one of them.

Slowing down, it turned out, wasn't half bad. Not with Lucy in his arms. It was more necessary than oxygen to hold her close, to share less than an inch of space between them. He kissed her, and then kissed her some more, pulling her down to the couch with him. Quickly, it got hot and desperate between them, him holding her like he feared she might change her mind and run. She, clawing like she wanted to climb him.

"Wait," she said suddenly, right after crawling in his lap.

"Yeah," Beau said on a gasp, releasing the tight hold but not releasing *her*.

He'd never release her were it up to him.

"Maybe we…maybe we should talk."

God, weren't those the four *worst words* in the English language? *Maybe we should talk.* Beau felt his heart thud against the wall of his chest, like a caged wild animal trying to break free. Thankfully, Lucy didn't go far, digging her fingers into his hair. This talk wouldn't turn negative anytime soon, he guessed. And hoped.

"Did you really think I'd say yes to Levi if he asked me to marry him? Did you think that was even a possibility?"

He considered mentioning the roses, but he didn't want to point out how much better Levi was about those little romantic touches women loved. As a rule, Beau was a confident sort, but Levi was a weakness. Levi had been the only man to last more than a few months with Lucy.

"I thought, yeah, it was possible. Levi's a good guy."

"He is a good guy, and my friend. But I was done with him six months ago."

"You've been done with him before. I thought maybe he was the reason you were leaving. Because you were so heartbroken this time."

Lucy closed her eyes briefly and fluttered them open again. Tonight, they were the darkness shade of amber he'd ever seen. Like the night sky, lit up by a few golden rays of fading sunlight.

"No. I was leaving because of you."

"Me?"

"Because I couldn't stand to watch you with other women. And then, with the influx of ladies coming here after the *Mr. Cowboy* show, they all gravitated toward *you*. It wasn't so bad before, but it got unbearable after that."

"That's because they saw me all the time around the cabins where most of them live. I've been in the center of the tornado, that's all."

"No, that's not why. It's because you're an extremely charming, as well as hot, good-looking cowboy and they all have good eyesight. Those women are no dummies."

He was speechless for about two seconds. "And how long have you thought of me as *charming*?"

"That depends. How long have you wanted to kiss me?"

"Um." Beau studied the ceiling while he did the math. "For about five years?"

"Five years!" Her head swiveled back like a duck's. "*Five* years?"

"That first time you gave me a haircut and you needed a guinea pig."

"Ohh," she said as understanding seemed to hit her. "I *remember* that day."

"You give sexy haircuts. I need another one."

Like she wanted to tease him, she ran her fingers through his hair. "Every time I gave you a haircut, you disappeared for weeks."

"Because I was trying to talk myself out of kissing you and ruining our friendship!"

"You *should* have kissed me."

"I see that now. But…thing is…you're the only woman I've never wanted to disappoint."

She was quiet for a long moment. "I think that's the nicest thing you've ever said to me."

"So far."

He couldn't help himself. There went the wink. Well, she'd said he was charming. Time to step up.

She framed his face. "Yes. So far. I don't know what I'm doing here, Beau, but… I think I'm following my heart for the first time in my life."

"I know everything is more complicated now." He took her hand and brushed a kiss across her knuckles. "I have a kid I'll have to co-parent for the next eighteen years. I have to…I don't know…start a college fund. But I want to thank you for not crossing me off some imaginary list as someone who's no longer an option."

"I'm the last person who's going to discourage you from being involved with your daughter. She needs you."

"But you're going to need me, too. For a lot of things. I'm hoping."

"You're already so many things for me. It scares me a little to think how much more you could become to me."

"That makes two of us. I'm scared, too. Scared to lose you, scared to disappoint you… scared I'm dreaming this."

She smiled, the one that had always made him feel like he could conquer the world. Her smile held it all for him—his past, his future, and everything that had ever mattered to him rolled into one.

"You're not dreaming. This is real. We're doing this. You and me."

"God, finally." He removed her hand from his face and kissed the palm. "It's about damn time."

They kissed again, more like a long make-out session, the kind he hadn't enjoyed in years. But guilt clawed at him because this was arguably his best friend in many ways. He never lied to his friends.

She'd just removed his shirt, easing it off his shoulders when he realized that it was time to confess the awful truth.

"Lucy."

"Oh my god, look at this man chest. I saw it the other day when you opened the door without a shirt but I—"

"*Lucy.*"

"What?"

"I don't want to start this relationship with a lie. Unfortunately, and this is killing me, but you seem to think I sent you those red roses."

"But you did."

"I wish I had."

"But you…"

"I thought they were from Levi and, honestly, I didn't want to talk about it. Then, tonight, I got snoopy after you called and got a look at the note. They were from me. But I didn't send them."

"Ohhh." Understanding crossed her face but lucky for him she didn't seem upset. "I think I'm starting to understand something here. You don't want to get ahead of yourself with the love part. That's okay, we can take it slow—"

"No. That's not what I meant. I did not send them. At all."

She didn't look disappointed, thank you Jesus, instead she looked truly puzzled, canting her head to the side. Until understanding seemed to strike her.

"*That's* interesting. First, the roses. Next, my place has to be tented and no one else has room for me. Even my own mother. Do you see what's happening here?"

Not really, but he was a dumb guy. "A mistake at the flower shop?"

"No, dummy. They're *all* playing matchmaker!"

It was an outstanding moment for Beau. Sure, it made sense to arrange a romance for Lucy, so she'd at least consider staying in town. But he'd have thought they'd play matchmaker with anyone but him. Frankly, the idea they'd thought of him for Lucy was flattering.

"Sadie, your mother, my own mother, Lenny. I thought it was weird she decided to paint my room on a whim. I bet the whole town is in on this!"

"Trying to matchmake? You and *me*?"

"Keep up."

"But—"

This was news to him. It was one thing to try to fix him up with one of the new women who'd arrived after the reality show. But to fix him up with arguably the best woman in town, their "miracle" baby, was unthinkable. Beau had no idea anyone held him in high enough regard to do him this favor. No one but his mother, and possibly Sadie.

"You do realize what we have to do?" She grinned.

"Sure, we have to tell them their evil plan worked. And I'll personally need to buy everyone a gift certificate or help with someone's construction project. Maybe I'll have a raffle and build someone a new house."

"Or…you know…we *could* mess with them."

It had been years since they'd worked together like this. With no idea what she had in mind, he could only grin at the smile in her eyes that said, "trouble ahead."

Chapter 16

Of all the dirty, underhanded, rotten things to do to a person. First, fake the red roses sent from Beau. That one was probably Sadie, Lucy would bet. She knew better than most how much Lucy loved it when a guy sent her flowers. It was Levi's one redeeming grace, even when he couldn't help but stare longingly in Jo's direction if she happened to walk by, then later apologize. But hey, she got the weekly flower delivery. It didn't hurt that she had the same kind of meh attitude about him.

But pretending her house had to be tented? She almost hoped that wasn't *also* a lie, but looking back, it was classic Lenny. So, they'd somehow forced her to move in with Beau. She could hear them thinking *either they will kill each other, or fall in love*. But what if this had all gone horribly wrong? They obviously hadn't considered *that*. Instead, everything had gone terribly right and for that she probably owed everyone involved a vow of eternal gratitude.

But not so fast.

She tapped her chin. "There are so many ways to play this. I'll have to think how best to mess with them."

"I love it when you talk dirty." He tightened his hold on her again. "What did you have in mind?"

"We could have fun with this. I could tell them for the first time in my life, I hate you because I've had to live with you."

Beau frowned. "Seriously?"

"And you hate me, too, of course!"

"I'm not that great of an actor."

"The point is, we can't let them know we're together."

"So, we fake *not* being together?" His brows knit together. "Isn't it usually the other way around?"

"It just makes me so mad my mother is still trying to control me."

"It isn't just her. Throw in Lenny, I assume. He's always treated you like another daughter. They all just want you to be happy, Lucy. That's all."

It was true. And if not for this silly arrangement, and if not for Levi, she wouldn't be here at this moment. The fact it had taken her all this effort to figure out that she had a thing for Beau that was never going to go away, well, that part was not exactly their fault.

"And I know Sadie means well."

Beau squinted. "You think she had something to do with this, too?"

"She's been bedridden this week and probably bored to tears."

"And let's face it, like me, she wants you to stay."

"Do you?" The words hadn't actually been said before. "You really want me to stay?"

"I want you to be happy. If I thought Seattle would make you happy, then I'd want it for you. You know I want everything you do. I'm always on your side. But if you're asking me if I want you to stay, if I'm asking you to stay…

well, yeah, the answer is yes. And I will fight for you, Lucy, if that's what you want."

The thrill of delight hit her again, the same one of moments ago when she'd kissed Beau. When she'd discovered that the fantasy of all this time fully met up with her expectations. The kiss was electric. Passionate. Feverish and desperate. Everything she'd ever dreamed. Beau was an incredible kisser, following her lead, and taking over.

He wanted her to stay.

She could tell him that he'd simply had to ask but that wasn't entirely true. Truer was that she'd never given him the room to ask. But now he had the space, and to see him pressing his advantage was nothing less than she'd hope.

"Please stay, Lucy." He kissed the palm of her hand, trailing soft and tender kisses up the length of her arm and to the column of her neck. "Stay with me."

Oh, he was so good at this. So good at drawing her in, at getting her attention. Keeping it.

Everything else was forgotten. Nothing mattered but their two mouths fused together, tongues tasting, needing each other like the sweetest wine. Years of untapped desire and longing were unleashed. Lucy almost couldn't breathe she was so caught up in this moment. It had never felt like this with anyone else. He lowered the strap of her bra and kissed bare, fleshy skin. She was on fire for him.

Beau picked her up and she discovered that a man who built homes for a living had a natural strength in his arms. He carried her into his bedroom and shut the door, and for the next few hours, they learned the geography of each other's bodies.

And on the threat of death, Lucy couldn't honestly tell you whether his sheets were 1,000 thread count or not.

She didn't notice.

· · ·

WHEN LUCY'S eyes fluttered open, she was spooning with Beau. He was dead asleep, his strong and heavy arm over her waist, his front pressed into her back. She shifted slightly and caught a baby staring at her. Charlotte was awake in the porta crib next to the bed, closer to her side, and she'd rolled over on to her stomach. The cute thing didn't seem at all traumatized and hopefully she'd been asleep all night or she'd seen some uh…stuff. Because she and Beau had been rather creative last night. Let's just say they'd crossed the friend zone with guns blazing. They'd leapt over hurdles and slid into home base. The friend zone was a dot in the distance. Ha.

"Well, hello," Lucy said to Charlotte, bringing up the sheets to cover her naked body.

"Hello," Beau mumbled softly.

"Not you, silly. Charlotte is awake."

"Oh." He raised his head and then lowered it to the crook of Lucy's neck. "She's awfully quiet for a change."

"I should get her a new diaper." She nudged Beau. "Give me your robe. I don't want her to see me naked."

He snorted. "She's a *baby*."

"I know, but I'm paranoid. Whatever she sees she'll never unsee. Even if she never remembers it."

"Yeah, sure, that makes sense. What about me?" He rolled on his back, the sheet covering only the lower half of his body. "I, too, am very naked."

"Yes, I noticed." She smiled and laid a hand on his waist.

Last night, she'd read his tattoos and he'd been impressed to see the three little hearts on her hip. He'd kissed them at length, one at a time, then told her how unsurprised he was that she'd been the only one with enough courage to go through with it.

"I'll just wrap the sheets around me."

She gathered them together, wrapping them mummy-style.

Beau splayed his hands behind his neck and gave her a slow smile. "Love that look on you."

"The toga look? Yeah, I totally rock it. I'll be right back." Lucy went into the adjoining bathroom and stared at herself in the mirror.

So, this was it. *This* was the look of utter and complete satisfaction. Her eyes were a bit bleary and her lips pink and bruised. And yes, there was a bit of beard burn on her neck. She'd been marked by him. Funny how she didn't mind. And her hip tattoos? Well, they, too, had a little beard burn from where he'd nibbled on them.

As much as she'd love to go back to bed with Beau, there was a baby. It was an odd situation. Finally getting together with a man you'd lusted over forever, and then becoming a bit of a makeshift family for a few days. She thought of how far Beau had come with the baby and hoped that he wouldn't be disappointed if or when the mother came back for Charlotte. Lucy could see how he'd changed in the tender way he held the baby. He had very real emotions for her now. Lucy was a bit worried. Despite the mother's careless drop-off, Charlotte was a well loved and cared for baby. One way or another, she would be back for her.

But if Rachel thought for one second she could later deny Beau his parental rights, she had another think coming.

Lucy showered and quickly washed up, coming out of the bathroom in a towel, depositing the sheets back on the bed. She'd change the sheets and make the bed later. Beau and Charlotte were already up, and she could hear them in the kitchen. Charlotte was babbling, probably from her high chair, and she could hear Beau singing one of Jackson's hit songs.

"Never over you, got me feelin' blue. Girl, I'm never over you," Beau crooned, beautifully off-key.

Lucy strolled into the kitchen, finding it difficult not to smile. "Jackson wrote that song about Eve."

Beau turned from the stove, where he was cooking eggs. "His first number one hit."

Coming up behind him, Lucy wrapped her arms around his waist and pressed her face into his strong back.

"Let me take over. You go and shower and do what you have to do."

"I'm having breakfast with my ladies. That's what I have to do."

"Alright then." Lucy kissed him, then took a seat at the table next to Charlotte and they both watched him at work.

The phone rang a few minutes later and Lucy picked it up.

"Lucy? It's Mom. Listen, you can't come over for dinner tonight. I'm sorry."

"Oh, I can't come over for dinner tonight?" Lucy said this loudly, catching Beau's attention. "And I was so looking forward to it. Why *not?*"

"Remember I was painting your room? Before I knew what happened, I was also painting the kitchen. So, I can't cook tonight. We'll do it another time."

"Oh, gee, mom. It's so interesting that you suddenly want to paint your entire house."

"I've been watching that home and garden show. It's time I made some improvements around here."

"That's alright, I'm kind of getting used to being chained to the stove every night. Though I was looking forward to a break."

"What do you mean, chained to the stove?"

"And to think I used to *like* Beau. As part of my work here, I have to cook both him and the baby three squares a day. And these are full meals, with all the trimmings. If it's not good enough, Beau makes me throw it out and start over."

Beau's eyes widened and he scowled. He shook his head, waved his hands, and mouthed, "No."

"What? I don't believe that! Not Beau."

"At least I'm learning a lot. I'm a hard worker as you know. I might as well learn how to cook the way a man likes. That's the way to their heart, isn't it?"

"Lucy, I'm surprised at you. Tell the man to make his own dinner! You're only there for the baby."

"That's alright. He doesn't know it, but I might slip a little something extra into his dinner tonight to make him sleep well." Lucy winked. "Honestly, I can't stand him."

Beau dropped the spatula and stalked toward her.

"Lucy Lorenzo!" her mother shouted. "Don't you—"

"Gotta go, Mom."

She managed to hang up just as Beau reached her, grabbing her by the waist and spinning her around like a top.

"It's all part of the plan," Lucy squealed. "We agreed."

"You made me sound like a Neanderthal." He set her down.

"Aw, she'll figure out it's not true. But first I have to mess with her a little." She reached up to tousle Beau's hair. "And you still need that haircut."

"Oh yeah. Great. More foreplay." He lowered his head to nibble on her neck. "I gotta admit. I don't like hearing you tell your mother you can't stand me, even if it's a lie."

"But I do like you." She curled one of his hairs around

her finger. "I like you *a lot*. How many times did I *like* you last night?"

"Three?" He gave her a lopsided grin.

"Hmm." She kissed him. "Now let's see how well *you* cook eggs."

It turned out that for a bachelor, Beau was not terrible in the kitchen. She'd been at the house before for cookouts, of course, but that was grilling. All men could grill. Putting together meals was another type of skill. This morning Beau cooked eggs, bacon, flapjacks, and potatoes. And she had to confess it was a bit surreal to sit at the table casually eating breakfast with Beau and a baby. For a second, she pretended it was their baby. They'd been married a couple of years-ish before she'd gotten pregnant and had their baby. A baby girl, of course, in Stone Ridge would be ideal even if boys tended to rule the day.

If it seemed as though they'd skipped a few steps along the way she didn't care. This was either a quick courtship or the slowest burn in history. Depending on which way you wanted to look at it.

After breakfast, Beau went out to tend to the animals and when Lucy encouraged him, he agreed to take his new horse for a long late-morning ride.

He came back with the new horse's name. "Tonto."

"Um, no." Lucy shook her head. "That's not appropriate."

"It's a *horse*, Lucy."

"A female. You know *I* didn't like a man's nickname. What about Princess? Or Queen?"

But she was only kidding. She'd name an animal Princess only as a joke.

Beau mimed throwing up.

"What about Victoria?" Beau suggested. "I don't *hate* that name."

Charlotte cooed and kicked her legs.

"I think she likes it," Lucy said. "I say it's a contender."

"Alright, that's a maybe."

Then something happened after lunch that surprised them both.

Lenny showed up.

"What's up, Len?" Lucy waved him inside. "Everything okay with the house?"

He wasn't wearing his exterminator's jumpsuit, but instead just casual wear, jeans and a pearl-button top. His eyes shifty, he appeared to check out the house, possibly looking for whips and chains. He'd been sent by Lucy's mother, no doubt, who wasn't going to let her daughter become an indentured servant. Good to know.

"Well, now, the house was tented but then I saw some vermin so I *should* spray again. If that's okay with you. Wouldn't want you to come across the vermin when you're *alone*."

"Oh, how interesting. Beau, did you hear this? Now I've got vermin in the house."

"*Vermin?*" Beau said, biting back a smile. "What kind?"

"That's right, you must also know your vermin, being a contractor and all." Lenny tipped back on his heels. "I'm afraid to say I believe it's the *R* word."

"Ew! Rats? In my house?" The phantom vermin was a lie, no doubt, but Lucy still cringed at the very idea.

"Well, don't worry," Beau said. "She can stay here as long as she likes."

"Good, good," Lenny said. "Because this could take a while."

"Of course, of course," Lucy said, biting back a smirk. "You definitely don't want to take shortcuts with vermin."

"Nope, definitely not," Lenny said.

"And I'm sure Beau appreciates having a built-in

babysitter for all the dates he's been going on lately. You know, with all the women."

Beau didn't seem to appreciate this new direction and paled a little. "Right. Lucy has been a big help."

"What *women?*" Lenny scoured the place with his eyes, like one of these women might be hiding in plain sight.

"All the ones after him, of course," Lucy said. "The new ones in town who don't know about him yet."

"I thought you might be ready to settle down now, son. And I thought you two…didn't I sense something going on here?" He wiggled a finger between Lucy and Beau.

Lucy burst out laughing. "Oh, no! That's hilarious."

"Truly funny," Beau added, but didn't laugh.

"I don't understand young people," Lenny said. "Enjoy your youth, both of you. Because when you get to be seventy, everything goes south and not for the winter. I mean, it *stays* south. Catch my drift?"

It was more information than Lucy ever wanted to have about old age, so she assured Lenny she'd be fine for a few more days and shuffled him out the door.

Chapter 17

Sadie hung up the phone, close to tears. This might be the worst week of her life.

Lucy's mother, and then Lenny, had called to inform her their plan hadn't worked. Although Levi had asked Jolette Marie to marry him last night (that news was all over town) it would appear that Lucy and Beau were no closer to kissing than they were before this whole mess started. And according to Esperanza, this whole idea might actually be backfiring. Because there was a real danger that Lucy would never think of Beau the same way again. Lenny had just reported they'd both laughed at the suggestion there was anything more than friendship going on between then. He did, however, advise that he'd gotten a few more days for them to be together by lying about vermin in the house. Good ol' Lenny.

The next part of the plan would take place this afternoon and Mom was ready.

"Do you think I should call them first?" Sadie's mother asked.

"Absolutely not. This has to be a surprise. We don't want them to have time to make up any excuses."

"If this doesn't work, I don't know what will."

"This is *going* to work," Sadie said. "It has to. We're running out of time. Lucy has to change her plans and soon."

"I don't see how they can resist grandma coming over to take her grandbaby for a while. It actually helps, when you think about it, that you're not supposed to get out of bed. This way I bring the baby to you."

"You're right. It's perfect except for the fact Lucy might just take off when she doesn't have to watch the baby." Sadie tapped her chin. "But I'm betting she won't. I think Beau will use his charms to get her to stick around."

"According to Esperanza, he's got her doing all the housework and cooking, too."

"Well, if that's true, at least it will keep her there."

"It's not ideal."

But nothing was ideal at this point. Sadie didn't know what else she had to do to get these two idiots together. Spell it out for them? Knock their heads together? Pass them a note in class?

"Either way, I'd like things to get back to normal around here." Sadie's mother went hands on hips like she meant business. "Your father is out at the cabins every day with some problem or another. These girls were under the impression they would have Wi-Fi out at the lake and can't seem to accept that they don't."

Sadie didn't have to wonder where they'd received that impression. She'd bet that Beulah laid out advertising copy worthy of a politician's preelection promises.

"Your poor father. Hard physical labor all his life and it's these young ladies who are about to do him in. You should have seen him last night. 'Good golly, Wanda, these ladies are not like the ones we grow in Stone Ridge. You'd think no Wi-Fi is the end of all existence.' And I told him, to them, it probably is! I'd like things to go back to the way they used to be."

"Mom, if this is Beau's daughter, nothing is *ever* going to be the same."

Granted, Sadie was the only one who hadn't seen the baby, but she'd been thinking of the remote possibility this might *not* be Beau's child. She couldn't imagine a woman who would lie about this, but she also couldn't fathom leaving her baby with a total stranger, biology be damned. She was wise enough to realize a bunch of cells and DNA strands had nothing to do with the human condition. A real family was about a lot more than that.

But if Charlotte wasn't Beau's daughter, then everything might go back to normal, which would be nice. The future would be wide open for him to marry whomever he wanted without feeling guilty about Charlotte's mother. Without feeling responsible for his child. Because she understood that Beau, despite what his past signified to some, had always wanted to live up to the honorable ways of the men of Stone Ridge.

"Hand me my laptop before you go?" Sadie said.

One of the many things Sadie had spent her spare time doing, from her bed, was research on the custody laws in the state of Texas. It was slow going with their internet connection on the ranch, but she was making progress. She knew enough now to tell Beau to ask for a DNA test, then to ask for visitation rights. If he was *actually* the father. More and more, Sadie had her doubts. It didn't make sense that the mother would drop her baby off so randomly, but she also might have heard about their town through Beau himself. Knowledge of their respect for women of all ages in Stone Ridge went far and wide. Plus, looks weren't everything. Everyone said the baby looked like Sadie, but growing up and going to school in Kerrville, Sadie had at least three other girls in her class with her same coloring. It wasn't exactly rare.

Sammy ran into the bedroom, clutching his blanket. "Go see Uncle Boo. I ready, Nana."

"Good boy! Well, Sammy and I are off to get your niece." After handing over the laptop, Mom bent to tuck the covers in for Sadie as if she was still ten. "Be sure not to get up while I'm gone."

"Sure." Sadie rolled her eyes. "I'll stay *right* here."

After all, where was she going to go?

YOU COULD HAVE KNOCKED Beau over with a feather when his mother showed up late in the afternoon with Sammy. He ran past Beau like a dervish.

"I'll take Charlotte to see Sadie. The pictures Lincoln took were so good, but she can't wait to meet her."

"Seriously? Because that would be great."

This was better than Beau could have hoped. To have alone time with Lucy, especially now, was the drug he craved. He could use a break and so could Lucy. It wasn't that he didn't love the cute little bug, because he was shocked to find out that he already did. Babies made it so easy.

Most of the time, Charlotte was a happy baby, batting her hands in the air, kicking her feet. And her toothless smiles were adorable. He would challenge the hardest heart not to melt when she smiled. It couldn't be done. Beau thought she was possibly the most beautiful baby he'd ever laid eyes on, and he included Sammy in that mix. He was a cute kid, but a bit out of control. You needed to keep your eyes on that one.

"Put that down," Beau said, taking the remote control from his nephew.

Sammy then moved to the swing where Charlotte sat.

"Baby!" he pointed. "Baby, baby, baby!"

"That's right," Beau said. "This is Charlotte, your cousin."

Maybe. He didn't know when he'd begun to doubt that Charlotte could be his but the sense of relief at the thought was no longer there. Now he was worried. He'd be damn lucky to be her father.

"That's right, Sammy. And soon you, Mommy and Daddy are going to have a baby of your own." Mom surveyed the house as if expecting to find Lucy chained to the stove. "And where's Lucy?"

Damn. She was *in* on this. Should he have his own fun with her for all this matchmaking? Or simply promise an extra special Mother's Day gift this year? He didn't know whether he should be mad about her conspiring or relieved. For one thing, if she had wanted him to be with Lucy, why couldn't she have said or done something sooner? If she was conspiring now, she could have done so much earlier. Then maybe he wouldn't be in this hot mess.

But on the other hand, it was good to know his mother approved. Good to know she wouldn't guilt him into marrying a woman he didn't love. There was honor, there was sacrifice, and then there was being miserable for the rest of your life due to one mistake. It wouldn't be fair to anyone, least of all Rachel.

"Someone called for a ride, so she took off."

She made a face. "Is she still doing that rideshare thing?"

"You know Lucy. She does a little bit of everything."

"She gives great haircuts, that's for sure. I always thought she should focus on that."

He'd have to agree on the haircuts though he didn't relish the idea of her giving any other men a haircut.

"You know, son, she's trying to raise money so she can *move*. Did you ever stop to think you're helping her leave town by hiring her as your nanny?"

"I've always thought Lucy should do whatever she wants. I want her to be happy."

He turned to see Sammy was pushing Charlotte in the swing. With a little too much force in Beau's opinion. Charlotte's eyes were big as saucers, but she wasn't wailing.

"Hey, take it easy there, slugger." He stopped the swing's momentum. "She's just a baby."

"Play, Uncle Boo! Play!"

Like the whirlwind that he was, Sammy ran through the house, which was fun to do once he realized Beau was chasing him. Once again outsmarted by a kid. Sammy upended everything in his path. Diapers went flying in the air, plastic toys, pacifiers, and clothes he and Lucy had just folded. He'd never noticed before this moment that his nephew was a menace.

"Hey, little bugger!" Beau said, picking up the squirming boy, who giggled like they were both playing this game.

"Oh my. It's like stepping into a time machine," his mother said. "That was you."

"You're kidding." He set Sammy down. "How did you ever put up with me?"

Charlotte was so sweet and calm. Of course, she couldn't really get around yet. This was apparently what he had to look forward to. No wonder Linc always looked exhausted.

A few minutes later, he'd helped his mother pack a few things and strap Charlotte into the car seat and then he waved them off. It was a good thing for his mother to start bonding with her latest grandchild. He'd use this time wisely as soon as Lucy got back. No time to waste.

The first thing he did was drive to the flower shop in town. Not to be outdone by Levi, Beau was going to get a *few* dozen red roses. His plan was to use some of the petals and make a pathway to his bedroom, where on the bed he'd have dozens of petals. She could either brush them off or they could roll around on them.

Bet Levi never did that!

He strolled into the new shop in town, Buttercup Blooms, located a few storefronts down from the Shady Grind. One of the new ladies in town had opened it with her mother and they both ran the place. There was a short line when he arrived, and he wasn't shocked to see Levi in it. For a horse wrangler, he sure had disposable flower income. For his part, Beau was going to have to make a stop at the feed store after this. He might have been gifted the horse, but not the upkeep. Eve was scheduled to come out for routine vaccines, too.

"Hey, there." Levi turned when he caught Beau in line.

"Congratulations." Beau clapped him on the shoulder. "Heard all about it."

"It's exciting. I feel like I just jumped off a rock into the Brazos river."

Beau blinked. That sounded far more suicidal than exciting. "Really."

"Maybe that's a bad analogy but Jo just has a way of making me feel spikes of adrenaline rushing through me. I guess a better analogy would be, well, for lack of a better example, when a wild horse is coming at me. Not sure what she's going to do but I know whatever it is I'm ready for it."

Beau still didn't understand. He quirked a brow.

"Guess I'm not a wordsmith." Levi shook his head but

the smile on his face was big enough to break it. "I'm just…"

"In love." Beau finished his sentence. "And it's exciting."

For him, Beau had come to realize, love was a quiet kind of thing. Real love wasn't all about a head rush. For a long time, he'd thought that was the case. But that intensity had never lasted. It had never become something deeper than a surface attraction. Now, he believed love was finishing each other's sentences, and wanting the best for each other. Love was knowing someone almost better than you knew yourself. It was about always taking each other's sides no matter what. Lucy had been that for him and more for years.

"Yeah." He lowered his lashes and glanced up at Beau. "And I'm sorry if I stood in the way of um…something between you and Lucy. "

"You didn't."

Beau liked to think if he'd gone after Lucy, he could have taken her away from Levi. Now that he knew how she felt about him, it was clear he could have. He just hadn't seen it before.

"Are you really going to let her go off to Seattle?"

"I can't keep someone here who doesn't want to be."

"You could do it, even if no one else could," Levi said. "All I'm saying is, sometimes you need to be clear about your intentions. Your feelings. Girls like that sort of thing. Flowers. Big declarations of love."

"Okay, Levi. I think I've done fine so far."

"Yeah, but…you've never been in love before. Right?"

Beau swallowed hard, unable to meet Levi's eyes. Every time he'd felt close to the feeling before, it faded, and he was terrified it would this time, too.

Then the florist called out for Levi's turn and his standing order. They weren't roses, but bluebonnets.

"I try to mix it up a little."

Beau bought red roses as he'd planned. Two dozen and he cleaned the florist out.

He waltzed out of the shop carrying what felt like a large bush in front of him and ran straight into Sarah.

He almost didn't recognize her away from the setting of the cabins. And it felt far more like a few weeks instead of a few days since he'd last seen her. So much had changed in a short period of time. He practically had whiplash.

And he'd forgotten they had a date tonight. Shitfire!

"Beau! Are those for *me*?"

"Um…"

"You were probably trying to surprise me, and I ruined it! They're beautiful. And *red*?" Sarah batted her eyelashes.

He barely knew the woman. She'd have been lucky to get yellow roses from him.

"No, hey…um, sweetheart, hey, I'm really sorry but… yeah…a lot has changed in the past few days. I'm going to have to break our date tonight."

"Then who are those flowers for? Honestly, I'm not used to this kind of treatment! Standing me up? *Me?* Why would you do that?"

For this, he had a good excuse for once. A dayum good one. "Well, I've recently become a father."

"That's not funny."

"I didn't think so, either. But there you have it. I'm a father now, with a baby girl, and a whole new set of responsibilities."

"Well…I do like children."

Great. She wasn't going to make this simple. "I'm sorry to say I need to focus on my family right now."

"You're the worst liar in history!" With that, she grabbed one of his bunches of long-stemmed roses from his hands and hit him with it three times. "Go away, Beau Stephens! Never speak to me again!"

Beau would love to say this was the first time this sort of thing had ever happened to him. Unfortunately, he'd be lying. He had no idea how many disappointments this made as he'd stopped keeping track a while ago. Fortunately, he'd just met her so he couldn't have done much damage.

He brushed rose petals out of his hair.

"Those were expensive," he shouted, and she flipped him off as she strode into the Shady Grind.

"Hoo boy." Pamela Ann stood outside the veterinary clinic across the street, a little dog on a leash next to her. "What have you done *now*, Beau?"

"Just…exist."

"Well." Pamela Ann crossed the street. "You sure have a way with the ladies."

"Yeah, thanks. I'm a work in progress."

"I see." She did a long slow slide, zeroing in on the roses. "I hope those are for Lucy."

Beau remembered Pamela Ann had a mouth the size of Texas on her. He was supposed to pretend he wasn't with Lucy, which was insane. Everyone pretty much already suspected, he imagined, but with the roses…he better start explaining. He hated that Lucy wanted to pretend they weren't together, as if maybe she was embarrassed by the way she felt about him.

"Yeah, well, we've been fighting."

"I've never known you to be a flower-for-an-apology kind of guy."

"It seems to work well for Levi."

"Levi isn't apologizing. He's just being who he is."

"And that is…?"

"A romantic man, of course!"

"I can be romantic, you know!"

"Don't try to be someone you're not." Pamela picked up her little black dog. "Don't try to be a King Charles Cavalier when you're a Labrador Retriever."

"Listen, I'm not in the mood for your riddles. As you can see, I'm carrying so many roses I almost can't see you."

"Oh good grief." Pamela Ann put the dog back down, lowered the bouquets, and met Beau's eyes. "You are a Labrador. Everyone loves you and you love everyone. Fetch, wag tail, smile. Which is great! Fantastic."

"It doesn't sound so great when *you* say it."

"I'm trying to make a *point*." She went hands on hips while her little dog made circles around her. "This shouldn't be difficult, so try to keep up."

"Is that your dog? Because—"

"This is Jimmy's dog. Stop changing the subject. The problem is you've never treated any woman special. Above the rest. And when you do, look out, she's going to melt. You've never done that before, have you?"

He was trying, for the love of God. If only people would stop giving him advice.

"Maybe I'm doing that right now."

"I saw your baby the other day. She's very cute. Lucy gave me a ride to the vet. Did she tell you?"

"No."

The little dog was distracting him. She kept going in a circle, obviously looking for a place to urinate, or worse, but Pamela Ann was oblivious. Some people shouldn't be dog owners.

"Listen, buddy, she's been in love with you for years. But she's never going to tell you that. Know why?"

He was still focused on the "in love" part, enough so

that he hadn't fully heard the rest of her sentence. She'd asked him…something.

"Fine, I'll tell you why. It's because she's *Lucy*. Our Lucy, tough, and strong. But some part of her still believes she's not wanted. She doesn't belong. How she could believe that everyone is simply being *kind* to her for over thirty years is beyond me, but maybe some things are so internalized they can't fully be explained?"

She'd said something similar to him the night they'd talked about Charlotte, and whether or not he wanted her to be a part of his life. Lucy didn't know where she belonged, which didn't make any sense to him. She belonged *here*. He didn't know how many times he'd have to say it. Just because someone else was stupid enough to give her away didn't mean anyone else would be. But maybe Pamela Ann was right, and it was that psychic thing Lucy talked about the other night. A kind of pain not easily described.

"I know you've probably told her a million times that you care, but sometimes you have to *show* a woman how you feel. Flowers are a good start, but that's just scratching the surface. Dig deeper. It's not enough. The things that really matter come from the heart." She touched her chest.

"Thanks for the advice. I'll keep it in mind."

He turned to go and that's when Pamela Ann's dog pissed all over his boots.

Chapter 18

When Lucy got back from taking her passengers home from their trip to Kerrville, she didn't see Beau's truck. He'd mentioned briefly that he'd have to go to the feed store so he must have decided to brave it with Charlotte in tow. With him gone, Lucy went to the barn to check out his new horse. Dating a horse trainer, and simply growing up in Stone Ridge, Lucy knew horses. She'd learned how to ride early. Her parents couldn't afford a horse of their own, mostly due to boarding and upkeep. But she'd had plenty of opportunities, nevertheless.

"Hey there," she said, coming up to the horse's stall. "I hope you know your owner is happy to have you. What a magnificent beast you are. You are truly beautiful."

Despite the unfortunate timing of getting both a horse and a baby in the same week, Lucy was happy for Beau. He deserved this. She'd be the first to admit how hard he'd worked over the years. She'd never known him to indulge in fancy trucks or thrill-seeking vacations. He had a goal and she'd watched as he single-mindedly worked toward it, going to college, coming home to work for his father's company, and eventually building his own home and barn. The last part, the prized horse, had materialized unexpectedly but it had also come from hard work and dedication to his craft.

She'd always deeply admired him for knowing exactly who he was.

"What should he call you?" She petted the horse's white forelock. "The name has to be perfect, just like you."

A name could be important. Hers had come with her, and she was grateful to the only tie she had to her former world. It linked her, somehow, to her origins. *Someone had loved her at least enough to give her a name.* She was grateful her parents had kept the name because she *felt* like a Lucy. Names should say something about a person. Something true. In Spanish, Lucy was translated to Lucia which meant "light." Her father had told her she was the light of their world.

Beau was the word for "male lover or sweetheart" and couldn't have fit him better. For years, he'd been everybody's sweetheart.

"Maybe *your* name should be True," Lucy said. "True for honesty, for genuine beauty, and true for the man who gave you away."

"Want to go for a ride?"

The deep male voice almost made Lucy jump. Had she really been so caught up in her thoughts over the last few minutes that she hadn't heard Beau pull up? Apparently.

She looked past him and around him. "Where's Charlotte?"

"My mom came by to take her to see Sadie, who said she couldn't wait another day before she saw her niece." Beau gave her a slow smile. "But obviously, this is just more of their matchmaking attempts. Giving us time to be alone. I, of course, said, please, take her. We both need a break."

Beau curled his arms around her from behind, drawing her close.

Lucy melted into him, far easier than she would have ever thought possible. All it took was a baby, a fake termite-and-vermin-infested house, and she was already willing to forget about her plans for Seattle. She didn't want to do this again, didn't want to flake on another plan. There had been many good reasons to stay in the past…but Beau. Well, he'd been her first plan hadn't he? No, not plan. Hope. *Dream.* A silly young girl's crush for something more from a man who didn't seem to want or need a woman for anything other than recreational purposes. And that was never enough for her.

"I thought of a name for your horse." She settled her hands on the big, callused ones wrapped around her. "How about True?"

"Hmm, True." He lowered his head to her neck, whispering in her ear. "I like it. Like true love."

"And short for Truehart. A connection and a way to honor him."

"Good point. True it is."

"Oh, that simple? You don't want to argue for Tonto or another Marvel character's name?"

"Nah, True feels right."

She turned in his arms and tugged on that long unruly hair. "Haircut."

"I want a haircut from you more than I want oxygen, but do you want a ride first?" He gave her a sheepish grin.

She quirked a brow and he laughed.

"A ride on *True.* She'll do fine with both of us. She's a dream to ride and you need to see it to believe it."

It was a perfect way to spend the early part of the afternoon. Both she and Beau brushed True, checked her shoes, and saddled her. He got on first, then offered his hand to Lucy, who settled behind him into the rear part of the saddle, so they were closer than close. They rode True all over Beau's acreage and the horse trail nearby, quieter than they'd ever been together. There were no teasing jokes, no mock put-downs. Just him expertly steering his horse, occasionally laying a hand on her thigh. She rested her head on his strong back, feeling the muscles bunch. Almost too perfect.

Beau stopped at the top of the hill for the view.

"Lucy, I have to be honest with you." He squeezed her thigh.

Oh no, here it comes. She got ready to hear the words Beau had likely said to women for years: I'm not ready to commit. I want to take things slow. Or worse: I think maybe you and I made a mistake.

Whatever it was, she needed to hear it and now was as good a time as any.

"Please. Go ahead and be honest. Now's not the time to start lying to me, I don't care if we slept together. We *have* to be honest with each other. That can't change no matter what else does."

"Well, okay, here it is: I don't want to mess with Sadie *or* Lenny, or anyone else who tried to throw us together. In fact, I'd actually like to name my horse in their honor, but that name would be too long."

"What are you saying?"

"I'm saying that I want everyone to know we're together. That, for whatever reason, their stupid plan worked."

"But—" This was definitely not what she'd expected to hear.

Beau seemed to hesitate. "Are you ashamed to be with me?"

"Beau! Are you kidding me? *Ashamed?*"

"Remember, we have to be honest. Especially on a horse named True." He turned to face her. "I have a bad reputation."

She heard the anguish in his voice.

"Beau. I never saw you that way. All I know, all I've ever known is my friend, the one who always took my side, the hardworking man. The cowboy."

"And…you hate cowboys."

She shook her head, fighting a smile. "That's not entirely true."

"Is it a little bit? Because you know me. Take me as I am. I can't change for you or anyone else. I might always be a Labrador Retriever—"

"Excuse me?"

"You know, friendly, a little bit flirty. Easily excitable? That's the kind of dog I'd be if I were a dog."

This conversation had taken a strange turn.

"I honestly never thought of you as a *dog*."

"Don't forget Labs are loyal." He said this as if defending his Labrador Retriever heritage.

Lucy was trying hard not to laugh because he seemed so serious. "*Most* dogs are loyal, I think."

"Anyway," Beau continued as if talking about himself as a Labrador was the most normal thing in the world. "I have to say something right now and it isn't easy."

"Just say it. It's just me."

He let out a deep sigh that sounded as if suddenly it wasn't "just her" but something much bigger.

"I think I'm falling in love with you."

"Oh, Beau." She didn't know what to say to that.

It seemed too fast. Maybe Beau was mistaking an infatuation with real love this time because it was her. And he'd always loved her in a different kind of way. They'd never been this close and the confusing feelings…

they were getting to her, too. She'd always loved him, sure…

"No, that isn't true." He turned away and looked over the horizon. "There isn't any 'think' about it. I know that I love you, Lucy. I love you."

"I *know* you love me as a friend. But you know better than to say those words to me. Don't confuse love for infatuation. You've been in love many times."

"No, I haven't ever been in love. Because this is different."

"This is just the first time you've felt this way about *me*."

"If you don't want to believe me that's fine, but I'm not taking it back. You belong to me. I love you, damn it. I always have."

She shook her head, caught between the fear and exhilaration that this was happening. She'd had more than one man tell her he loved her, Levi included, but she'd never returned the words. They meant too much to her and she knew when she told a man she loved him, she'd never take those three little words back.

Love, to her, was eternal. You never abandoned someone you loved, not if you truly loved them.

"*How* do you love me?"

"Is this where I list all the things that made me fall in love with you? Because I've got them. I wrote them down, but I don't need a list." He thumped his chest. "All the reasons are right here. I love that you're brave, I love that you're kind, you're funny, and you *finally* opened up to me. I think that was the missing part. Now I'm in love with you and there's nothing you can do about it."

Lucy bit down on her lower lip to keep from smiling too big. "What makes you think I want to stop you?"

"Because you don't believe me? Because you're leaving

and this could complicate everything? Because I'm a father now?"

"I think becoming a father has been good for you. It's like you grew up overnight."

"That's true and it was a little late. I'm sorry that I disappointed you," Beau said. "I tried never to do that."

"You've never disappointed me. You must be thinking of someone else."

"I have." He lowered his head, studied the ground.

"No. You never lied to me, you never led me on, you never tricked me. You were always a friend, always on my side. How could you have disappointed me?"

"I made you wait."

A long breath of silence sat between them.

"Some people are worth waiting for." She forced him to turn his face back to hers. "It remains to be seen if you're one of them."

Again, she'd made him laugh. She hoped that would never change. Ever.

"Keep teasing me like that, no matter what else happens."

"You got it."

"I don't pretend to understand how you feel, and I swear I'm not trying to fix this for you anymore. But…you and I can make our own family. Children who are going to know who they are and where they were born and that they have two parents who love each other. Please tell me you know you're wanted right here with me."

"You've given me a lot to take in."

"Listen, you don't have to say anything. I wanted to tell you how I feel because, well…for a while there, I wasn't sure I'd have the chance."

"Our timing has always been off. Even now, I'm not sure…"

He took her hand and brushed a kiss across her knuckles. "I know you could have any cowboy you want. But I doubt any one of them will love you like I do. Maybe I'll have to be sure enough for the both of us."

"Beau," she said softly.

He was saying all the right things. Her heart was tugging and shifting and changing with every word coming from his lips. Words that sounded like they were coming straight from his unwrapped heart. She thought she'd always wanted this…him…but now it felt too big. Too much to hold in her heart at once. Charlotte and her mother made everything so much more complicated. Beau was a father and that truth had changed him, and while the change was welcome, Lucy was probably not the one who should benefit from it.

"I will fight for you, Lucy. You've been given fair warning."

With that, he turned, and right hand still on her leg, led True back home.

AFTER TELLING LUCY HIS FEELINGS, Beau felt unburdened. He'd held on tightly to his thoughts for so long that giving them away almost made him feel lighter. The intensity had scared him off once before and until he risked losing her for good, telling her the truth hadn't been urgent. On some level he believed Lucy would always be here. Someday, he figured they'd be together, after she came to her senses and realized she belonged with him. After she'd had her adventure in Seattle or wherever she chose to go.

He hadn't wanted to risk losing her by chasing her before either of them was ready. Now he was ready, and she was not. Timing, again, had proven to be their nemesis. But he'd just have to chase her and show her, day by day, that he'd changed in more than one way. He wasn't Beau Stephens flirting and chasing after all the women. Now he understood what he wanted, and it was her.

People might think Charlotte had changed him, but the change had been happening internally for some time. He thought of the night a year ago when he and Lucy had exchanged a laugh. When she was no longer looking at him, he'd lingered, watching the soft tilt of her neck. Watching the way her upper lip curled when she laughed, and her eyes crinkled at the corners. She always covered her mouth when she laughed, like her bubbly laugh was so big it might fall outside of her.

He'd had a random thought then: *This is the woman I'm going to marry. If she'll have me.*

But the fear grew from being so invested and knowing the possible outcome was not in his favor. She'd been dating Levi at the time, and Beau proceeded to be miserable as he watched her date Levi yet again, break up with Levi, and then immediately make plans to leave Stone Ridge. He pretended not to know she planned to move. Pretended it would never happen. She'd seemed to be heartbroken, and he'd left her alone with her thoughts. They'd never talked about their love lives with each other. If she ever mentioned anything about Levi or another man, Beau tuned it out. He wasn't a masochist.

But she wasn't getting away from him this time. This was his moment. He meant everything he'd said: he would fight for her.

Lucy went inside the house while he unsaddled and brushed True. He hadn't the chance to do much with the roses when he arrived. No petals strewn and lining a path to the bedroom. Romance was tough. It would be even tougher with a baby, but Beau figured he wouldn't have

Charlotte all the time. They'd have to make some kind of visitation arrangement and he'd see if he could at least get her every other weekend. Rachel lived in Kerrville, which wasn't ideal, but they'd have to work something out. When she got back, he'd tell her all about Lucy and how he would have to rescind that marriage proposal.

Lucy met him at the door with the roses. "Tell me these are from you."

"Yes," he said. "I confess. They are *literally* from me this time."

"Red roses."

He shrugged. "I already said I loved you."

She held all the bouquets up. "But this confirms it."

"Well, I had to make a statement."

"I get it. You had to show you loved me harder than you *thought* Levi loved me." She touched a petal from the first bouquet. "Honestly, I suspect Sadie sent these."

"I definitely love you way more than Sadie does. If I had managed to beat you home, I had plans for those rose petals."

"Don't tell me." Setting the roses down, she pressed a finger to his lips. "Save it for another time and surprise me."

He took her hand and pressed a kiss to her palm. "You know…we have the entire afternoon together. I'm pretty sure they'll keep Charlotte a while just to give us time. Time for us to figure out we like each other a lot. Little do they know."

Lucy shoved the hat off his head and proceeded to curl her long fingers through his hair. "Time for a haircut, I'd say."

"Dear God, yes. Please. Naked?" He gave her a hopeful smile.

She scrunched up her nose. "No. That would not be as fun as you might think."

This led him to believe she'd tried it before, but if so, Beau didn't want to hear about it. At least it sounded like an unpleasant experience. He vowed never to give her an unpleasant experience while the two of them were naked.

"Like sex on the beach." He winked, because of the drink she'd served him.

Sex on the beach was not fun, take it from him. He'd been to Galveston.

Leaving his embrace, she found her bag and dug through it, pulling up a case and unzipping it.

She held up her scissors. "Are you ready?"

No fool, Beau hurried off to find the closest chair.

Chapter 19

Some things, Lucy mused, always remained the same. Beau was never quite as antsy as when she had a pair of scissors near his neck. But for the first few minutes he sat on the kitchen chair, she didn't have to remind him to stop squirming. He closed his eyes and groaned a little when she tugged on both sides of his hair, pulling up the strands to check length.

"This mop is out of control," she said.

"*You're* out of control." He smiled with his eyes closed.

She snipped and used the comb to check the next strands. "Why do you always wait so long?"

"I think that's pretty obvious. I wait for the Lucy Lorenzo special."

"Looks like I'm going to have to start cutting your hair more than once a year."

She leaned in close and pressed a kiss under his ear. Gratifying all those old urges was proving to be as fun as she'd imagined.

"If you kiss me like that again, don't expect me not to

reciprocate. I don't care if you put a machete to my neck, you're getting kissed."

"Noted." She snipped again. "Oops."

One eye flew open. *"Oops?"*

"Don't worry, I think I can fix it." She bit her lower lip to keep from laughing and giving herself away.

She *never* made mistakes, even with a squirmy cowboy.

"You *think?*" He quirked a brow.

"No problem. It's just a little uneven, so I'll cut it shorter to match the other side."

"How much shorter?"

"Um, military short?" She tilted her head. "That okay with you?"

He sighed. "Yeah, what do I care? It's only hair. It will grow back."

"Now, that's what I call a good attitude."

She continued to spritz his hair with water, cutting and styling, working her way around him, turning his head to the left and right. Tipping his chin.

"I don't hear any buzzing." He opened one eye.

"You let me worry about that."

She finished, removing the towel, brushing him off, then handing him the mirror to see the finished product.

He grinned and lowered the mirror. "What happened to the crew cut?"

"Your hair is too beautiful to chop it all off." She lowered herself on his lap, straddling him, fingers sinking into his lush thick hair. "And to think all these years I've been making you attractive for other women."

"When you could have been enjoying the fruits of your own labor."

"Oh, but I have. From a distance."

He kissed her, then kissed her again deeper. Longer. More tender than she could have imagined possible. Beau managed to make her feel both sexy and yet somehow still…delicate and precious. It surprised her how much she enjoyed this sensation. She wasn't weak or helpless, far from it, but it was also okay for him to be strong. It was okay for him to want to take care of her. She could be strong enough to be weak at the right time.

And the fact that he loved her was far more than she'd ever hoped for. He'd told her he loved her, not expecting anything in return. That's how confident Beau was in his own skin. He could put himself out there with the kind of courage she didn't have. More than anything else, she found this attractive. More than his gorgeous hazel-green eyes that said so much, the strong jawline that could cut glass, or the amazing hard body. She loved how funny he could be, how carefree, and yet how ambitious when he needed. He was kind and protective and she loved that about him, too.

She loved him for who he was without her, and who he was with her.

Kissing him, she lingered to truly taste the sweet flavor of mint on his tongue. How marvelous, how amazing, that this felt so natural and yet it took them so long to get here. Timing was everything, someone once said, and for once theirs seemed to be in sync.

He stood, carrying her with him, as if lifting no more than a seven-ounce bag of potato chips.

Setting her down near the couch, she slid down the length of him, like gliding down the rough crag of a mountainside.

"Beau?"

"Yeah?" The word was rough and sinewy, ripe with desire. She felt it rumble through her as much as she heard it.

"Take me to bed."

He didn't say anything, but just gave her a slow and sexy smile. Lifting her into his arms, he carried her there.

A FEW HOURS LATER, Lucy lay once again wrapped in Beau's arms, feeling absolutely spoiled and decadent. She hadn't lain down in the middle of the afternoon since the last time she was sick with the flu.

This was so much better.

"Why didn't we start sleeping together a long time ago?" Beau said now, twirling a loose curl of her hair around his thumb.

"I don't know. You were stupid, I guess."

"Ha! You're right. Are you saying you would have slept with me?"

"I probably would not have been able to resist you, no. But it's for the best."

"That's your opinion. I feel like I have a lot of time to catch up and not enough hours in the day to do it."

"Where there's a will, there a way. You can give up a few hours of sleep, for instance. That won't kill you."

"Right. Let me do the math. So, if I give up two hours of sleep every night and instead bang you silly…I might have made up for all that time in about…ten years?"

"We really can't count the teenage years."

"Why not?"

"I wasn't having sex, for one. You *know* my parents. If it were up to them, I'd be a virgin bride."

"Well. I wish I'd been your first."

"Setting the standard that high at the beginning might have been cruel."

Beau snorted. "You're good for my ego."

Lucy rolled on top of him. "And a lot of other things."

"Show me." He slid her a slow wicked grin.

And she showed him everything for the next several hours.

BY THE TIME Beau's mother arrived, Beau and Lucy had showered and dressed. She helped him straighten the house and remove all evidence of their afternoon delight. His belt, boots, Lucy's panties, and bra. He wasn't hiding a thing, but he also didn't think it appropriate to shove the evidence in his mother's face. She was smart enough to figure it out on her own.

"Hope she wasn't too much trouble." Beau grabbed the handle of Charlotte's car seat.

"She's a darling angel baby," Mom said. "Sadie really appreciates the visit. She should be off bed rest soon, Lord willing. Lying in bed all day and night is driving her up a wall. And I'm sorry I haven't been much help with Charlotte."

"There will be plenty of time to spend with her," Lucy said, coming up behind him.

"Oh Lucy, sugar! You're still here." His mother smiled smugly. "I would have thought maybe you'd take a break with Charlotte gone."

"No, I…stuck around."

"We hung out together, took a ride on the new horse." Beau unbuckled Charlotte from the car seat. "And where was she going to go when she now has vermin in the house?"

"Vermin?"

"How'd you arrange for that?" Beau said. "Is Lenny now on the Stephens payroll?"

"I'm not sure what you mean." His mother's cheeks turned a bright pink. "Why would Lenny be on our payroll?"

"Beau…" Lucy said but then didn't complete her thought.

"Save it, Mom. We get it now. You were trying to get Lucy and me together. Good job."

"Beau Stephens! I was trying to do no such thing. Why, I—"

"Thank you." He smiled, letting his mother off the hook. While he could have kept her going a while longer, yanking her chain, he didn't enjoy frustrating his mother like he thought he might.

"Um, *thank you?*" Mom looked from him to Lucy and back again. "For…?"

"Everything." Lucy smiled. "I'm just glad there isn't an actual rat in my house. *Or* termites."

"It was all Sadie's idea!" Mom threw up her palms.

"Aha!" Beau said. "I thought so. The roses?"

"She called them in, along with the note," Mom admitted. "I told her not to, to stay out of your business, but you know Sadie. When she's bored, she will find things to do. From her bed, there wasn't much she could do and feel accomplished."

"It's okay," Lucy said. "We figured it out the other night. Beau thought Levi had sent me the roses. Because he knew *he* didn't. I assumed he had so we didn't talk about it."

"This almost backfired on y'all. I thought Levi wanted to get back together with Lucy, so I didn't think I had a chance."

"You didn't think you had a chance?" Mom's head was on a swivel, going back and forth between him and Lucy. "You mean you *wanted* a chance?"

"I'm only going to say this once so listen carefully. I love Lucy." Beau put his arm around her and drew her closer.

"Wonderful!" She clapped her hands. "Sadie was right. It was just waiting to happen. And now we won't lose Lucy to Seattle after all!"

Beau felt Lucy stiffen beside him. "I guess that will be up to Lucy."

"Of course you'll stay!" Mom grabbed Lucy in a momma bear hug. "I've always wanted you for a daughter."

"C'mon!" Beau rolled his eyes. "No pressure."

"It's just…well, Beau has a lot going on right now and I did make plans," Lucy said.

"Plans were made to be broken. That's what love does," Mom said. "It rearranges your world and shapes it into something better. Brighter. Given time, you'll realize this is where you belong."

Beau couldn't agree more but he kept his thoughts to himself. Later, after his mother had left, Lucy packed her bag. The case with the scissors that had cut his hair. Her clothes. Beau tried to ignore the pounding heartbeat in his ears. It made sense for her to leave now, and Rachel would be back soon for Charlotte. But Charlotte wasn't the issue either anymore. He could handle her, sure, but he didn't want to without Lucy. He didn't want to do much of anything without Lucy. She calmed him, made him believe he could do anything. He needed her in a way he never had before.

"Don't go," he said, taking her wrist. "Not yet."

"But…I should get home. There's no excuse for me to be here anymore."

"You need an excuse?"

"What will Rachel think if she shows up and I'm here? How will that look? Like you've been shacking up with a girlfriend when you should have been watching Charlotte."

She had a point, but it didn't matter. "I don't care. Besides, I don't think she'll be back until Monday."

"We've been playing house for a few days already. Maybe I should go now so you can miss me."

The words made him smile. "Please." He threaded his fingers through hers. "Just one more night."

Beau didn't usually have to work this hard to convince a woman to stay. In fact, usually the work was done for him. This time, he'd never wanted anything more in his life than for Lucy to wake up next to him tomorrow morning. The rest they'd figure out. He was sure of it. The confidence came from knowing these feelings hadn't just come out of nowhere. Whether or not she wanted to admit it, she felt this, too. It was scary and unexpected, and he got it. She was torn between going through with her plans to move and staying because of him. But he'd wait for her if that's what it took. She could go, but she would come back.

"All right, you smooth talker." Lucy wound her arms around his neck. "You convinced me."

Chapter 20

For once, Beau's life was close to perfect.

Lucky for him, Charlotte was a good sleeper. Last night, they'd put her portable crib in the spare bedroom Lucy had been occupying. Lucy set up the video monitor and they went to bed without a baby watching them. He had to admit that seemed a lot more fun for everyone concerned. Even if he hadn't paid any attention to Charlotte while she was sleeping, not having her in the room seemed to unleash something a little bit wild in Lucy. And he was the happy recipient.

The next morning, he woke to the sounds of Charlotte fussing through the monitor. He let Lucy sleep, quickly threw on some clothes, and went to get the baby.

"Hey, how are you doing, sweetheart?" He picked her up, switching off the monitor first so he wouldn't disturb Lucy.

Grabbing a diaper, he quickly changed her while she made babbling and cooing sounds. She was a good baby, and he definitely saw the Stephens resemblance. Maybe he hadn't exactly *wanted* to see it before. It would have been better to have a child with the woman he loved but he had a daughter now and couldn't regret it. It would all work out somehow. His sunny Labrador nature had him believing they could be a blended family. Lucy would come around and reconsider Seattle. He hadn't missed the goofy grins she gave Charlotte, too, like she'd already fallen in love with her.

"Let's get you a bottle."

He strapped Charlotte into the swing so his hands would be free. Just as he reached the kitchen the doorbell rang. Beau practically did a soft shoe dance to the front door, expecting no one in particular.

He found Rachel. In tears.

"I thought you'd be here Monday. Is everything okay?"

Beau moved aside when she tried, unsuccessfully, to shove him out of the way.

"My baby."

"She's *fine*."

Sure, he might have sounded slightly defensive but who would blame him?

Even as he said the words, Rachel was unbuckling Charlotte from the swing. She held her close. "I missed you so much."

Charlotte kicked her legs in earnest, like she did when particularly excited, Beau had already noticed. She recognized her mother. The reunion was sweet, and he should be happier. He should be relieved. Rachel was back. She *hadn't* abandoned her baby.

But he had so many questions. *Where have you been* topped the list, though it probably wasn't any of his business. Obviously, they had much to discuss. And they should get started, but he felt self-conscious with Lucy sleeping in the bedroom. She'd probably heard the commotion and would be out any minute. And wouldn't that look lovely for him. It was what she'd warned him about last night, but at this point he didn't care what Rachel thought. She'd been the one to dump their daughter here without any warning.

He found himself fervently hoping Lucy would sleep through all this. Then later he'd wake her and tell her what happened.

Rachel was rubbing Charlotte's back. "Did she cry much after that first day when you called me?"

"We got her to calm down after you refused to come back."

"We?" She turned with a half smirk on her lips. "See what I mean? I knew you'd have help."

"In all fairness, you left me here to sink or swim. Yes, I had help. My mother. Her friends, my friends, and everyone who cares about me. They didn't want me to struggle the way you must have wanted."

"That's a lie. I knew you would be fine with her, or I wouldn't have done this. But just think of having to do this entirely on your own, without any help. That's what I had to do when she was a newborn."

"You could have asked for my help."

"You gave me no indication you were the type. A rolling stone, so to speak. We hardly bonded that one time."

"Regardless. We have a lot to talk about."

"Yes, I guess we do. I'm sorry I ran out on you but believe it or not, it was tough to leave her. The thing is…I knew if I didn't get a break I was going to *explode.* And then I wouldn't be good to anyone, least of all her."

"A phone call or a heads-up would have been nice. You just showed up and rocked both of our worlds."

She bounced Charlotte in her lap. "On the other hand, a phone call might have also given you time to run."

"I *wouldn't* have done that."

"Yeah, well, I see that now." She glanced around the room. "I don't know how, but somehow you have more baby stuff than I do."

"It was all donated."

"Somebody jumped the gun. Too bad you won't be able to use it anymore." Rachel's voice strained a few decibels above normal.

He edged his tone to match hers. "Isn't that something we should talk about?"

"Having her for these days wasn't enough for you?"

"No. I want to be involved in her life, if I'm her father, as you said."

"I only said there was a good chance. She probably is your daughter."

"Probably. Now it's *probably*?"

Rachel glanced at something over his shoulder and without turning around Beau knew Lucy had emerged from the bedroom.

"I heard yelling," she said, rubbing her eye with the back of her hand.

Rachel stood. "This isn't much of a surprise to me. I see you recruited help. Was my baby a *chick magnet*?"

"Lucy, this is Charlotte's mother." He made the introductions. "Rachel."

"You came back for her," Lucy said.

"Of course I came back! I *said* I would. I hope you two didn't get any ideas playing house. This is just probably another one of your many girlfriends, Beau, but this is our *child*."

"Now she's my child again?"

"Well, maybe. You know what, I should leave now. I'll call you later. We can arrange a DNA test. Nice to meet you, Lucy. Thank you for helping take care of my daughter."

But she didn't sound grateful. She sounded snippy and short and rather pissed. Which was incredibly rude to Lucy, considering how much she'd helped with the daughter Rachel had dropped off.

"Wait," Beau said. "We should talk first. When can I see her again?"

"We'll have to see about that." Rachel started to strap Charlotte in the car seat.

"Listen, I'm going to go now and give you two a chance to talk," Lucy said.

"No." Beau stopped her halfway to her bag, grabbing her arm. "You're not going anywhere."

"Actually, maybe it is a good idea," Rachel said. "If we're going to talk. Co-parenting is between you and me. No offense, Lucy. You seem like a nice person and all, but you probably don't know Beau *like I do*."

Lucy snorted, but she had the presence of mind not to say anything. She could read a room better than almost anyone he'd ever met.

Beau continued to clasp Lucy's hand tightly. "Lucy isn't going anywhere. Whatever happens, she's a part of it. She's here to stay."

Rachel whipped her head up and met his eyes. "Funny, you didn't mention her when you asked me to *marry* you."

"When I *suggested* we get married for the sake of the baby. You're the one who turned me down. Now, I'd not only like to rescind that offer but I'm going to need some evidence that Charlotte really is my daughter. And then we can talk about visitation."

"Beau, I really—" Lucy said, tugging on his hand.

He understood how awkward this had to be for her. But he didn't want to make it any worse than it already was and Lucy leaving at this point would be much worse. For both of them.

"If you want to go back in the bedroom and wait for us to finish talking, that's okay. But you're not leaving." He quickly corrected himself because he knew Lucy. Almost too well. "I mean, I don't want you to leave. *Don't* leave. Please."

Lucy exchanged a look with him. He read in her eyes a fierce determination that told him she didn't want to leave him, either. She wanted to stay here and fight with him. But it was better for him to handle this alone.

"I'm going outside to the barn."

He let her go, watching as she walked out the sliding glass doors to the patio.

"She doesn't seem like your type." Rachel sniffed.

"I've known Lucy since I was a kid. She knows me almost better than I know myself."

Rachel quirked a brow. "I guess I misspoke then. Was she shocked to find out you're a daddy now?"

"I think it's safe to say everyone was."

"I tried to leave you out of it. It's not like either one of us planned for this."

No, but when you played, you paid. Beau had stepped up and done more than he'd ever thought possible. He'd changed a baby's diaper, bathed her, rocked her to sleep, fed her a bottle, and somehow survived the week.

And in the process he'd fallen fully in love with his best friend.

"What do you want to do now?" Beau said, trying to get back to the subject. "I'd like to spend time with her again."

"Naturally. She's a perfect baby." Rachel smoothed the back of Charlotte's head and she cooed with a big drooly smile.

"There are things we have to talk about. Things we have to settle."

"Like *child support?*" Rachel smirked, as though he'd been derelict in that area.

He had, of course, but through no fault of his own. "Exactly."

"We've done fine without you."

"Up until a few days ago," Beau felt compelled to add.

"My mother fell and had an injury so my support for the past few weeks was gone. I think I lost my mind for a little while."

"Where did you go?"

"Not far. I went to visit some friends."

Beau wondered whether this was none of his business when he realized that she'd left their child with him and took off for days. It was very much his business.

"But where *were* you?"

"Not that it's any of your concern but I went to see my ex. It turns out he wants to be a family. He'll raise Charlotte like she's his own."

"That's going to be a little bit of a problem because she's my daughter, or so you said."

"I thought she was. Maybe now I'm not so sure."

"Really? You're going to pull this now? You said she looks like me!"

"Look, let's face it, life will be much easier for both of us if Charlotte is not yours. We can move on, with our respective partners. We can be happy."

Yes, it would have been easier if Charlotte wasn't his but *easier* wasn't the point. He loved the little girl now and the thought she might not be his own was like a sharp knife in his chest. His breaths were coming short, and pain pressed between his temples.

"This isn't fair."

Rachel stood. "Maybe it isn't fair but it's the truth. You had a few days with her. I've had *months*."

"And whose fault is that? Either way that has nothing to do with this. If she's my daughter, I want to be a part of her life."

"Well, you sure have changed your tune." Rachel went hand on hip. "You didn't want her, admit it. I had to hoist her on you."

All he could think of was Lucy, a tiny baby left behind in the cold. Thank God Lenny had found her when he did. Lenny, who thought of her as a daughter and had always looked out for her. Lenny, who found the note, too. Who claimed the note had said her name was Lucy. Beau didn't think anyone else had actually seen the note, but he couldn't remember now.

"I didn't know about her, and what you did wasn't fair to either one of us. Charlotte cried because she must have thought you abandoned her."

"I didn't *abandon* her."

"You're lucky I didn't call the police. Lucy thought I should."

At this, Rachel's cheeks flushed, and Beau realized he may have gone too far. If he'd called the police then, now he'd have a say in the matter. Maybe. Or Charlotte would have gone into the system until they figured it all out and they'd have all been worse off. But now that she was back, Rachel clearly had the upper hand. Beau would have to go through her to see his daughter.

"She wasn't the only one," Beau lied. "I thought maybe I should, too. But you claimed you'd be back, and I wanted to believe you."

"And as you can plainly see, I am."

"I appreciate that. I know she missed you. And I'm sorry that you felt so overwhelmed. You should have had more support."

Rachel seemed to relax at the acknowledgement from

Beau. He understood the closeness between mother and baby and didn't intend to intervene. But he also wouldn't have another man raise his child. Beau folded up the pack-and-play crib Rachel had brought and carried it to the trunk of her car. He watched as Rachel buckled their baby into the back seat and drove away, little Charlotte with her.

And just like that a little piece of his heart was gone.

He walked, meeting Lucy halfway between the barn and the house.

"What happened?"

He explained everything, leaving out the parts where he'd stupidly mentioned Lucy wanted to call the police.

"I thought I'd be happy to see her go." He wrapped Lucy in his arms, needing her warmth and touch.

"You love her." Lucy held him close, speaking softly into his ear. "Because that's the kind of man you are. You're going to be a good father."

"If she lets me."

"She will." Lucy framed his face with her hands. "I love you, Beau."

"Yeah?" His voice sounded like a croak of surprise and amazement.

"I do."

Beau felt a grin split his face.

Sometimes the sweetest words were the ones most worth waiting for.

Chapter 21

"You should have seen him." Lucy barely held back tears. "He won't say it, but I know. He's devastated."

After she and Beau straightened up the house and put away all the baby detritus, the place looked empty. Desolate. It was back to being a bachelor's house. Beau didn't have much to say for a change. He walked around for a while looking dejected and lost. She told Beau she'd be back later and made her excuses because she didn't want to get all weepy in front of him. He was the one who'd had the loss, not her. And yet it felt so personal because it had happened to Beau. She loved him so much she *felt* his pain.

Anyway, it was about time Lucy came to see her other best friend. They had a few things to discuss, not the least of which was her matchmaking. Lucy was shocked to see how big Sadie had grown. It was as if her stomach was this huge mountain. Like…Mount Everest. Lucy chose not to ask if they'd made a mistake and Sadie was actually having twins. It was difficult to believe only one baby was housed in there.

Lucy squeezed her hand. "I probably shouldn't have told you this today. You're going to be extra emotional."

"She's my niece." Sadie's lower lip quivered. "I already miss her."

"We've got to do something to help Beau. You surely have the free time on your hands to figure this out. Time enough to arrange for red roses to be delivered for your brother." Lucy cocked her head, smirked, and made her "gotcha" face.

"Fine, I admit it. It isn't because I wanted you to stay in Stone Ridge, although I do." Sadie huffed. "But you and Beau belong together, and I've known it for a long time."

"I wish you'd have told me."

"The timing had to be right, but he's *always* loved you. In our house, it was always Lucy this or Lucy that. Once I told him he should just go ahead and *kiss* you and get it over with." Sadie cocked her head, as if remembering. "I think I was sixteen. He yelled at me, told me to get out of his room, and that was the end of that."

Lucy laughed at the image. "You'll be happy to know that all your efforts worked."

Sadie smiled. "They did?"

"Yes, not that it's any of your business."

"Of course, it's my business! It's my brother. And my best friend." Sadie clutched Lucy's hand. "Please tell me."

"Well…we're together."

Sadie squealed, making Lucy feel a bit embarrassed.

"It's about time!"

Yeah, sure, it only took about two decades. Lucy could discuss all her feelings but that was one other way in which she was more like a guy. She didn't indulge in girl talk the way Sadie and Eve did. And they had more important matters to address now.

"Do you know anyone who could help Beau? I was

thinking we could call Riggs. God knows he's busy but he's an actual attorney and can give Beau some advice on his rights as a father."

"That's a good idea. I'll call him and make a list of action items." She picked up her pen and paper nearby. "For a couple more days, I'm stuck here."

"Is this where you've been doing all your scheming?"

Sadie, born teacher and organizer, flipped through several pages of her notebook.

"I've had so much to think about as I lay here and twiddled my toes. I can't see them anymore, you know that?"

"I'm…not surprised."

"Hey! Wait until you're eight months pregnant and then let me know."

Once, that image would have scared the stink off Lucy. She didn't know her own parents' biology or what kind of DNA cocktail she'd bring to a child. Now, her thoughts went to the man who might just someday be her baby's father. She knew him, his family, and that was enough for her. He would love his child at first sight. Her baby would have a ready-made family who would adore him or her. And as for her DNA, maybe that wasn't everything. She had her parents, and they were wonderful.

After leaving Sadie, Lucy went back to her house. Her non-termite-infested, non-vermin-occupied house. Everything looked different. The boxes were still stacked where she'd left them, the one containing the old newspaper still sliced open. She reached inside and held the paper between her hands again, reading the small text that announced life-changing news. Her own special kind of birth announcement, her mother had called it. The small-town paper ran birth announcements and landmark birthdays of the town's residents such as when Mrs. Mary had turned one hundred last year. Unfortunately, by press time she was no longer alive but, regardless, she'd made it to a hundred.

Well, there was something else Lucy had to do, and she'd put it off long enough. Whether or not Beau was Charlotte's father wouldn't change the way Lucy felt. They'd work it out one way or another. She'd always be there for him and he for her. No point in fighting facts any longer. She loved him with all her heart.

And they couldn't have a relationship with thousands of miles between them.

Lucy dialed Dottie in Seattle.

"Lucy! I'm so excited. Are you all packed and ready?"

"Um…well…"

"Oh, no! Not this again. What is it this time? Your mother claims she's dying? Sadie needs you to be her doula? Lenny wants you to take over his exterminator job?"

Lucy couldn't blame her. It could have been any one of those things. Every time she talked about moving, in fact, it was Lenny who needed something. It had never been Beau keeping her here before. Her life had changed and not in a small way.

Lord, she'd been so lucky. Lucky to wind up in a town like this one, with her found family, her friends, and neighbors. With the solid men of Stone Ridge. It could have all been so different. A few hours one way or another and she might not know all these people. She would have been raised by someone else. But she had wound up here and was now with one of the best men she'd ever known. It felt as if she'd known him her entire life and that it couldn't have ever been any other way but this one. Falling in love with her best friend. Having the opportunity of a life with him.

She was different from anyone else she'd ever known but somehow that was a good thing now. She didn't know when she was born or exactly where, but instead…she had this. It was more than she could have ever wanted or dreamed.

"It's nobody else this time. It's just me. I don't want to leave anymore." Lord, it felt good to say it out loud and most of all believe it. "I'm sorry. This is where I belong."

"I thought you were sick of cowboys."

"Yeah, but I found a good one."

BEAU DROVE out to meet his father at the lakeside cabins where, according to their office manager, he'd gone to attend to some maintenance. Something weighed heavy on his mind and if he was right, it meant confronting someone who'd never been anything more than kind to him. So much had happened in the past week but what was on his mind now could be the most significant of all. The fact it had all jelled together in his mind only a few hours ago made it feel urgent.

His father was walking out of Sarah's cabin when Beau arrived and caught up to him. Interestingly, no half-dressed woman followed *him* out the door. For the first time in his life, Beau looked forward to being the kind of man every woman understood was "taken." Like his father, a family man.

"Hey," Beau said. "Everything going okay?"

"You were right about these city folk." His father shook his head. "Wi-Fi is all they got on their blessed minds. I tried to explain to these young ladies that if they want to meet a cowboy they best get outside in the fresh air."

"That's good advice. Why didn't I think of that?"

His father clapped him on the shoulder. "You've been

busy. There's also something about babies that seems to suck out your last brain cell. That's what your mother always said."

Beau updated his father on the latest with Charlotte and Rachel.

"It's good you want to be involved in your child's life. I'm proud of you. A lesser man would take the opportunity she handed you to walk away."

They ambled to the lakeside, enjoying the dappled afternoon sunshine through the willow trees. Beau and his father used to do a lot of fishing back in the day, and they should do that again.

"That's just the thing," Beau said. "Can you tell me why someone would walk away from their own baby?"

His father blinked. "Well, she did come back."

"I'm…not talking about Rachel." He met his father's gaze. "I mean Lucy. I never spent much time wondering about her past. She was always just Lucy Lorenzo to me. Not surprisingly, I guess, I discovered it's pretty important to her to know where she came from. Her *real* birthday."

"Well, we all know that story. It started out as a tragedy but wound up an uplifting story. Lucy couldn't have done better than to wind up here with Esperanza and Arturo."

"That still doesn't answer my question. *Why* did someone abandon her?"

"We might never know that. But I'm thinking the usual reasons. No resources. Overwhelmed. Possibly someone quite young."

"You were around back then. How hard did y'all try to find her parents?"

"I don't know. Lenny seems to be the repository of all that information. He was our 'roving reporter' at the time." His father made air quotes.

"Right. And it is interesting that he found her, too."

"I suppose. But you know Lenny. He's got his hand in so many deals. I imagine he was coming home from work that morning and just happened upon her. He used to clean the church, too, I believe. And it was a Sunday when she was found."

"It was a *Sunday*?"

He nodded. "That's the way I remember it, but you have to understand. It was a long time ago, I had you—a toddler—and your mother pregnant with Sadie. I was in that crazy stage where I got very little sleep and was functioning on fumes."

"It just…seems strange. Lenny has always been so much a part of Lucy's life. I guess I never noticed that before."

"Well, he couldn't raise her himself, but he definitely bonded with her, having found her. It makes sense. Lenny had a house full of kids and grandkids or he might have taken her in himself." His father paused. "Why? You think Lenny knows who the mother might be?"

The odd feeling kept creeping up on Beau. There was only one thing left to do. He wanted answers and for that he had to talk to Lenny.

Chapter 22

Beau called Lenny using the satellite phone and a few minutes later he arrived at the lakeside cabins.

He pulled up in the golf cart he used for his rideshares and eyed Beau's truck parked nearby. "Did your truck break down?"

"Yeah," Beau lied. "I just need to get over to Daisy's auto shop in Kerrville for a part."

"Oh, I can't take you that far in this! Why don't you just call Lucy? We split the calls and she takes all the long-distance rides."

As if Beau didn't already know this.

"Just take me downtown and I'll give her a call when I get there." Beau hopped on.

Now, to find a way to bring up an awkward subject. How exactly did you accuse someone of lying the way Lenny had? More and more, Beau realized he *had* to know a lot more about Lucy than he'd claimed. But bringing it up wasn't going to be easy.

"Speaking of Lucy." Beau cleared his throat. "Whatever y'all were up to, it worked."

"What in the Sam Hill are you talkin' about?" Lenny turned on to the road, driving along the shoulder as he did with his golf cart.

They weren't getting anywhere fast, so best to start the conversation off without accusations.

"Yeah. The termites? And the vermin? Might as well fess up. Lucy and I figured it out."

"You have to understand." Lenny shook his head emphatically. "I was under a lot of pressure from the women. Lots and lots of stress. I do what's asked of me because I know who actually runs this town."

"Right. The women do."

"You got that right, son. I'm sorry if I was out of line, but hey, a little push or shove in the right direction couldn't hurt."

"No, it didn't hurt at all. I have to thank you for that."

"Oh hell, now, I'm a romantic. Otherwise, I wouldn't have been married three times. You know how hard it is to get married three times in a town like ours? Hard enough you have to work at it!"

"It doesn't hurt to have married the same woman twice." Beau snorted.

"Well, that's true. But the worst thing is to marry someone you don't love. Did that once so maybe that's why it's a trigger of mine. You'd be on borrowed time."

"I tried to do right by Rachel, but I'm in love with Lucy."

"I'm truly happy for you."

"So, that's why I want to find out who abandoned her and why they never came back."

Lenny steered off the road. "Oh now, hell. Why would you want to do that after all this time? Just leave well enough I say. The point is, Lucy was raised by Esperanza and Arturo and she's had a great life. Why would you want to mess around with that? I mean, what if it's someone who didn't want her and still doesn't want her?"

"I get it. She belongs here with us, but I don't think we will ever lose her. I know I won't. Now that I finally have her, I'm hardly going to let her go. She knows *where* she's wanted. But every child deserves to know where they came from, don't they? Their origins and biology?"

"Well, sure, but…"

"Just pull up over here." Beau pointed to the Shady Grind once they'd crawled into town. "Let me buy you a cold beer."

Lenny blinked. "Well, I should really go home and check in with the family. You know how it is."

Beau had never seen Lenny turn down a cold beer. It took a little effort on his part, but Beau finally managed to get Lenny inside. The place was already a bit slammed. Still, they found a spot at the bar and Levi set them up.

"Congratulations again, Levi," Beau said.

"Thanks. Hey, no hard feelings." Levi set a beer in front of Beau. "I feel like I stole Lucy from you for a while. Lots of wasted time there for us both."

"Don't worry about it. You didn't steal her."

"I should have realized it wouldn't work between us when she talked about you so much. Beau did this, and Beau did that. I've known for a long time she was crazy about you, but it wasn't up to me to be the one to tell you."

They were interrupted by several well-wishers congratulating Levi on his engagement.

"Congrats, Levi! Way to nab the richest woman in town!"

"Hey, better make sure you hog tie her on wedding day. She's been known to run!"

Jeremy clapped Beau on the shoulder. "Where have you been, man? I haven't seen you for a while."

Until then, Beau hadn't realized how often he'd dropped by the bar. It had only been a week, after all.

"He's a father, that's what happened!" Lenny chuckled.

He probably felt somewhat relieved the subject matter had changed but Beau wasn't done with Lenny yet.

"Lenny, tell us the story of how you found Lucy," Beau said. "I've been thinking a lot about it lately."

"That's always a good one," Jeremy said, though he quickly lost interest when a group of women entered the establishment.

Lenny lit up at being the center of attention. He told the story just as he always had before, no variations. Got off work, found the baby, called the police. Wrote the newspaper article. All's well that ends well.

"So, you didn't clean the church that morning before services?" Beau said.

Lenny, now on his second beer, scratched his temple. "Well, now, I can't actually remember what job I'd been working that day. You have to understand, this was more than thirty years ago. It sure wasn't the post office job."

"Right. Because it was a Sunday. It's just you remember everything else so well and with such detail."

"I've told the story many times. That's the way it goes."

"When you saw Lucy, was she crying?"

"Crying? Oh, uh no, just a sweet little angel in her basket. Just like I said."

"So, then you just picked her up and what did you do then?"

Beau had already heard it, but he hoped Lenny would slip up and say something more. Something he hadn't mentioned before. Something different. A clue.

"Like I said a *thousand* times before, and this is what I told the police. I saw the basket and noticed Lucy in there. So, I tried to…" He stopped talking midsentence.

Beau quirked a brow. "Tried to what, Lenny?"

"Now I'm gettin' all confused." He scrubbed a hand down his face. "It was a long time ago and I was just trying to help like I always do. You have to understand. I didn't want her to get in trouble."

"Who? *Who* didn't you want to get in trouble?"

This was the truth, buried in an old man's memories. Lenny was an old-timer, and when he was gone, so would be the story.

Lucy's story. And Beau wanted this for her more than anything because she deserved to know the truth, no matter what.

Lenny glanced around as if to make sure no one else was listening in. As it worked out, everyone seemed fascinated with the group of women who were showing off their matching tattoos of a cowboy.

"She was young. Only sixteen." Lenny bent close to speak softly and shook his head. "I didn't want her to get in trouble. So, I helped. I always, *always* help."

"*Who* was young?"

"Jacqueline. My daughter. Lucy's mother."

Chapter 23

Lucy was in the middle of emptying another box when her landline rang. She fully expected a rideshare request from the Shady Grind from someone who'd had their keys taken away but not until later tonight. So she wasn't surprised to hear the loud din in the background, the sound of a pool cue hitting the balls and silverware clinking.

She picked up the phone. "Alright, who's day drinking over there?"

"Lucy, it's me," said Beau's voice. "Wanted to make sure you're home."

"I told you I would be."

"Good. I'm coming over right now, and don't *go* anywhere."

"I'm not going anywhere. I'm unpack—"

But he'd already hung up.

Lucy told herself the urgency in his voice, the rapid-fire words, the hang-up, didn't have to mean bad news. He hadn't even taken the DNA test yet so it couldn't have anything to do with Charlotte. For one second, she allowed a sense of panic to lace through her. Something might be wrong with Sadie. Maybe she'd been rushed to the hospital with contractions. Lucy had just visited with her earlier and to be honest, she'd looked ready to pop but supposedly had a couple of more weeks to be considered in the safety zone.

She busied herself tidying up the house, putting away clean dishes and folding some of her laundry. The boxes she'd already unpacked she broke down and stacked in a corner. She hoped the settled view of her home would send Beau the message loud and clear: she wasn't going anywhere. She would stay in Stone Ridge but now with a sense this was her place. Her home. Unless this was simply about her heart.

Maybe *Beau* was her real home.

When he hadn't arrived thirty minutes later, the actual distance from downtown, she questioned whether he'd gone somewhere else first. But he'd be here, she was sure of it. He must have something to tell her. Well, obviously. They'd already said, "I love you" and for Lucy, there was nothing more to say. She didn't want to move in with Beau too quickly and hoped he didn't want to convince her to save money by doing that. There was so much to work out with Charlotte and her mother. Lucy didn't want to get in the way of a smooth transition for Beau to have visitation rights if he wound up being the father.

So many possibilities of why he didn't want her to go anywhere crowded her mind they bubbled inside, and she almost couldn't hold them all.

Finally, an hour later, Beau's truck pulled up outside. She ran outside and was halfway there when she saw Lenny pull up behind him.

"Lenny." She went hands on hips. "If this is about the termites and vermin, it's fine. You're forgiven. I'm frankly just grateful you were lying about it."

"Sweetheart, that's not it." Beau took her hand. "Lenny has something important to tell you."

Lenny nodded and looked like she'd rarely seen him before: lowered head, hands stuck in his ever-present utility work pants, appearing quite dejected.

"Let's go inside." Beau led her back to the house, hand low on her spine as he steered her.

What on earth had Lenny done now? It wasn't like he hadn't been the adventurous sort in the past, hence the termite-and-vermin lies. Married multiple times, she'd seen him as someone who occasionally skirted the edges of polite society, so to speak. But that was many of their older cowboys and Lenny was always so kind. Retired long ago from the post office, he at least kept quite busy, doing good for the community by offering free rides when Lucy normally charged her passengers. He had a lot of children, about seven or eight, and seventeen grandchildren last she'd heard, scattered all over Texas and beyond.

"Would y'all like some iced tea?" Lucy offered once they were inside.

"Yes, I would," Lenny said. "Please."

"Best get on with it, Lenny," Beau said. "We'll drink tea later."

Dear God, what was going on? She plopped down on the couch, anxiety and fear pressing down like a vice. "You're scaring me. What's *happened*?"

"It isn't terrible news." Beau took her hand in his, squeezing. "I'm here."

"I don't know where to start," Lenny said, swallowing heavily.

"Start what?" Lucy demanded, but instead of looking at Lenny, she turned to Beau.

He was her strength right now. Her rock. But he wasn't giving her words, just steadily keeping his gaze on Lenny.

Lucy pointed. "Go ahead, Lenny. *Talk.*"

"Okay! Do you remember hearing about my Noelle Lee?"

"We've all heard about your first wife."

Lenny talked about her from time to time, making her sound like a movie star that had accidentally wound up in Stone Ridge.

"Yeah, well, we married after knowing each other for a month. I'm sure you've all heard the story. Marry in haste, repent at leisure, they all say." He cleared his throat, practically bug-eyed. "Anyway, before we divorced we had a daughter. I don't talk about her much, but her name is Jacqueline. Noelle Lee wanted one of those fancy names, like the former first lady. She always thought she was better than toasted bread, that one."

"Lenny, get on with it," Beau said.

"Yeah, yeah. She left Stone Ridge, like so many women do, and took our little Jacqueline with her. They lived in San Antonio, and I hardly got to see her much, aside from the occasional weekend here or there. She grew up into a beautiful girl, just like Noelle Lee. Well, one day she showed up and wanted my help. She…she had a little baby with her. A girl." Lenny's voice shook.

Lucy's breaths came in short and uneven because she feared where this was going. Her hand flew up over her mouth and then she lowered it.

That was her, *she* was the baby. And Lenny was her *grandfather*?

"Why did she just leave me at the church? Why not leave me with you?"

"She did leave you with me."

"*What?*"

"I wanted to keep you, but my wife didn't want Noelle Lee's grandchild. And our house was already overflowing.

Kids, grandkids. Not one of them can hold a job. I knew Esperanza wanted children desperately. And Cal and Marge Henderson were right here in town, so good with fostering kids. They had the room on that big ranch of theirs, too."

"Why would you leave me *outside* all night to be found?"

Beau's hand went to Lucy's leg to still her.

"I didn't."

"That's just the story he told," Beau said quietly.

"I wrapped you up in a warm blanket, put you in a basket and called the police. You were never actually sitting alone outside the church. But you see, I couldn't tell anyone about Jacqueline. She would have been in a lot of trouble, especially with her mother. Eventually she heard I couldn't keep you and she just trusted me to do the right thing."

"Which was to lie for over *thirty years*?" Lucy's throat felt like a thousand needles were stuck inside, making it difficult to swallow. Or breathe.

"Lucy." Beau's voice was soft.

"No!" Lucy stood, letting go of Beau's hand, and pointing to the door. "I don't want to talk to you anymore, Lenny. Or should I call you 'grandpa'? Just…just *get out*!"

"Don't you have questions?" Beau said. "This is the time to ask them."

"I told you this was a bad idea," Lenny said. "But you wouldn't listen."

Lucy stomped out of the room and slammed the door of her bedroom shut. She paced across the length of the floor, hardly aware of her surroundings. Inside, anger boiled over. All this time, right under her nose! How dare they, how dare they all make her feel like this special darling baby when she was anything but that.

She was the unwanted daughter of a teenage mother. How predictable. Pathetic. God, her mother's name was Jacqueline. Jacqueline.

And Lenny was her *grandfather*? What in the ever loving hell…two seconds later, she threw open the door. Thankfully, both Beau and Lenny were still there. Beau, his arms crossed as he stared at her with his intent eyes. Waiting. He wasn't letting Lenny go before she got her answers, and he knew she'd want them. Some answers more than others.

Her mind still wasn't clear, but she had her first question. The most important one.

"Did my parents know? Have they been lying to me, too?" Her words caught on a sob.

Beau reached her in two steps, and she was in his arms, her face brushed against his warm neck. He held her tightly and over his shoulder, she raised her head to meet Lenny's gaze.

"That's all I want to know right now. And then you can go."

"They have no idea." Lenny shook his head. "I was going to take this secret to my grave but after everything that happened with Charlotte…Beau explained what it meant to you, just to know. It isn't that you weren't wanted, Lucy. You were very much wanted. Jacqueline brought you to me. Someone she could trust. Noelle Lee wasn't going to let her keep you and Jacqueline wouldn't just give you up to anyone. She wanted to know where you were and that you were safe. That's why I kept you close, why I never wanted you to leave town. I saw that you were always provided for and taken care of even if I couldn't do it myself. It's not something I'm proud of. No one else knows. I swear to you. And they never will, only if you want them to."

"Oh my God. Beau. I can't believe this is happening."

Lucy clutched at his shirt, fisting her hands in the material. She clung to him like she'd fall down without his holding her up. "I-I thought I w-wanted to know. But I didn't want…this."

Beau slid one arm up and down her back. With the other arm, she could swear he was literally keeping her from sliding to the floor.

Chapter 24

A few hours later, Lenny had left, and Lucy thought most of her tears were gone. She'd cried for hours. First in Beau's arms, then she'd locked herself in the bathroom, slumped down against the wall, and cried some more. Alone. The big ugly cry. All the while, her mind focused on her new reality: Lenny was her *grandfather.* Her mother was in San Antonio, not even that far, and her name was Jacqueline. But what about her father? Beau was right. She had plenty of questions now that Lenny was gone. Too many.

She'd always had many skills and never quite settled on one. Apparently it was hereditary. She was just like Lenny, a person with more than one job, flitting about and good at everything. An expert at nothing. It was surreal. She could even recall once, many years ago, quietly wishing Lenny was her grandfather instead of having one like her mother's father, an old-school, uptight man who didn't want her to ride horses because it wasn't "ladylike."

She stayed in the bathroom so long she thought Beau

would get the hint, get bored, and leave. But Beau wouldn't go. He wouldn't leave her.

And she wouldn't have left him, either.

Lucy emerged from the bathroom, wetting her swollen eyelids with a washcloth.

"Let me show you something." He led her to sit beside him on the couch and swiped at his phone. "I took this photo from one in Lenny's wallet. It's old and a little faded but…"

A younger woman with long dark hair, smiled hugely, her arms around Lenny. The stranger looked like her.

"That's Jacqueline. She's beautiful. Remind you of anyone?"

Lucy nodded. "It's so strange to find this part of me I didn't even know existed."

"Did I do the right thing? It's upset you so much. I pressed Lenny, and I was the one who didn't stop until he slipped up. But maybe it was all better left a secret. You're clearly miserable." His slightly downturned eyes were especially tender and soft today.

"It's because of you that I know something that's always been in the back of my mind. You did this for me. How did you even figure this out?"

"It just all came together in my head and suddenly I couldn't see why we didn't all figure it out right away. I mean, Lenny found you because he was supposedly working that day. He also wrote the newspaper article. We all accepted that because he had so many jobs, he was everywhere all at once. I had a talk with my father, and he remembered that no one had actually ever seen the note. This was all Lenny, trying to help. It sounded so much like him. Trying to make it all better. The only question was why and now it all makes sense. He wouldn't tell anyone the truth because otherwise your mother might be in trouble for abandonment."

"She did abandon me, but I'm telling myself that at the very least she cared what happened to me. She must have loved me and took good care of me for a while. And when I think of a teenager raising me, or even growing up in Lenny's overflowing household with a woman who didn't like my mother to begin with…"

"One way or another, we would have still met. I would have still fallen for you." He pressed his forehead to hers.

"I imagine I definitely would have been able to sneak out of that house much easier had I lived with Lenny." She chuckled.

"You had good parents."

"The best. They put me first in everything. I can't believe I took them for granted all these years. I mean, look at what my life might have been instead."

"Do you want to meet her?"

It was a good question. She thought of Charlotte and how happy she'd been to see her mother. Maybe that had once been her, too, as a baby, instinctively reacting to the person who brought her into the world. They were connected at that time through pure biology. But too much time had passed. Jacqueline may have given her life, but her real parents had kept her alive and thriving. They'd showered her with love and dedication and never once walked away.

Not walking away and not ever giving up on a mouthy teenager. That was huge.

"I always thought so but now…I need to think about it."

It would depend on her mother. If she felt at all threatened by Lucy meeting her biological mother, she wouldn't do it. But something told her Esperanza wanted whatever

Lucy wanted. And the thought made her want to cry all over again.

"I'll support you whatever you do."

That night, Beau stayed with her. In bed, they reached for each other, their movements ranging between desperate—her—and tender—him. In the morning, she woke with his arm slung around her waist possessively. She'd already grown to love sleeping with him. His body was always warm and hard, and he held her like he owned her…but in the best of ways. Like she was his, but more importantly, he was hers.

As usual, Beau was right, and she had questions for Lenny, but she'd sent him away in anger, shock, and frustration. While Beau finished showering the next morning, Lucy put on a robe, grabbed a pen in the kitchen and made a list.

Questions for Lenny and my mother:

1. When is my actual birthday?
2. Who named me Lucy?
3. Where is my father?
4. Are there any medical conditions I should be aware of?
5. Who else knows about me?

And at the end of the list, the last, scariest one of all: Do you think Jacqueline would like to see me?

She wouldn't blame the woman for not wanting to see Lucy again. There would be some fear of repercussions and anger. Maybe, it was possible, her other family didn't even know about Lucy. She might want to keep her teenage shame—Lucy—a secret forever.

Beau emerged from the bathroom a few minutes later in a puff of steam wearing nothing but a towel, his newly cut hair still curling at the ends. It was the way she personally liked it. A little long and a little wild to match the man and his heart.

"Hi." She set down her pen, her attention completely removed from the list.

He had a way of doing that to her. Making her want things. So *many* things.

"What are you smiling about?"

"Oh, I'm remembering the day you came to the door without a shirt on."

He smiled and quirked a brow. "I probably did that on purpose."

"Like a mating call?" She stood and walked toward him.

"Maybe. For you, anyway."

"I've got news for you, baby. You are a walking, talking, official mating call."

He reached for her, pulled her close. "I hope that's a compliment."

"Oh yes. As long as I'm your only mating call, I don't care how many others hear it. I don't blame them. You're *loud*."

Beau's skilled hands untied her robe and slid inside to her naked body.

"I don't have any appointments for another hour."

"That's good, because I have plans for you." Arms circled around his neck, she kissed him, slow and deep with promises of more.

No matter what else happened to her life, Beau was that one constant. He'd always been her best friend and now was much more. *Everything.*

The man she loved, who would always stand by her.

·   ·   ·

LATER THAT MORNING, Lucy went over to her childhood home. She had so much to tell her mother, not the least of which was that she and Beau had started a relationship. That she was truly in love for possibly the first time in her life. But the toughest thing would be telling her about Jacqueline. Because this wasn't something she could hide from her parents even if she wanted to keep it from everyone else in town. Little by little, she'd reveal the truth to those she knew best but for now, Lucy would rather continue to be known as Lucy Lorenzo, daughter of Esperanza and Art.

"Lucy!" Her mother said, hugging her. "I didn't expect you."

"How's the painting going?" Lucy smirked.

"Oh, it's all done." She threw up her palms. "I changed my mind."

"That's convenient."

Lucy followed her mother into the 1970s-style kitchen her parents had never updated. The orange-and-brown paisley counters were old school, but her mother always kept a clean and tidy home.

"I should tell you something. The funniest thing happened. You know how I couldn't stay here because you were painting so I wound up staying with Beau? We fell in love."

Well, that was the short story.

"You're kidding!"

"It's funny. Suddenly he was there, all good-looking like he'd always been but this time with a baby. It changed *everything.* I was lying about being chained to the stove, by the way." Lucy picked an apple out of the fruit basket and took a bite.

"I figured that."

"You can fess up, Mom. Everyone else already has."

"I was just trying to help. But if I'd asked you to stay in town for Beau's sake, you wouldn't have believed it. You would have expected me to want you to stay for me and your dad. So, I went along with the game. You and Beau simply needed a little push."

Lucy didn't even want to bother telling her mother the real push had been Levi, choosing to go after what he truly wanted. Showing Lucy that it was okay to love someone even if it wasn't convenient. If not for him, Lucy might have simply been a live-in nanny for a few days. But she'd taken that risk and it had paid off.

"That's not really what I'm here to talk about." Lucy lowered her head and studied her fingernails.

"Is something else going on?"

"Quite a few things."

Slowly, she explained what Beau had discovered by talking to Lenny and asking a few probing questions. Her mother's face turned pink, then red, then a bit pale.

"Lucy, are you okay, honey?" She reached for Lucy's hand.

Leave it to her mother to make this her first question. She'd know how difficult this would be.

"It's hard," Lucy admitted. "Mostly, the lie. *All* the lies over the years."

"I didn't know. How could Lenny *do* this?"

Lucy's resentment was fading slowly, like slowly seeping air out of a balloon. It helped that she'd always known Lenny to be a good man who often made mistakes.

"Easy. He was trying to protect someone he loved."

"I certainly understand what that's like. We've always tried, maybe a little too hard, to keep you safe. But it was because of what we thought were your tough beginnings. We didn't know who we were dealing with, and whether it could be a truly irresponsible and dangerous person. I worried she might snatch you back in the same irresponsible way she'd left you. Now it seems it was just a young and troubled lady."

Lucy sympathized and always had. But it wasn't until she'd cared for Charlotte and then watched her go with her mother, a woman Lucy wasn't sure should be trusted, that she really understood. Loving a baby was not for the faint of heart. Speaking of risk, Lucy had once heard Sadie describe her feelings about Sammy. *It's a little like watching your heart walking around on legs.*

Esperanza had all the questions that Lucy should have asked Lenny. Ironically, almost verbatim from her list.

"I was upset with Lenny last night, so I threw him out of my house."

"Lucy, this is your chance." This time, her mother took both of her hands in hers. "You can discover your past. Your biology. You can meet your birth mother."

"You don't mind?" Lucy's voice shook with emotion.

"I know who you are and you're mine. You were mine when you had colic and I walked the halls with you all night. When you first smiled that toothless smile. The first time you called me 'mama.' I feel sorry for the woman who gave you up. I prayed for her every night that she'd know she did the right thing. Little did I know she had someone watching over you from close by."

This is what Lenny had essentially done. Which meant Lucy's birth mother knew everything about her while Lucy knew almost nothing about her.

Her father ambled in the door, on his lunch break, no doubt. He still worked forty hours a week even though he'd turned sixty-five last year. "I can't. They wouldn't know what to do without me," he said whenever anyone suggested he retire from his job as a land surveyor.

"Hi, Daddy." Lucy stood and went into his arms.

"Hello, Button. Fancy seeing you here. You never come by."

"I was here two weeks ago," Lucy said, reminding him.

"Oh, that's right. Sue me if I like seeing my daughter every day."

She and her mother exchanged a look. Later, they'd tell him everything. *Later.* For now, Lucy wanted to spend some time with her family.

"I want to thank you," Lucy said to her father, "for realizing even before I did that Beau was never 'just Beau.'"

Chapter 25

Beau scheduled the DNA test for the following week.

But they wouldn't have the results for weeks, and some-times it felt as if his entire life hinged on the answer to *one test*. What if she wasn't actually his daughter, after he'd become attached to her? He might never get to spend time with Charlotte again. Rachel, back with her ex, still wasn't interested in giving Beau any time with her until she had to. When he'd called to inform her when he'd scheduled the test so she could arrange for Charlotte to go, she made excuses. She also made excuses when he called to suggest a date he might see Charlotte again, while they waited. Doctor's appointments, family events, work. She seemed to at least understand, on some level, that Beau could have made her life difficult and chose not to, but this apprecia-tion only extended so far.

Even if he found himself dipping into melancholy, surprised how much he could miss a baby, he pulled himself out. He had Lucy. They had each other. It was Lucy's situation that made Beau reconsider his feelings about Charlotte. He didn't want his daughter to ever experience the doubt and the questions Lucy had about her own biological family. A child deserved to know both parents in her life, even if it couldn't always be the idealized version of a family. Beau would be there for his daughter. Because he was certain, maybe on that psychic level Lucy had talked about, that Charlotte was his.

He was back to work, at least, and had an appointment today with Colton and Jennifer Henderson. A couple of months ago, they'd come to him and described exactly what they wanted. Colton had returned from his stint at the Army to rejoin the family ranching business. He'd been staying with his wife in a small house perched on a hill, waiting to get started on plans for his own home. Each brother had built on the land they'd inherited from their adoptive parents, Cal and Marge Henderson.

Lucy almost wound up on this ranch and would have lived here if she'd been adopted by the Hendersons. She would have been raised with three cowboy brothers. Either way, Beau was certain they would have met, and everything would have been the same. Their friendship over the years, growing into something deeper, stronger, and settling into what they had now. Something truly unbreakable. He was certain there would be a lifetime of love ahead of them. Even if there were bumps ahead, and Beau was fairly certain there might be, he would never give up on her.

Colton and Jennifer were eagerly waiting for him outside when he arrived, blueprints in hand.

"Hey there," Beau said, ambling toward them. "How are y'all?"

"I'm excited," Jennifer said. "I can't wait to see the plans."

"She just wants to make sure we're putting in those his

and hers sinks in the master bathroom." Colton made a move with his hands and added, "She likes to spread out."

"I come with product. Skin, hair, teeth. I don't know what it's like to wake up in the morning already looking gorgeous." She hooked her finger toward Colton.

He laughed and pulled her into his arms. "Yes, you do."

This kind of thing used to make Beau want to gag, but now he only thought of Lucy. Speaking of someone who woke up looking gorgeous…she didn't wear or need any makeup. A natural beauty.

Beau spread the blueprints out on the hood of his truck. He'd designed the home they wanted with everything vital in mind. Colton wanted to use the land for horses and the new cattle he would be raising. There would be a barn and stables and a ranch-style house at the center of it all. Beau had made good use of every inch of square footage.

He pointed. "Here are the bedrooms. Four like you wanted, with the largest one right here, your bedroom."

"And the children's bedrooms nearby," Jennifer said, practically bouncing.

"Are you pregnant?" Beau grinned.

"No, but I bet I will be soon."

Colton put a protective arm around her and he seemed to grow three inches in height, his chest practically bursting. This might be what it would be like to have a baby with the woman you loved. Beau hadn't yet experienced that, and he wondered how quickly he could talk Lucy into having babies.

First, he better marry her.

Beau went on to point out all the features he'd designed for a modern and energy-efficient home, relieved to meet with their approval. In his experience, he had to make a lot of changes on the design before breaking ground. But Colton and Jennifer weren't like Mr. Truehart, who wanted high-end everything, sparing no expense. They were willing to cut corners where it saved them money and still got them the end result. A home where they could grow into and raise a family.

"This is perfect," Colton said, admiring the design. "When can we get started?"

"Next week too soon for you? The materials have already been ordered and so have the appliances. Sometimes those take a while, so we'll get started with the foundation next week."

Colton fist bumped him, but Jennifer gave him a big hug.

As Beau drove away, he thanked God he was lucky and blessed enough to do what he loved for a living.

He still had a few errands to run, but when he got home, he planned on taking True for a ride.

SO MUCH WAS right in Sadie's world, but her stomach wasn't one of those things. She had cravings like she'd never had with Sammy. No sooner did she eat than she was hungry again.

Her mother had served her lunch, then taken Sammy to the park. It was a good thing because her boy was bouncing off the walls lately, as if he understood big changes were coming. Lincoln would be coming inside a couple of hours from now for her appointment later today, to check and see if all this bed rest had helped and she might now go back to normal.

Until the time of the exam, Lincoln was outside tending to a cow having a difficult labor and had left her the satellite phone to reach him. Sadie figured it was fine to get up and walk a tiny bit more than she had in a week. Carefully, she stood and made her way down the steps toward the kitchen. She could still smell the sweet aroma in the air of the chocolate chip cookies her mother had baked for Sammy earlier.

It was cruel to have only given Sadie one. Her baby gave her a swift kick from inside as if she sensed the sugary treat coming, too. More and more Sadie was certain she was having a girl. Maybe that weird concoction her mother offered when she and Linc were trying to get pregnant again had actually worked. She and Linc were still arguing about a name, but something told her she'd get her way. Her baby girl would be named Faith, a name Sadie had loved since she was a little girl.

Sadie reached the cookie jar and took out a soft cookie, still warm, the melty chocolate dissolving on her tongue. She paired it with a glass of milk chock full of calcium, good for the baby. Sure, these were extra calories she didn't need, but she was already big as an apartment building. Might as well enjoy the cookie without guilt.

A pain wrapped around her back and went straight to her stomach, the cramp nearly doubling her over. Oh no. Really? She was being punished for this cookie? This couldn't be happening. No, she wasn't going into labor now because she couldn't be. But the sensation was too familiar. The tightening around her belly. After a few seconds it went away and sheepishly Sadie went to the couch and sat down. She swore to herself that she wouldn't get up again and regretted the hubris that made her think one cookie wouldn't hurt. It obviously *had*. When the second pain came seven minutes later, Sadie knew that was too soon. She was in labor. The pain was excruciating, too, coming in waves fast and too hard. The baby was coming.

Sadie could almost feel the head pressing down on her pelvis. No. Too fast. Stop it now!

She had to get to Lincoln, but she'd left the satellite phone upstairs where he'd put it. No way would she get up there now, so she went for the landline phone. Her mother wasn't home, and Lincoln was out in the fields. She called Eve but her voice mail went off, meaning she could be tending to an animal. She called Lucy, then Beau, but neither of them picked up.

"Doesn't anyone ever answer their phone anymore?"

A second later, Lucy called her back. "Did you just call me?"

"Yes!" Sadie gasped, her breaths coming in sharp and pained. "I need help."

"What's happening? Sadie? Are you okay?"

"I'm…in…labor…and I can't…get…" She groaned as the cramp took hold.

"I'll be right over."

Sadie clutched the handset phone. Help was coming. Maybe she wouldn't have to deliver this baby on her sofa.

Sadie was panting now, remembering the Bradley method. This was how cows gave birth naturally and without painkillers, the childbirth method said, and if it was good enough for a cow it was good enough for Sadie. For a while, she'd considered giving birth at home, but Lincoln nixed the idea. She hoped he wouldn't come home and find out she'd done it anyway.

Lucy burst through the front door a few minutes later. "Sadie!"

"Hello," she said. "Thank you for coming."

"Where's Lincoln?"

"He's somewhere in the field, taking care of a cow in labor."

"How ironic."

"Lucy…don't make jokes."

"I'll go find him for you."

"The satellite phone is upstairs, but we don't have time for that."

Lucy's face turned ashen. "Wh-what? Why don't have we have time?"

"I'm having this baby, like *now*."

"No! Sadie, you can't do that." She went to her knees beside Sadie. "Please don't. I can't handle this."

"Oh yes, you can. You're going to be an auntie soon." Sadie tried a smile, but it was probably more of a grimace. "The question is, do you want to deliver your niece, or do you want Trixie the midwife to do it?"

"Those are my choices? Of course, I want Trixie. She's a professional!"

"Then you have to drive me. *Now.*"

Sadie had to hand it to Lucy. She managed to half carry, half steer Sadie's hefty body to her sedan and plop her in the back.

She held up her palms. "Please, please don't have the baby in my car."

"I'll try," Sadie said. "It's not *my* first choice, you know?"

Before leaving, Lucy had phoned the clinic to alert Trixie that they had an emergency and were coming in. The groans of pain were scaring Lucy, so Sadie bit down on her lower lip to keep them inside.

"Don't worry, we should be there soon," Lucy said, turning on to the main road. "I don't want to get into an accident, or I'd drive faster."

"That's…okay…" Sadie panted. "Smart."

"Lincoln would kill me if I got us into an accident. Ha! Remember the time I borrowed my mother's car without permission? I knew how to drive. I just didn't have my license yet. It was Lincoln who pulled us out of the ditch."

"I remember."

"He didn't rat on us, but he sure read *me* the riot act."

"Well, you were driving."

"Yeah, but he was mostly angry that I almost got *you* hurt." Lucy laughed. "I knew then how much he loved you."

"Oh, that's a sweet memory."

Tears brushed against Sadie's lashes. There were so many memories. She didn't know about him, but she'd loved Lincoln from the time she was ten.

And he might miss the birth of his daughter.

Chapter 26

As Lucy drove to town, only one thought kept her from losing her mind. The unfairness of this generational situation. The biology.

"I really don't think it's fair only women have to do this part."

"Which part?"

"Childbirth! Nature should have planned this better. It should be something that a couple takes turns doing. Doesn't that sound fair? I mean, y'all take turns getting up in the middle of the night. Giving the kid a bath. Stuff like that."

Sadie made a strangled noise that sounded like a laugh. "Oh my lord. Stop trying to make me laugh. I think I peed."

"I'm not trying to make you laugh! And a little pee is what you're worried about?"

"I would rather not lose all my dignity. I'm barely hanging on here to about three percent of it."

"Don't worry about dignity! Who cares? You are strong and you are powerful and only you are capable of this. Do you think Lincoln could give birth? Of course not! That's the thing. Men aren't built to have babies, are they?"

"No uterus," Sadie said between moans. "Hard to do."

"I'll bet they couldn't do it even *with* a uterus. It's too much pain. They wouldn't have trouble handling birth control if *they* had to give birth, let me tell you." She snorted and slapped the steering wheel. "Oh no, then the prophylactic would be whipped out right on time, every time, you betcha!"

"Are we there yet?" Sadie said between pants.

"Just about. One more turn. Hang on."

Lucy turned on the street leading to the women's clinic, built only a few years ago with donations from the Ladies of SORROW and a grant from the famous Winona James.

Both Trixie and Dr. Grant stood outside the clinic waiting. Dr. Grant came right up to the rear passenger seat when Lucy pulled up and shut the car off.

"How's our patient?" he said.

"I'm a little early for my appointment."

"In more than one way," Dr. Grant laughed. "That's okay. We're ready for you."

Sadie replied with a spine-tingling groan.

"Oh boy," said Trixie. "Let get her inside, Judd."

Lucy helped and all three of them carried Sadie inside to one of the exam rooms.

"We've got it from here." Dr. Grant closed the curtain, leaving Lucy on the other side.

But she could still hear them, trying to calm Sadie down, then rustling that sounded like they were removing her clothing. From here, panic began its slow and silent attack. This wasn't good. Sadie was having her baby. Right now. And the high blood pressure? It must be breaking records at the moment.

"Maybe I should call for the heli." This was from Dr.

Grant. "They can get the baby to the NICU in Kerrville in five minutes."

"Not necessary. We have a good-sized baby here, even early. Trust me," Trixie said.

"Her blood pressure, Trix. It's too high."

"Somebody call my husband," Sadie moaned.

Lincoln! Lucy could do that. He would single-handedly reduce her blood pressure. Lucy didn't want to leave Sadie and drive back to the ranch to look for him, but she could start the phone tree. This time, the job would be simple: get a few good men to get Lincoln and bring him to the clinic. He was probably just now thinking about going back to the house to check on his wife. If she wasn't there he was going to have a cowboy-sized meltdown.

"Beulah? It's me, Lucy. Alert the men."

"Oh Lucy, dear! How are you? You *never* call."

"This is an *emergency*. I don't have a cow stuck in mud or a fence to repair but I need one or two men who are closer than I am to go get Lincoln at the ranch. He's out in the field and doesn't know I had to take Sadie to the clinic. She might be having the baby!"

"Consider it done."

Next, Lucy called Beau. Not just because it was his sister in trouble but because she, Lucy, needed comforting. The entire ordeal had shaken her to the core. Sadie and her moans and groans. She would never *unhear* that. Her friend was suffering, and Lucy couldn't help her. Why did women always have to carry the heaviest burdens?

Well, probably because they *could.*

It wasn't a big leap when her thoughts ran to her mother, a teenager, going through this ordeal, possibly all alone. Maybe she'd cried out for her mother. Or her father. How scared she must have been of the pain, her body contracting and pushing out a child she wasn't ready to have.

Beau didn't answer his phone, but Lucy texted him on the off chance he might be somewhere downtown with decent Wi-Fi.

Help!

Two seconds later, he texted back:

Sure. With what?

Good. He probably wasn't far if he'd replied. Somewhere with good reception, at least.

I had to take Sadie to the women's clinic. She's in labor!

There was no reply for several seconds, three dots appearing but giving her nothing. Lucy waited for him to say he was on his way. Nothing. She texted again:

Hurry. Please come. I need you. I'm really scared.

Why would he choose this moment to ignore her? If this was how it would be, with Beau failing to show up when she needed him…even to the point of ignoring her text message. It just didn't sound like him.

Then the door to the clinic flew open and Beau stormed inside.

"Lucy!" He held open his arms and she almost flew into them. "I was at the bank when I got your text. I came right over."

"She was alone and by the time I got to her she said it was too late for me to find Lincoln. Too late to wait for him. So, we called Dr. Grant and I drove her over. She's in so much pain. I hate this so much."

Lucy pressed her face to his chest, clinging to him.

"Don't worry, my sister is strong, and she'll get through this."

"Her blood pressure…it's too high again. I heard the

doctor." Lucy fisted Beau's shirt, clinging to him. "I don't know what that means but it's not good."

Beau just kept whispering in her hair and rubbing her back telling her that it was okay, and the doctor would take good care of Sadie. She didn't know how much time had passed when Lincoln nearly tore the door off its hinges getting inside.

"Where is she?"

Beau stood and moved in front of Lincoln. "Calm down. It's under control. She's with the doctor and I doubt there's anything you can do."

"Get out of my way or I swear I'll shove you into next week," Lincoln growled.

Beau didn't move and the two men squared off. They were both about the same size and Lucy didn't honestly know who would win this fight. She was about to get up and get between them, but the doctor peeked through the curtains.

"Come on back, Lincoln. You're about to be a father again."

"Oh, shit." Beau stepped aside and Lincoln moved like a cheetah toward the doctor.

A COUPLE OF HOURS LATER, the waiting room was filled.

Beau's mother arrived not long after Lincoln, without Sammy, whom she'd dropped off with Riggs and Winona, who had kids about the same age. Word spread quickly and Daisy, Lincoln's sister, arrived with Wade and their grandmother, Lillian, in tow. Eve and Jackson, Lincoln's brother, were seated nearby, Eve looking just as distraught as Lucy.

Lucy was in his arms, finally calm to the point where she snoozed softly, waking only every time someone new arrived. He supposed the emotional weight of the situation had taken most of her energy. As for him, he was wide awake and alert. They'd all heard the sweet sounds of a baby crying but it had been increasingly tense since that moment. A lot of activity was going on in the back, where they'd wheeled Sadie shortly after Lincoln arrived. But Lincoln hadn't come out to announce whether they'd had a boy or a girl, which seemed ominous. Beau's mother was about to break the door down if they didn't let her back soon.

"Mom, calm down." He tried to get her to meet his gaze. "She's *going* to be okay."

"I won't know that until I get back there and see for my own eyes." She stood and went back to pacing.

Sean and Bonnie Lee Henderson showed up with a basket of muffins from the General Store. Bonnie went around with the basket, being her honest-to-goodness self and not the badass head of the Irish Mafia she played on a streaming show.

"Hey, the last time there were this many people in the clinic waiting room Winona had been shot. She was pregnant at the time. With twins! Speaking of panicking, I think Riggs shaved a few years off his life that day. But hey, she was fine. I'm sure Sadie is going to be just fine, too," Sean said.

A gunshot versus high blood pressure. Way to show them things could always be worse. Beau couldn't accept that his sister was going to be anything but fine. His mind just wouldn't go there.

"You know what I was thinking?" Lucy whispered to him. Her head was on his shoulder, and she lifted to meet his eyes. "How much harder it must have been to do this all alone."

"You're thinking of Jacqueline."

"Yes. My mother said it's okay with her if I want to meet her. I wasn't sure, but now I do. I have so many questions."

"Lenny might have some answers for you." Beau couldn't help it, he felt sympathy for the man.

Lenny did a lot for this town, and he obviously loved Lucy. Something told Beau it was no surprise he'd become a clown so he would be invited to children's birthday parties, including Lucy's. He'd stayed on the sidelines of her life, watching her grow up without being able to tell her who he was. Because he'd made a promise to his daughter, which he chose to honor. It meant he'd had to let another man be her grandfather while he stayed just a friend.

"He might. But I'm still not talking to him. The only words I want to hear from him are Jacqueline's name and address."

"Yeah?" Beau tugged on a lock of her hair. "No forgiveness yet?"

"I'm not sure he deserves it. All these years, lying to my face. I had biological *family* in this town the entire time, and I didn't even know it. Maybe if I'd known I wouldn't have felt so…I don't know…different."

"We never knew you felt that way."

"With you and Sadie, I always felt like myself. But it's hard not to feel different when you're dubbed the 'miracle baby.' When I was younger I thought it was fun. And then I discovered I didn't have an actual birth certificate until my parents went and filed one with the little information they had. It was…weird."

"That makes sense."

He considered that Charlotte's birth certificate might have to be changed, too, and what would she think about that reissued certificate? No. He had to stop thinking like this.

"If I'd known I had one relative in town, maybe I'd have felt more connected. Do you think Lenny knows my real birthday? He must."

Every sound in the room came to a halt when Lincoln entered. It was as if all the oxygen had been sucked out of the room. Lucy sat up straighter, turning her entire body toward Lincoln. She gripped Beau's arm so tightly he could feel his heartbeat through his arm.

"It's a girl." Lincoln broke into a smile. "She tiny, but she's good."

There were cheers all around, him included. Beside him, Lucy stayed fairly quiet.

"But how is *Sadie*?" she spoke up.

Like a real friend would. Beau draped his arm around her waist.

"That's what I'd like to know!" Beau's mother pushed forward. "I want to see *my* girl!"

Lincoln held up his palms. "Look, nobody panic but an ambulance is coming soon for Sadie and the baby."

"What?" Lucy said. "Why?"

"Calm down," Lincoln said, sounding like Beau had a couple of hours ago. "Believe me, I had the same reaction. But I asked the doctor and it's just to check her out. They're worried about postpartum preeclampsia, and she needs medicine they don't have here."

"But she's okay?" Beau's mother said, wringing her hands.

"Yes, very happy, and can't wait to introduce y'all to Faith Stephens."

Everyone filed out, Beau's mother staying behind so she could ride with Lincoln when he followed the ambulance to Kerrville.

"Wow, what a day, right?" Beau walked Lucy to her car, parked directly in front of the clinic.

"You have no idea."

"Want to grab dinner later?"

"Sure," she said, winding her arms around his neck. "Thank you for being so patient with me. I kind of lost it there for a while. She's my best friend, and—"

"I thought I was your best friend."

She smirked. "You were, too. Now you're my…"

He made a face when she hesitated. "Your *boyfriend*. And don't forget it."

"I'm too old to call you my boyfriend."

"Fine, I'll go straight to fiancé. I'm tired of waiting for you anyway."

She blinked. "Beau…is that a proposal?"

"Don't worry, I'll do it better. Give me time. There will be flowers and fireworks. Maybe a choir."

"Let's not get crazy." Lucy laughed.

He grabbed her hand and brought it to his lips. "Yeah, *let's* get crazy. Let's do it up right. I'm ready for everything."

"Me too." She lowered her lashes. "But…"

"There's a but?"

"I hope you don't mind but I'm not too sure about children anymore, especially after what I witnessed today. That was…scary."

"So glad you said that. If having a baby means I might risk losing you, I'm not ready, either. When I saw Lincoln's face, and the fear in his eyes…well, let's say I'm in no rush."

"Okay, we're agreed. No children for now."

"Except for Charlotte…maybe."

"Right. Charlotte, because you already have a daughter."

Great job, idiot. He had a gift for bringing down a romantic moment, but he wanted to remind Lucy he now came with baggage. And a third party they'd have to co-parent with for *eighteen years*. It didn't make him her most attractive option in a town of which Lucy had many, that was for certain. He wouldn't blame her if she decided being with him was far too much trouble.

When Lucy's gaze pinned to just over his shoulder, Beau turned and saw Lenny, a bouquet of flowers in his hand.

"I…I just heard about the baby."

"I'll take those," Beau said. "Thanks, Lenny. I'm sure Sadie appreciates this."

"Is she okay?" he said.

"They took her to the hospital just to get checked out because she was a few weeks early. She had a girl," Beau said. "Faith."

"A girl! Congratulations to you and the family."

"Yeah, thanks." Beau looked at Lucy, possibly to elicit some response but got nothing.

Lucy stood like a statue next to him. She was acting like she'd never seen Lenny before. Like he was some odd creature she'd come up on in the wild. A snake with two heads. A wild boar. A tarantula.

"Lucy," Lenny said. "Can we talk?"

"No," she said, a word that came out easily enough, and then spoke to Beau. "See you later."

Then she let go of Beau's hand, hopped in the driver's side of her car, and took off. Beau and Lenny both watched her drive away.

"Do you think she's ever going to forgive me?" Lenny said, the sound of his voice a croak.

"Yeah, you know Lucy. She will. Just give her time, okay?" Beau clapped Lenny's back.

"I got time, I guess. But not much. In case anyone forgot, I'm old." Lenny shook his head slowly. "I really blew this. Big time."

"Something tells me you did what you had to do, and you meant well."

Yes, he should have told Lucy sooner. He shouldn't have kept something that huge from her for over thirty years, especially when he stayed in her life, but on the outskirts of it.

But Beau, of all people, was in no position to judge the man.

"She wants answers, and you have them for her. Such as her actual birthday."

Lenny canted his head. "Fourth of July."

"You mean that's her *actual* birthday? How did you…I mean, I'm sure you…but…"

"I'm nothing if not resourceful. I was the one who suggested we celebrate it on that day, the birth of our nation and all. Thankfully she wasn't born on an obscure day."

Beau shook his head. "Yeah. You certainly are one of a kind, Len."

"Here." Lenny handed Beau a piece of paper. "That's Jacqueline's phone and address. I've already told her what happened. She wants to see Lucy."

"Seriously?" Beau unfurled the paper with an address in San Antonio.

"She's always wanted to. You need to tell Lucy that. She stayed away so she wouldn't cause issues. Jacqueline wants to talk to her, to explain."

Beau could imagine, too, there was a fear of judgement from others for what she'd done.

"Of course."

"That's what I wanted to talk to her about. Maybe you could tell her instead."

"Sure."

Beau's chest tightened in sympathy for the old man. For a moment, he saw himself in Lenny. Lenny, too, loved women, given his many marriages and children. Lenny also tried to do the best he could not to disappoint those he loved.

But, as Beau had begun to suspect, that wasn't possible if you were human.

Chapter 27

A week later, Sadie came home from the hospital with Faith.

The doctor pronounced her healthy, the eclampsia never materializing, thanks to early intervention. Her blood pressure had lowered to normal levels and Faith, while tiny, had rallied even if four weeks premature. After the first day, she'd even started nursing like a champ. But once more, between Lincoln and her mother, Sadie wasn't allowed to do anything but lay in bed and nurse Faith. At least now she could see her feet. Every now and then, she wiggled her toes just because.

Unfortunately, both her mother and Lincoln still felt eternally guilty that they hadn't been around when she went into labor. Now, her mother entertained Sammy at home with puzzles and games instead of taking him to the park to decompress. Lincoln came in from the field every chance he had and was relying more on Jackson, their father, and other ranch hands.

Lucy was sent gift cards and flowers in thanks for

simply answering her phone, let alone getting Sadie to the clinic.

"Don't you worry about a thing," her mother now said at the door just before she closed it. "I won't be far."

"Hey, sweetheart."

Lincoln entered seconds behind her mother. He now regularly came upstairs and ate his lunch with Sadie and Faith.

"Hi," Sadie said. "Mother and baby are doing fine."

"More than fine." Lincoln bent to press a kiss on her temple.

He checked in on Faith's bassinet next to their bed. "What a cutie."

"She's your daughter, what did you expect?"

"Do you want some of this?" He grinned and offered half of his sandwich.

"Mom just fed me lunch." Sadie crossed her arms. "Linc, we need to talk."

"Uh-oh. What did I do now?" He plopped down on the bed next to her. "Leave the seat up again?"

"Nothing, cowboy. You are perfect and I love you."

"Is there a *but* coming?"

"Yes. I'm sorry if this sounds ungrateful, *but*…the thing is, I want my life back." She set her hand on Lincoln's thigh.

Lincoln quirked a brow. "Your life?"

"You know, where I fix breakfast, lunch, and dinner and take care of my children and my husband all by myself. Like a boss."

"You want *me* to tell your mother to go home?" The look on his face was priceless.

"No, I'll do that."

"Well, she's not going to like it."

Sadie was sympathetic. As a mother now, she understood how difficult the ordeal must have been for her. She'd been at the park with Sammy when Lenny found her and drove her in his golf cart to the Henderson ranch to drop Sammy off. Lincoln and everyone else told her how scared she'd been. How she and Lillian Carver held hands and prayed.

"She has her own life and business and it's been on hold for a couple of weeks now. Of course, she won't say anything. But being a full-time grandma/nanny is not her thing. We're really taking advantage of her."

"I guess you're right."

"And while I appreciate your visits, I want you to rest easy. I'm going to be fine."

"I know that."

"No, you don't. You keep looking at me like I'm going to break, and you want to be there to pick me up off the floor."

"You better believe I'm going to be there. I'm not going to miss another minute."

"Yes, but…just don't forget, you were there in time to watch Faith be born. The hard part is over. I want you to relax."

He set down his sandwich. "*Relax?* This isn't the time to relax! I have two children, Sadie, and I have a wife who I'd die without. For the longest few minutes of my life, I thought I might lose you. And if I lose you I may as well not exist."

"Oh, Linc." Sadie lowered her head to his chest, listening to his strong heart. "I love you and I'm not going anywhere."

"You better not. Because I can't live without you." His arms came around her, squeezing her tightly.

"I can't live without you, either. So, I don't want you to stress. You have a partner in me. It's time for me to pick up where I left off and help run this ranch." She raised her head to meet his gaze.

"Already?"

"Yes! I don't expect to be doing cartwheels but I'm not going to stay in bed anymore. I feel fully recovered. And after this, I'm going downstairs and having this talk with my mother."

"But—"

She put a finger to his mouth. "I know the last time I got up I went into labor but that won't happen again. See? She's right over there."

"Ha, funny girl. You might not go into labor but what about something *else* going wrong? You just had a baby."

"I'm young, and I'll be careful. Plus, I had plenty of rest. Almost too much. I went stir-crazy and ordered roses for my brother to give to Lucy. I had Lenny pretend Lucy had termites."

"Yeah, I'll be glad for all that mess to calm down."

"No more matchmaking." She crawled into his lap and threaded her fingers through his thick hair.

"What are you doing?" He gave her a slow smile.

"I'm getting ready to kiss my husband."

Lincoln's arms wrapped even tighter around her, and he deepened the kiss until they broke apart in a mutual gasp.

"I missed you," he said, pulling her closer, pressing his forehead to hers.

"It's been too long."

"I'm counting the weeks."

"Me too. Want to make out while the baby is sleeping?"

"God yes."

So, Sadie made out with her husband, and afterward walked downstairs to send her mother home.

. . .

TWO WEEKS LATER, Lucy drove to San Antonio to meet her mother.

When Beau had given her the address and phone number he'd obtained from Lenny, he'd asked her once more to please forgive Lenny.

He was only trying to help.

She heard the refrain frequently, from Beau, her mother, father, and even Sadie. They'd all quickly forgiven Lenny for his "miracle baby on the church steps" story and word spread through town. She wasn't so much a miracle as she was the granddaughter of a resourceful man.

And here's the thing: Lucy understood what he'd done on an intellectual level. Emotionally, different story. Lies were toxic. They hurt people when telling the truth would be simpler. All these years, her grandfather had been in her life but not fully *in* it. He'd stayed to the sidelines and hadn't helped raise her or contribute financially. Her parents had never been flush with cash and at any turn could have used help. Not that they would have accepted it and, granted, in a small town like Stone Ridge where everyone took care of their own, basic needs were always met. Lucy had never gone without essentials, and looking back Lenny was always in her life, at birthday parties and graduations, always particularly proud of her. She hadn't ever quite noticed it other than the fact she'd already been singled out by the entire town as the "miracle baby" so it didn't seem unusual. They all had a false sense of pride in her. In the end, Lucy was simply the daughter of a teenage runaway. So plain and ordinary. In a way, it was a relief.

And she was luckier than most to discover her origin story.

She pulled her car into the parking lot of the coffee

shop where they'd decided to have their first meeting, her stomach in tight knots. This was the moment she always thought she wanted, but now that it was about to happen, Lucy thought of turning back and aborting the mission.

Last night in bed, she and Beau discussed how she'd handle this moment.

He'd helped her plan and wanted to drive. Lucy had almost let him. She needed the support and he'd been her rock through all this. But in the end, she wanted to do this alone. If the reunion turned contentious, Beau wouldn't have to feel protective and intervene. It was time for Lucy to have a private moment with a woman she hadn't seen since the first months of her life.

Because she hadn't talked to Lenny, Lucy didn't actually know what she'd be walking into. The little she'd talked to Jacqueline over the phone, she sounded normal and encouraging about meeting. So, Lucy had no idea if Jacqueline had an entirely new family with children and a husband who might be feeling equally protective over her.

A woman waved to her from a table when Lucy walked inside, someone she would not have recognized if she had to pick her out of a crowd. She looked nothing like the young woman in the photo with Lenny years ago. Of course, she would be older now, about forty-eight. Esperanza was actually fifty-five and still looked younger than this woman.

The rich smells of coffee and pastry hung in the air as Lucy approached, palms sweaty and heart pounding.

"Lucy." Jacqueline had long, dark hair streaked with gray, wore little makeup, and her smoky voice was a bit of a surprise.

"Hello. Nice to meet you."

With no awareness of protocol, Lucy didn't know what to call the woman. *Mom* didn't feel appropriate. She wasn't her mother, the woman who'd stayed up late when Lucy had a fever or sewed a third Halloween costume when she'd changed her mind about two others. Yes, she'd carried her and given birth to her, and Lucy had a particular recent awareness of how difficult that must have been. But unfortunately, it wasn't everything. It was just the beginning.

"I was so glad when Daddy called to tell me he told you the truth. It was time."

"Maybe it was *past* time. I wish I'd known I had a blood relative in town. Someone to ask about health conditions and such."

"Please don't blame him. He would have done anything for me. I asked him not to say anything."

"But you were *sixteen*. Maybe you shouldn't have been allowed to make the decision."

Lucy considered how many times her conservative parents had vetoed her decisions because, according to them, she hadn't the maturity to make them. That's how Lucy never wound up with a nose piercing that might have made her look a bit like the cattle raised in Stone Ridge.

"Good point. But you know my father. He just wanted to help. Things were tough at home, and this was what I wanted. I thought one day you'd put it together and we could tell you the truth."

"I didn't put it together at all. I moved on and lived my life. If it wasn't for my…for Beau, I might have never known about you."

"The truth is, I wasn't quite ready to meet you until a couple of years ago. I had a lot of work to do on myself. But it's hard to believe you didn't figure it out. I guess Daddy can keep a secret."

"He can. I'm sure you've heard the story."

"Genius. He made you special. A miracle baby."

The waitress came to their table and poured coffee into their mugs.

Lucy cleared her throat, fisting her hands under the table. "I don't know anything about you."

"I wish I had great things to say about myself, but I've been in recovery for the past five years. It's been a long road."

Recovery. Okay, so her mother was an addict. No wonder she hadn't aged well. It was a shock but not an unexpected one. But she was prepared with questions.

At dinner and during rides together in late afternoons on True, she and Beau had discussed every possibility, so she'd be prepared.

What if she's been married five times?

What if she's never been married?

What if she's been married for twenty-five years to her college sweetheart and has five other kids who know nothing about you?

That one, honestly, bothered Lucy. The thought she'd raised children after Lucy, but never thought to contact her firstborn child would have been disheartening.

"You know, you could always talk to Lenny first," Beau had said.

Lucy ignored that. She still wasn't speaking to her grandfather.

"You have to be okay with all of it, sweetheart."

Now, there was silence from Lucy, so Jacqueline took the lead and kept talking.

"My father didn't raise me since my parents divorced fairly young. I didn't get to see him much over the years. In the city, I got into drugs, drinking. I was arrested. After I gave birth to you, I went off the rails for a while."

"Oh. I'm...sorry."

Lucy definitely hated to hear that. It sounded as

though Jacqueline held her responsible, partly, for spiraling. And maybe she was.

"First things first. Your birthday. It's really the Fourth of July."

That made sense, since Lenny would have known her actual birthday.

She understood he was sorry, but this was a difficult thing to forgive. Her lack of forgiveness would have been further extended to her mother, but having been a teenager, she got a pass. Lucy had made bad decisions as a teenager, too, so she understood.

"Daddy wanted to keep you but…well, I'm sure you heard the story. The next best thing, in his opinion, was for you to grow up nearby so he could keep an eye on you. So, he arranged for that to happen. He had connections, some even at the sheriff's department. In the beginning, I admit, I was happy he took over. Handled my 'problem.'" She made air quotes. "But I missed you almost immediately. Maybe that's why I went wild, not that it's an excuse. Had I had my act together enough, I might have tried to get you back. I know Lenny would have helped me, too."

Just the idea made Lucy's hackles come up. What a disaster that would have been.

"Just so you know, I had good parents. I was an only child and they doted on me."

"I'm sure you're wondering…no, I never had any more children. Never married. I've had trouble keeping relationships. Always picked the wrong men." She studied a fingernail, bitten to the quick. "I know you probably wanted a better story, but this is all I have. I'm being honest. It's essential to my recovery."

"And that's…that's going okay? Your recovery?"

"Daddy checks in with me often. He had his own struggles…well, that's not for me to say. I suppose addiction can be hereditary, but it seems to have skipped you." She tried a smile.

"Does my biological grandmother, Noelle Lee, know?"

"Of course, yes, but she's turned into a bitter woman since time proved physical beauty isn't lasting. You look like her when she was young, but much prettier. She wanted to leave you in the past and I guess I'd made her life difficult enough by being the kind of daughter I was. I'm sorry."

"Maybe it's an obvious question, but what about my father?"

For the first time Jacqueline frowned. "He was never involved."

"You've lost touch with him."

"Yes, if you want to put it that way. I can't encourage you to look him up. He was…older than me and took advantage of the situation."

The very idea that Lucy's blood coursed with someone who sounded less than honorable made her stomach turn. This was, at least, one possibility she and Beau hadn't even considered. They should have.

"Don't go down that road, Lucy." She reached across the table and patted Lucy's hand. "Please don't forget my father is also your blood. Your biology. He may have made a mistake, but it was with the best of intentions. He'd never hurt me, you, or anyone else. He's a good and honorable man."

"I'd still like my father's name, in case…well…if I ever need medical information."

"If you ever need a donor, you wouldn't do well to ask *him*." Jacqueline took a breath. "But yes if that's what you want. I'll get you his information. On our side of the family, besides my addiction, there's only been the typical stuff like high blood pressure and cholesterol, but mostly we're healthy. Just take care of yourself and you should be fine."

The platitude made Lucy's skin prickle. So far, this wasn't going well. Jacqueline was perfectly nice, however, even if she wasn't Lucy's idea of a mother. It made her homesick. For *her* mother. For Beau. For Stone Ridge and all the residents who had basically been her very large, highly intrusive, extended family.

She'd never been more grateful for each and every one of them.

"I guess my last question is, who named me Lucy? Was that you?"

It was, she'd always believed, the only part of her past that came with her.

Jacqueline smiled as if this brought up a pleasant memory. "Daddy wanted to name you that, based after that song? 'Lucy in the Sky with Diamonds.' He thought your amber eyes shined like diamonds in the sky."

For the first time, Lucy had to bite back a laugh. Leave it to Lenny to accidentally name her after a song the Beatles wrote about LSD.

At least, she was fairly sure it was an accident.

Lucy smiled and exchanged a look with Jacqueline. A moment in which it seemed they both thought of the hapless but good-natured man who was their common ground.

Once upon a time, Lucy thought she'd been left on the church steps, and no one had ever cared enough to come back for her.

The truth was, as always, far more complicated.

But one thing was certain.

There was one person who'd never left her.

Chapter 28

After an exhausting afternoon filled with framing Colton and Jennifer's house, Beau headed home. He had what might seem like ambitious plans for tonight, at least for the likes of him. Given his last attempt at romance, he would have to call this idea a reach. Grandiose. No rose petals this time, but he was *cooking dinner* for Lucy. He could cook the hell out of a steak, but Lucy wasn't fond of meat, an irony that never failed to make him smile. He had a freezer stock full of rock fish he caught during the year, scaled, and stored, but he only knew how to grill those, too. The other night, when temps dipped into the forties, warm-blooded Texan that he was, Beau declared it too cold to grill.

His plans had required a call to Sadie.

"Linc's right here," she said. "Let me get him for you."

"I want to talk to *you*," he said. "I'm cooking Lucy a romantic dinner and I need an easy recipe. Something I can handle."

"Oh, dear."

Beau rolled his eyes. "Seriously, you got anything for me?"

"It's too cold to grill."

"Yeah, I know! So now you see my dilemma."

After much hesitating, Sadie declared Beau "worthy" of her Taco Salad recipe. "It's her favorite."

"Is that romantic enough?"

"Lucy loves it."

Women were easy to please sometimes, at least when it came to a meal. A salad. Simple.

Now, Beau picked up his mail and headed inside, already thinking about dinner. Dessert was the apple pie he'd picked up at the General Store. He had white wine, too, Lucy's favorite.

All he had to do was put the chicken breasts in a pan and while they fried, chop lettuce, tomatoes, boil corn cobs, and slice the kernels off. He had the salsa he'd mix with ranch dressing to give it a kick. It all sounded too easy, so he'd probably screw it up in an original way.

On the counter, the corner of an envelope stuck out and Beau recognized it as being from the place where he'd taken the DNA test a couple of weeks ago. Pulling it out, he sliced it open and held his breath before reading it. If not for Lucy, he would have thought of this moment every hour of every day. As it was, he only thought of it once a day, interspersed with thoughts of how he'd ever get Lucy to forgive Lenny. He blamed himself, of course, even if Lenny wasn't one to hold a grudge. If not for Beau, and the way he'd pressed for the truth, his relationship to Lucy would still be one big secret.

But secrets could be toxic.

Beau unfolded the page and read the results:

The alleged father is excluded as the biological father of the tested child. This conclusion is based on alleles…

Beau read it three times to be sure he hadn't made a mistake. But no, he had read it right the first time.

He was *not* Charlotte's father.

Not. Her. Father.

It took minutes for the news to sink in. Whole minutes in which he stared at the piece of paper in his hands like it might bite him. Beau walked to the couch and fell rather than sat. He ran a hand down his face. Damn it all. At one time, this was *exactly* what he'd wanted. What he'd hoped for because he didn't want the responsibility of a child. He wasn't ready and he didn't want to share a baby with a woman he simply tolerated.

But that was before he'd spent time with the little girl. Before his *entire family* had been introduced and based on a passing resemblance to him and Sadie, assumed she had to be his. They'd all become attached to her. Not just him. The anger that pulsed through him made him want to hit something. Instead, he crumpled the paper in his hands until it was practically dust.

His mother would be so disappointed. So would Sadie. But Lucy…well, maybe not so much.

The phone rang and caller ID showed Rachel's name.

"I do not want to talk to you right now," Beau said when he picked up. "It's better for us both that I don't say anything, believe me."

"Listen, I'm so sorry," Rachel said. "It was a simple mistake. But it *could have* been you. If it helps, I wish it were you."

"It doesn't help." Beau hung up.

He was such an idiot. Should have listened to Lucy in the first place and called the police. He wouldn't have been putting his own daughter in the foster system but might have taught Rachel a lesson. *Don't go dropping your baby off where she doesn't belong.* Not everyone was as kindhearted, or *foolish,* as Beau. Now he would have to explain to his entire family that he was a complete idiot. He'd made it too easy for Rachel, ready and willing to be a father to Charlotte, like a total chump who fell for the ruse. Maybe Rachel had never really believed Charlotte could be his. She'd simply used him. The possibility rang true.

Forgetting dinner, Beau went for a ride on True to decompress. That took an hour and when he still wasn't calm enough, he grabbed the keys to his truck and took off for the Shady Grind.

It was Saturday night, and the place was slammed as usual. He'd forgotten there was a mini concert here tonight, too, headlining Jackson Carver and Winona James, who didn't often grace a stage these days. No wonder it was packed. Someone at the door told him there was a Nashville film crew who would film and broadcast on a streaming show later.

Beau eventually muscled his way to an empty stool at the bar and settled in. "I'll have a beer."

Levi served him the usual. "What's up? You look like you just lost your best friend."

Not a best friend. A daughter.

"I'm fine," Beau said, vaguely aware he sounded anything *but* fine.

"I haven't talked to Lucy in a while," Levi said. "Is she still, you know, pissed with Lenny?"

"You could *say* that," Beau said, now acutely aware of how lies destroyed relationships. "I mean, he's her grandfather and she never knew."

He couldn't believe he hadn't been more sympathetic to Lucy and the lies she'd lived with for decades.

"Sure, but I mean, it's good ol' *Lenny.* He meant well."

"Yeah but sometimes that isn't enough."

Jolette Marie, whose back had been to him, turned and Beau noticed her seated next to him for the first time.

"Congratulations," Beau said. "On your engagement."

"Thank you." She flashed the ring finger on her left hand and reached for Levi's hand across the bar. "I guess we'll be planning a big wedding. Of course, you're invited."

"I'll be there."

Knowing John Truehart, the marriage of his only daughter would be a big deal in Stone Ridge. If Jolette Marie managed not to run away from this one. But odds were, since the man was young and handsome like Levi, he stood a good chance. More than fifty-fifty. Beau would call it more like eighty-twenty or better. Unfortunately, numbers made him think of the ones he'd just read: 99.99999 or some long-ass number that screamed: no, you are *not* the father!

"And what's new with you? Where's Lucy?" Jolette Marie said.

"She went to meet her biological mother over in San Antonio."

"Oh." Her mouth formed a perfect circle. "That whole thing…it's amazing, isn't it? Lenny. Wow."

"Yeah. He should have really said something sooner."

At the moment, Beau wanted to find him, and ask him what he could have been thinking lying to Lucy for over thirty years. It was unconscionable. At least Beau hadn't been through over thirty years of thinking Charlotte was his only to find out the truth.

"What about your daughter?" Jolette Marie asked.

When Beau didn't answer, he saw her exchange a look with Levi. It was the kind of "save me" glance you gave someone when you stepped in a pile of crap and wanted them to help pull you out before the stink permeated every inch of you.

"He's still waiting for the test results. That DNA stuff

takes a while." Levi cracked open a beer and slid it in front of another customer. "Right?"

It wasn't unusual for everybody in town to know his business, but this time the idea burned. Nothing like being made a fool out of in front of the entire town. He supposed the entire county would be worse, but it was little comfort.

"Already got the results. Just today. Turns out I dodged a bullet. That's why I'm here celebrating." Beau raised his bottle. "I'm not that baby's daddy. Let's drink to that."

"Congratulations, I guess." Jolette Marie said. "I'm happy if you're happy."

Levi, smart man, had made his way down the other end of the bar to take care of some customers. Whatever his thoughts were, he'd keep them to himself.

"What's not to be happy about?" Beau grunted.

"Now you and Lucy can have a baby when you're ready," Jo said, taking a pull from her beer. "You don't have to co-parent with someone who will make life hard for you."

He nodded. It was all true. Beau *should* be happy, and he didn't understand why his heart ached.

SOME THINGS in life couldn't be tied up in a neat little ribbon. The end. This was one of those. A twist and turn to another road that had no end. Lucy headed straight to Lenny's house because despite the fact he'd lied to her for years, he hadn't done anything to disrupt her life. He'd improved it and given her a chance at a stable family. She'd been raised by two fully functioning adults who desperately wanted her. He'd never left Lucy, even if he couldn't raise her himself. Instead, he'd stuck around and had a part in her life. It could be said he'd been on the outskirts, not caring enough to breach her inner world.

It could also be said that he cheated himself by remaining on the outside, making sure nothing went wrong.

It was time to forgive.

She knocked on the door of Lenny's ramshackle farmhouse outside of town. The golf cart was gone so he'd probably gone to a rideshare, or one of his many other jobs. It was a gift, actually, to be good at many things. She was grateful for the same ability.

Lenny had affected so many lives. She pictured Lenny's funeral would have a long line of people she'd never heard of come from out of town to pay him his respects. He really didn't know how to say "no" to anyone.

One of Lucy's new relatives answered the door. Paula, apparently her aunt now, who lived with Lenny since his second wife passed away and helped around the house. She had three sons, if Lucy recalled. Her cousins. They had children. Her second cousins? This was something they'd all have to deal with later. She had nieces and nephews and cousins outside of town she'd probably never get a chance to meet. But all this would come at another time. Right now, she had to talk to her grandfather.

"Hey, Lucy. He's not here," Paula said.

Lucy wasn't asked inside, but that didn't come as a surprise. Lenny was the outgoing one in his family and everyone else managed to keep to themselves. The last time she'd been inside, about a year ago, the house wouldn't have been out of place on the show *Hoarders*. Lenny kept *everything*. Old decanters, stacks of old newspapers from the times he was a reporter, nuts, bolts and screws, a collection of lighters and every tool known to man. He could fix anything.

Just as she was leaving, the golf cart pulled up and parked near a grove of trees. Lenny got out, dressed in his termite-killer coveralls. Not seeing Lucy, he began to unload his equipment.

"Hey, Lenny," she said, coming up behind him.

He jumped, yowled, and clutched his chest. "Holy son of a macaroni, girl! Don't come up on me like that. You're liable to put me in the ground."

She bit on her lower lip to keep from laughing. "I didn't mean to scare you."

For a moment, they simply stared at each other. The hanging leaves from the branches above them curtained them with the sensation of privacy. Secrecy. It reminded her that some secrets, however misguided, served a purpose. To protect. To shield.

He set down the canister he'd been holding. "Did you see my Jacqueline today?"

Lucy nodded. "It was a good visit. I'm glad I went because I feel like I understand so much better now."

"You do?"

"I know you were trying to fix something. As you always do."

"But it's not true what they say about me. I can't actually fix *everything*. People…people are hard."

"Yes, that's true. They have to want to change first."

A moment passed and Lucy felt Lenny's pain through every wrinkle on his worn face. He'd had a daughter he'd tried to save from herself and her poor choices. He may not have been able to save his daughter, but he'd certainly saved his granddaughter.

"Exactly. Now you understand. I love my daughter, but…she didn't deserve you. Now, Esperanza did. She loved you like you were her own from day one. I don't care what biology says. It's just a clump of cells. Love can grow anywhere it's given room."

Those were wise words coming from her grandfather. She'd take them.

"I'm sorry, Lenny. Or, I mean, should I call you… grandpa?" Lucy winced. It felt unnatural. But she had one grandfather left, her mother's father. She called him "Abuelito," so it seemed there was room for a "Grandpa."

Lenny waved a hand dismissively. "I'm too young at heart for you to call me Grandpa. Call me Papa. That's what all the other grands call me."

"Okay, Papa. Hey, did you know that 'Lucy in the Sky with Diamonds' is a song the Beatles wrote about an LSD trip?"

He blinked. "What? No. It's about a beautiful woman with eyes who sparkle like diamonds."

Lucy laughed. Good to know it was an accident.

"Google it when you get a chance."

"I sure will, missy. And I'll prove you wrong. The Beatles were my favorite band. Those blokes knew how to croon."

"You're one of a kind, Lenny." Lucy reached for him, hugging him tight. His bony frame seemed particularly frail today. "I forgive you for everything."

Good people didn't live forever, and neither would Lenny. It was a reminder to forgive and move forward while she still could.

"Thank you for that, sugar." He patted her back.

Lucy stepped back. "And now I have to go find Beau and tell him everything that's happened. He wanted to go with me, but I wouldn't let him."

"I saw his truck over at the Shady Grind when I drove by on my way home."

Interesting. He was supposed to be cooking her a

romantic dinner. She'd laughed about it this morning as he set off for a job, promising her a night of good food and romance.

"You can't do anything but grill." She'd tousled his golden hair and kissed him.

"I'll figure it out. Dinner tonight at my place. Romance."

So, what on earth was he doing at the bar? A few pointers from the chef? It wouldn't surprise her.

A few minutes later, Lucy arrived at the Shady Grind. She almost couldn't find a parking space it was so packed. Jackson and Winona were performing one of their concerts tonight and that usually brought out about every resident in town. And yes, Beau's truck was parked in one of the front row parking spaces, indicating he'd been here for a while. It seemed odd to find him here, but on the other hand, a night of romance could be found anywhere and didn't have to include dinner or red roses. For her, she only needed the man she'd loved for years. And she particularly needed him tonight because she wanted to celebrate the reconciliation between old and new. Just like the two of them. They'd had a friendship that caught fire and changed them the way fire changes wood and welds metal into another shape. They'd been made into something new.

She'd loved him for so long that she had no doubt she would until her dying breath. It was the reason she'd understood and accepted that Charlotte would have to be *her* daughter, too. She'd have to raise the child of another woman and that was fine. If it was good enough for her mother, who'd loved Lucy without reservation, it was good enough for her. There were grooves and spaces inside hearts and enough room to love someone without holding back.

Inside, music blared as Jackson riffed on a guitar solo. The makeshift stage was crowded with onlookers and a few people waved at Lucy and nodded. Her head swiveled as she searched for Beau in the crowd. The song ended, and everyone clapped.

"This next song is Winona's single, the first one in about *five* years, am I right?" Jackson said.

"I've been a little busy as you know." Winona smiled and finger waved to the audience.

Jackson lightly strummed his guitar. "You call three kids in three years busy? Ah, c'mon. Keep up. Yesterday I tagged cattle *and* wrote a new song."

Everyone laughed.

Winona winked at the crowd, always the consummate pro. "Here's the best way to have three kids in three years. Throw in a set of twins, then have a daughter just because. Listen, buddy, I might not pull cows out of ditches, or tag cattle, but I wrote this song sometime between pouring juice and cutting sandwiches into triangles. It just flowed out of me like love does. I call this 'You Gave my Heart Wings.' Thank you, Riggs, for giving me my dream and mostly for loving me."

The crowd turned slightly as everyone acknowledged the built cowboy in their midst, Riggs. Someone patted him on the back and when he turned, Lucy saw it was Beau. As the song began—a beautiful ballad about a woman who found love just when she'd given up looking—Lucy made her way through the crowd, elbows jutting her in the stomach. She didn't care. At some point, Beau finally noticed her, and he moved toward her. It seemed easier for him to move through, as people gave him a wide berth and he sliced through the group like a sharp knife. He was far more noticeable, he of the golden hair and easy smile. Standing out from the crowd, he was her star. Her compass.

When she reached him, she melted into him, going on tiptoes to wind her arms around his neck. His arms immediately went around her waist, tugging her close. They were hip to hip in this crowd, but his smile was strained, eyes holding a world of hurt. She understood something was very wrong.

"I have so much to tell you." She tugged him down to her and whispered in his ear to be heard over the music. "But is something wrong?"

"Not anymore." He bent low to kiss her lips. "We'll talk later. I just needed you, that's all."

"You have me."

It wasn't until the song ended that Lucy realized they were still standing in the middle, simply staring at each other and a circle had been formed around them. People were smiling, pointing, talking. Someone sounding suspiciously like Jeremy may have charmingly said, "Get a room."

"Um…maybe we should go?" Lucy said.

Beau gazed at her from under hooded lids and raised her hand to his lips to kiss it.

"We should."

Then he picked her up and carried her out the bar to cheers from the crowd.

Epilogue

Fourth of July
Six months later

"Happy birthday, baby."

Barely awake, Lucy had staggered into the kitchen for a cup of coffee. Beau, as usual, was already up and about since before the sunrise. He looked as he always did, a little like the sun. While she wasn't feeling particularly glamorous at the moment, Beau pulled her into his arms and planted a kiss on her lips. He then opened the oven door and drew out a single cupcake with a candle in it. Naturally, it was a white cupcake with red, white, and blue piping. The candle had the appearance of a mini firecracker. He lit it and sang happy birthday to her in his deep bass, wonderfully off-key voice.

She laughed and blew out the candle. "If people are coming over later, I really need to get ready."

"No hurry. Aren't you going to take a bite?" He pointed to the cupcake.

"Not for breakfast." She made a face.

Lately, she'd been feeling out of sorts, her stomach churning at odd times. She hated to be sick on her birthday. Today she felt even worse, but she didn't want to tell Beau and ruin the grilling party today. Their families and friends were coming over and then later they'd drive to the lake to watch the fireworks.

Six months ago, she thought she'd be in Seattle meeting new men and starting a whole new life. The same boxes she'd already packed made their way to Beau's house two months ago, when he'd finally talked her into moving in with him. She loved falling asleep next to him every night. Neither one of them had ever lived with someone before this, so they were in brand new territory. Her mother wasn't crazy about the arrangement, thinking Lucy should only move in with Beau were a ring involved. But Lucy wasn't old-fashioned, and she wasn't exactly in a hurry, either. Six months ago, they'd both been through such life-altering changes.

The day of Jackson and Winona's concert, she'd later found out the terrible news that Charlotte wasn't actually Beau's daughter. For weeks, she'd seethed with anger at the woman who, in Lucy's mind, had taken advantage of a good man for a few days of "me" time. To someone else, it might have been a relief but not to Beau Stephens. He'd become attached to the little girl, not to mention how his entire family greeted her with open arms. Sadie cried when she heard the news, and so had his mother, Wanda.

But Lucy wasn't a crier. Never had been. She flew right into "planning the woman's demise" mode. All Lucy could say was she had better not run into Rachel anytime soon. It would take years to forgive this slight because it hadn't been against her. Rachel had hurt the man Lucy loved and she wasn't the forgiving type when it came to her man.

He tipped his hat. "I'm going to go out and check on the animals but don't eat that cupcake without me."

Lucy wasn't even sure she could stomach it at all today. She'd be lucky not to pitch her lunch. She showered, then dried off, and pulled the box from under the sink where she'd hidden it yesterday among all her hair products where Beau would never look. Better safe than sorry. It was an early home pregnancy test, which she was sure would be negative. The only reason Lucy was even taking the test was because of something that happened last month.

In a wild moment, all barriers were down, and she and Beau forgot about protection. They. Just. Forgot. But hey, it was only *once*. They were very good about that sort of thing for the most part, but that day he'd walked in after riding his horse looking like Rip from *Yellowstone* and Lucy attacked him.

It didn't mean she was pregnant because she wasn't the most regular woman anyway. And last week, she'd given a ride to Beulah, who came down with the flu the following day. It was just making its way through town, that was all. She was only the first to fall. Next week, she'd probably be nursing Beau through the flu, who would behave as though he were dying.

After the requisite minutes were up, Lucy checked the results. They were positive. She was pregnant. *Pregnant.* It was true what everyone said, it only took one time. The same thing had happened to Sadie. But Lincoln had already asked her to marry him. The planning was just out of order. This must be a Stephens family curse.

And if Lucy's mother didn't like the "shacking up together" look, she was going to *hate* the pregnant before marriage version. But damn it all, Lucy was thirty-three today and maybe it was about time she had a baby. Sure. Beau would be fine with this, too. He'd already been through this scare once before. Even if, okay, they weren't married, and this could rush things along. Lucy didn't want to rush things along and she did not want to get married because she was pregnant. Of course, she loved Beau, and he loved her. They were forever but just didn't quite feel ready for the marriage certificate. Well, she didn't. Probably. Beau would of course suggest they get married, at which point Lucy would always wonder if it was because of their baby. Their *baby.* They were having a baby. She looked at herself in the mirror.

"Ready or not, you're going to be someone's *mother.*"

Then something very unusual happened: she burst into tears. .

BEAU COULDN'T REMEMBER EVER BEING this worried. Lucy didn't seem to be having much fun today. She claimed her stomach was upset but then he'd catch her staring off into space. It was her birthday and nearly everyone was here at their home to celebrate. Spilling out into the patio, the kids kicking a ball outside. And still she hadn't touched the cupcake.

Beau had to keep his eye on it, seeing as he wouldn't want anyone else to eat it. That could be dangerous. Nestled among the blue frosting in a little protected plastic cove was the ring. A few weeks ago, he'd gone to Kerrville and sought out the best conflict-free diamond ring he could afford. It was a carat in the shape of a diamond, perfect for Lucy. When she'd told him Lenny named her after the Beatles song, he hadn't stopped laughing for a whole minute. Leave it to Lenny.

He'd wanted to marry her since the night she took him

home after Winona and Jackson's concert. After he'd told her everything, it was Lucy who made it all better. Lucy who washed the pain away. She hadn't needed to say a word, just the look of compassion in her eyes was enough for him. Far from what Beau had expected, nobody thought he'd been a chump. They were all pretty upset with Rachel, and Riggs even offered his services to have her brought up on abandonment charges.

It would serve her right, but Beau decided to move on. At least he'd learned a valuable lesson. Until then he had no idea how ready he was to be a father. Now, it could happen with Lucy. Someday. Neither one of them was quite ready, even if he felt a bit ahead of her. He was a couple of years older, so it made sense.

This year was an unusual one, because for the first time Lenny didn't tell the "miracle baby" story of finding Lucy on the church steps. Also, even though Lucy's mother had been invited to the celebrations, she still wasn't comfortable in coming to Stone Ridge. Worried she'd face too much judgement and that it would thwart her sobriety. Lucy didn't push the issue. She saw Jacqueline from time to time but not often. Instead, she'd grown closer to Lenny and the rest of his immediate family.

She had a forgiving nature so eventually he'd stop worrying she'd go after Rachel and wind up on an episode of *Dateline*.

They all sang happy birthday and Lucy blew out the candles on the sheet cake Esperanza had baked for her. It was the same one every year, the one she'd had since she was a kid. Gifts were exchanged, and Beau sat on his hands. He was sorely tempted to fish out that ring and give it to her now in front of everyone but then they'd lose their private moment. The surprise would be ruined.

"What's wrong with our girl?" Lenny said, stepping up to Beau while Lucy was opening presents.

"I don't know, but I'll find out."

"She looks a little…I don't know, green in the gills. Tired. Maybe she's got that flu bug Beulah had last week."

Yeah, that had to be the problem. Beau told himself it wasn't because she'd decided he was too much trouble, too much of a pain to live with, or worse, that her family didn't approve. The kiss of death. Esperanza wasn't crazy about their arrangement, but Beau planned on asking Lucy to marry him. He'd just been waiting for the right moment. And today was being robbed from him. It would have been perfect to ask on her birthday. Another way to memorialize the day as special since she was no longer the "miracle baby." She couldn't kid him. Lucy was missing that notoriety just a little bit.

Finally, it was time for everyone to pile into trucks and make the drive to watch the fireworks coming across the lake from the neighboring town of Nothing. They were famous for their fireworks show, and nothing else. Beau had blankets, a couple of chairs, and that damn cupcake. This was happening. Either that, or she was breaking up with him. He already had a speech prepared as to why breaking up wasn't a good idea.

Beau laid out the blankets and Lucy took a seat cross-legged. Before the show started and took the spotlight, Beau pulled out the cupcake. "Here."

"You still have that?" She practically gagged. "I'm sorry, I can't. I'm too full still."

"From what? You haven't eaten much today, not even birthday cake!"

"I know. I guess…I'm just not hungry." She sighed.

"What's wrong? Are you mad at me?"

"What?" She blinked. "Of course not. You're still perfect."

"Nobody's perfect, baby." He pulled her into his arms, between his legs. "You've got to tell me what's wrong. I know there's *something*. Remember, I know you. You're not feeling well. Are you sick?"

She hesitated a moment too long. "Nothing's wrong. Here, let me have that cupcake."

He handed it to her. "Be careful eating it."

She rolled her eyes, then licked at the icing.

"There's something…wait a second…I think someone left a utensil in this cupcake! Who made this? It's hard like metal…look, it's…oh my god."

She turned to him, a look of genuine surprise in her eyes. He'd done it. He'd stumped her. She was speechless. He was already on the floor, so it was an easy roll to one knee.

"Lucy Lorenzo, I've loved you for half my life. Will you marry me?"

"I…I can't believe this is happening. You have the most amazing timing."

"No, not really. I almost couldn't get you to eat this stinking cupcake. It's your birthday, how hard can that be?"

"I mean…you're really asking me to *marry* you?"

"Are you really saying *yes*?"

"Yes, dummy! Yes!" She pretty much screamed those words, which caught the attention of everyone in the vicinity.

Before long they were surrounded by family and friends. Sadie, Lincoln and their kids, Eve and Jackson and their daughter, a pregnant Daisy and Wade, Lillian Carver, Esperanza and Art, and of course his mother and father. One advantage of doing this on her birthday was already having the family assembled. Phones were out, snapping pictures.

"At last!" Beulah Hayes said, walking up to the commotion. "I never thought we'd get you married off, Beau Stephens! I'm here to tell you, as I live and breathe, there is a God!"

"Amen, Ms. Beulah, amen. Preach!" said Lenny.

Beau's proposal was punctuated by one of the most spectacular fireworks he'd seen in years.

Later that night, he got a shock of his own.

"You're going to be a daddy." She showed him the test with the double solid pink lines.

That's when he realized that indeed his timing was rather perfect for once. "Are you serious?"

"Yes. I hope…I hope you're happy." She chewed on her lower lip. "I know we didn't plan this."

"We couldn't have done this any better if we did." He took her in his arms. "I love you, Lucy Lorenzo. You're my girl, and you always have been."

The Residents of Stone Ridge

Beulah Hayes: President of the Ladies of SORROW

Sadie Stephens: youngest child of Wanda and Merle; married to Lincoln Carver

Beau Stephens: oldest child of Wanda and Merle; engaged to Lucy Lorenzo

Samuel "Sammy" Stephens: oldest child of Lincoln and Sadie

Faith Stephens: youngest child of Lincoln and Sadie

Wanda Stephens: mother of Beau and Sadie

Merle Stephens: father of Beau and Sadie

Lillian "Mima" Carver: grandmother, matriarch

Albert Carver: grandfather (deceased)

Hank Carver: father of Lincoln, Jackson, and Daisy

Maggie Mae Carver: mother of Hank's children (divorced from Hank)

Lincoln Carver: oldest son of Hank and Maggie Mae; married to Sadie

Jackson Carver: youngest son (middle child) of Hank and Maggie Mae; married to Eve

Daisy Carver: daughter (youngest child) of Hank and Maggie Mae; married to Wade Cruz

Wade Cruz: rodeo cowboy; married to Daisy

Eve Iglesias: local veterinarian; married to Jackson Carver

Lillian "Lily" Pearl Carver: oldest child of Jackson and Eve

Brenda Iglesias: Eve's mother

Ricardo Iglesias: Eve's father (divorced from Brenda)

Lucy Lorenzo: bartender at the Shady Grind; engaged to Beau Stephens

Esperanza Lorenzo: adoptive mother of Lucy

Arturo "Art" Lorenzo: adoptive father of Lucy

Leonard "Lenny" Gray: jack-of-all-trades; secret grandfather of Lucy

Jacqueline Gray: birth mother of Lucy

Noelle Lee: Lenny's first wife; biological grandmother of Lucy

Rusty Jones: old rodeo cowboy; biological father of Daisy

John Truehart: richest man in the county and horse breeder; father of Jolette Marie

Jolette Marie Truehart: only daughter of the wealthy Truehart family; engaged to Levi Cooper

Levi Cooper: horse wrangler; engaged to Jolette Marie

Calvin and Marge Henderson: (deceased) adoptive parents of Riggs, Sean, and Colton

Riggs Henderson: rancher and eldest Henderson brother; married to Winona

Sean Henderson: rancher and middle Henderson brother; married to Bonnie Lee

Colton Henderson: rancher; soldier; youngest Henderson brother; married to Jennifer

Winona James: Nashville superstar; ex-wife of Jackson Carver; married to Riggs Henderson

Joe "Joey" Henderson: twin son of Riggs and Winona; twin brother of Cal

Calvin "Cal" Henderson: twin son of Riggs and Winona; twin brother of Joey

Mary Henderson: daughter of Riggs and Winona

Bonnie Lee Wheeler: married to Sean Henderson

Jennifer Walker: married to Colton Henderson

Horace Walker: father of Jennifer; former military mentor to Colton

Dr. Judson Grant: one of Sadie's many suitors

Trixie Delacorte: midwife at the new women's clinic

Twyla: musician; protégé of Winona James

Jeremy Pine: single man of Stone Ridge and frequent suitor

Annabeth Dantzer: veterinarian; Eve's partner at the Lonestar Veterinary Clinic

Caroline: owner of Triple S catering

Shula Jackson: manager at the Wild Rose; owner of new flower shop, Buttercup Blooms

Lenora: Ellie's mother

Jimmy Ray: Sadie's student

Pamela Ann: mother of Jimmy Ray

Derek: father of Jimmy Ray

Ellie: Sadie's student

Bobby Joe: Sadie's student

Priscilla Beauchamp: owner and manager of the Shady Grind

Lloyd Hayes: husband of Beulah; owner of The General Store

Pastor June Marie: pastor at Trinity Church

The Ladies of SORROW: (Society of Reasonable, Respectable, Orderly Women)

Beulah Hayes: current President

Maybelle Wheeler: sister of Beulah; mother of Bonnie Lee

Birdie Ruth: only daughter of Beulah

Ada Armstrong: aunt of Dr. Judson Grant

Wimbreth Williams (deceased): founder of SORROW; author of the book *Men of Stone Ridge*

About the Author

Heatherly Bell is the bestselling author of over fifty-six titles under two different pen names. She lives for coffee, craves cupcakes, and occasionally wears real pants.

She lives in Northern California with her family and loves to hear from readers.

You may reach her at
heatherly@heatherlybell.com

Also by Heatherly Bell

LUCKY COWBOY

NASHVILLE COWBOY

BUILT LIKE A COWBOY

COWBOY, IT'S CHRISTMAS

MR. COWBOY

SOLDIER COWBOY

WINNING MR. CHARMING

THE CHARMING CHECKLIST

A CHARMING CHRISTMAS ARRANGEMENT

A CHARMING SINGLE DAD

A CHARMING DOORSTEP BABY

ONCE UPON A CHARMING BOOKSHOP

COMING SOON:

HER FAKE BOYFRIEND

30 DAYS TILL CHRISTMAS

For a complete book catalog, please visit the author's website.